D1431550

Love Finds You™

IN

Daisy

OKLAHOMA

Love Finds You™

IN
Daisy
OKLAHOMA

JANICE HANNA

summerside
PRESS™

Summerside Press™
Minneapolis 55337
www.summersidepress.com

Love Finds You in Daisy, Oklahoma
© 2012 by Janice Hanna

ISBN 978-1-60936-593-6

All scripture quotations are taken from the King James Version of the Bible.

The town depicted in this book is a real place, but all characters are fictional. Any resemblances to actual people or events are purely coincidental.

Cover design by Garborg Design Works | www.garborgdesign.com
Cover photo of model and sky © Susan Fox / Trevillion Images
Cover photo of daisies by iStock
Back cover photo and mountain photo on page 7 courtesy Oklahoma
    Tourism and Recreation Department
Photo on spine by Bigstock
Interior design by Müllerhaus Publishing Group | www.mullerhaus.net

Summerside Press™ is an inspirational publisher offering fresh, irresistible books to uplift the heart and engage the mind.

Printed in USA.

Dedication

·····················

Dedicated to the memory of my uncle, Gene Wyatt.

Special thanks to Ellen Doughten and the many
other Facebook friends who helped me come up
with hooligan-like pranks to include in this story.
I have to wonder what you were like as kids!

And to William and Jacob. "Snips and snails and
puppy dog tails" doesn't even come close.

Atoka County, Oklahoma

RUMOR HAS IT THAT DAISY, OKLAHOMA—LOCATED IN ATOKA County, just off of Highway 43—was named after a local girl named Daisy Beck. It was once a thriving community boasting a general store, a school, a post office, and other places of business.

Today, little remains of this once-upon-a-time town. If you blink when you drive by, you might miss it. However, the land around Daisy is as beautiful as ever. I know this from personal experience, having been through the area this past year. Rolling hills capture the imagination, and the trees are so green you might think they were painted onto the landscape with an artist's brush. On second thought, they were! The Lord Himself surely blessed this little patch of ground with an extra splash of beauty.

As I set out to write this whimsical tale, the melody to "Daisy,

Daisy, give me your answer, do" became my theme song. I couldn't help but use it in the story.

I pray you enjoy your trip to Daisy as much as I did. May you see the spirit of the people of Oklahoma on each page, and may the antics of the children remind you of your carefree childhood days.

Janice Hanna

Chapter One
....

Tips for Dealing with Unruly Young'uns—*The Bible commands strict discipline when it comes to the raising of children. With all the hooligans wreaking havoc in our little town, we have no choice but to come down on them with a firm hand. "Spare the rod, spoil the child"—that's my motto. Not everyone takes such a strong stance when it comes to Daisy's children, of course. I know I'm often alone in my principles, especially where the sheriff is concerned. 'Course, he's got his hands full with those two rapscallion boys of his. But, by gum, I plan to rid this town of childish nonsense if it's the last thing I do. And if it means tanning a few hides along the way, well, so be it.*

—Molly Harris, Daisy Resident and Chairwoman
of the "Fresh as a Daisy" Committee

Daisy, Oklahoma, Early September, 1912

The Atoka County jail housed no prisoners that Monday morning unless one counted the local sheriff. After the verbal thrashing he'd just received from Molly Harris, Gene Wyatt felt like hiding out in one of the cells for the rest of the day.

He pulled off his Stetson and hurled it at the hat rack. "Crazy busybody. Who does she think she is, anyway?"

For a moment, he wondered what it would feel like to toss the town's crankiest senior citizen into an empty cell and throw away the key. Wouldn't that make a great article for the *Atoka County Register*? He could almost picture the headline now: Local Woman Rethinks Her Meddling Ways from Behind Bars. Surely the other residents of Daisy would back him up.

On the other hand, they might turn on him. Stranger things had happened of late. Folks who'd once claimed to be his friends had turned cold shoulders to him after hearing Molly's repeated tirades about his boys. Many seemed to share her concerns.

Releasing a slow breath, Gene tried to calm down. Unfortunately, Molly's words weren't easy to shake off. They'd stung, worse than he cared to admit, but what could he do? His hands were already too full, what with raising the boys alone.

He made his way to his dreary office, eased his way into the chair behind his messy desk, and began to thumb through the mail, which he'd just fetched from the postmaster. Minutes later, he still found himself mulling over the elderly woman's criticism of his two sons. Sure, William and Jacob were a handful—there was no denying that—but did she really have to call them *hooligans*? They were only eight and ten, after all. Far too young to be accused of such nonsense. And that comment about how they might end up serving time was way out of line.

He paused. The way things were headed, they could very well end up going down the wrong road. If only they still had a mother to guide them, then maybe...

No, he wouldn't think like that. The two years since Brenda's death had been dreadful, but the pain of losing her lessened more with each passing day. No point in resurrecting it. The boys would be fine. He would see to it. In the meantime, he had work to do—plenty of it.

A familiar voice rang out from the front office, interrupting his thoughts.

"Son, are you here?"

He recognized his mother's voice at once. Gene did his best to shake off his concerns before facing her. No point in letting her know how he felt about Molly's accusations.

"I'm here," he managed.

His mother entered his office, the somber look on her face a direct contradiction to the cheerful yellow dress and matching flower-laden hat. "I guess you heard from Molly. She's wound up tighter than your grandfather's clock."

Gene did his best not to sigh aloud. "I think everyone in town heard her tirade. I wish she would keep her thoughts to herself. At the very least, she needs to learn to control her volume so as not to raise the dead."

"She's plenty worked up, that's sure and certain." His mother removed her fashionable hat, which left her upswept hair a bit disheveled. She pressed a loose strand of hair behind her ear, and the crinkles around her soft blue eyes deepened. "I've seen her frazzled before, but not like this."

Gene rested against the edge of his desk. "Not sure what to say in my own defense."

"No need to say anything. She's just a bitter old woman who loves to complain. But she does have a point about some of the boys—not just William and Jacob, but the boys from the orphanage too. She counts them all as one since they're comrades and coconspirators in mischief."

"I understand that. I really do." He felt his anger growing as Molly's words flitted through his mind. "But to call them rabble-rousers? Sounds like something she read in one of those ridiculous dime novels. And to say the boys are going to destroy the town if someone doesn't take action—what sort of talk is that? Does she have to be so melodramatic?"

"Slight exaggeration, but not by much." His mother gave him a thoughtful look. "William and Jacob and the other boys *have* been up to tricks again." She placed her hat on his desk then took to fussing with her hair once again.

"I know, I know." He thumbed through several papers on his desk, hoping she would change the direction of this conversation instead of elaborating. Surely she knew how awkward this was for him.

His mother leaned forward and whispered, "You do know they were swimming nude at Old Man Tucker's pond yesterday, don't you? Naked as jaybirds, all of them."

"Not a criminal offense," Gene said. "And why are we whispering?"

"Don't want folks to hear. It's so embarrassing."

"Embarrassing? Boys swimming without clothes?" He laughed. "Mother, you worry too much about what others think. You always have."

Carolina Wyatt had never been one to give up on an argument easily and she didn't this time, either. Instead, she flinched but then lit right back into the conversation. "True. But the way those boys run willy-nilly from here to there with no adult supervision, it's a wonder they don't get hurt. They tied a rope to that big tree in my front yard last Saturday, and William nearly hung himself with it. Scared me to death."

Gene shrugged it off. "They told me. But nothing came of it except a scraped knee when he fell. And if it makes you feel any better, he was fully dressed when the incident occurred. If you'd stopped by to report that he was climbing trees in his birthday suit, I'd be a little more concerned. As it is, he's fine."

A half smile crept across his mother's face. "Yes, he's fine; that's true." She took a seat in the chair opposite his desk. "But not everyone in town is fine with the children's actions. You heard what the boys did to Mrs. Wabash, didn't you?"

"What this time?" He looked her way, waiting for the inevitable story to unfold.

His mother leaned forward and placed her hands on his desk. "They snuck into her wardrobe and stole her unmentionables. Then they ran them up the flagpole in the square just this morning, along with a notice that the things belonged to her."

Gene stifled a chuckle as he forced the image of the orphanage's soon-to-be-leaving director out of his mind. "Oh, is that all?"

"Is that all?" His mother's cheeks flushed pink. "Clearly you know nothing about women, or you would understand the humiliation in that story. Mrs. Wabash feels she can't show her face in town. Not that she's planning on staying in town much longer, of course."

"I shouldn't think it would be her *face* she'd be afraid of showing." He couldn't help the laugh that followed.

His mother leaned back in the chair, the wrinkles around her eyes growing deeper as she gazed his way. "Honestly, you're as bad as the children."

At this, Gene sobered a bit. "I'm not excusing their behavior," he said. "But let's face it. Running Mrs. Wabash's unmentionables up the flagpole is hardly the equivalent of burning down the orphanage. And as for her leaving town, I can't say I'm altogether sorry. She's never cared much for the children, from what I can see. The director of an orphanage should at least pretend to care for the children she's supervising, don't you think?"

"Of course. But don't be so quick to judge her, Gene. You don't know what she's thinking or feeling. Besides, she gave more than a year of her life to those boys and girls and feels she's done her part."

"I suppose."

"And as for how she's feeling about the children, please keep in mind that they've tormented her almost from the beginning. That flagpole stunt wasn't their only injustice against her. The boys put a dead possum behind the heating grate in her room. From what I've been told, the stench was unbearable."

"Boys will be boys." He found himself ready to be done with this conversation.

"Yes, they will." His mother crossed her arms and gave him a pensive look. "I raised one myself. And he turned out pretty well, if you don't mind my saying so, so I feel confident I can speak on this subject with some authority."

"Well, of course." Gene squared his shoulders and prepared himself for another challenging conversation.

Her gaze narrowed. "Look, son, I know you feel caught in the middle where William and Jacob are concerned, but, in case you don't realize it, you always give the same excuse when the children act up."

"I do?" He looked her way, confused by her words.

"Yes. And it's true that boys will be boys, but there's a time and a place for boyish shenanigans. And you might remember how you got quite a few spankings when your pranks went awry. Your boys and their friends need good, honest discipline."

"I'm doing my best with William and Jacob. But without Brenda…" He pushed back the lump in his throat and shook his head. If anyone could understand this, it would be his mother. She'd walked this road with him. Knew how desperately he and the boys missed Brenda— her tenderness, her laughter, and her indomitable spirit. Every dream they had ever shared was swept away in that awful tornado. Now he was left alone to piece things back together, whether he felt like it or not.

"I know, son." His mother drew near and gave him a pat on the arm. "I don't mean to scold. Really. I'm just trying to offer a bit of helpful advice."

"Mm-hmm."

"They just wear me out, that's all. Wait until you hear what William did this morning."

"What's that?" he asked.

"Carried a mess of catfish into my house and asked me to clean them."

"I haven't had fried catfish in ages. Sounds good."

"Yes, well, he dragged in the stench of worms and mud all over my freshly mopped floor. But here's the kicker. He caught those fish in Old Man Tucker's pond. The poor old fella chased him off his property and all the way to my front door. I've never seen anyone so angry."

"Mother, boys will be—" Gene stopped himself from finishing it.

"The more time William and Jacob spend with their old friends, the more likely they'll end up in trouble. They need a woman in their lives to teach them right from wrong."

"They have you. You're the best grandmother in town."

She grunted. "Maybe. But even the best grandmother in town can't handle seventeen orphans and your two boys by herself. Once Mrs. Wabash leaves, those children will need someone who's still young enough—and hardy enough—to tackle the challenges they present. I'm old, and I'm tired. I don't have it in me to stay on top of their every move."

"You're doing fine."

"No, I'm not. They're faster than I am. You should've seen me following along behind Old Man Tucker as he chased William across the yard. Poor old fella was only dressed in his skivvies. Apparently they caught him unawares."

"I understand, Mother." He did, of course. But what could he do about it? Every attempt had already been made, every avenue exhausted. And speaking of exhausted, wasn't that the real issue here? He'd worn himself out trying to fix children who didn't care to be fixed. They simply wanted to be children. Rowdy, undisciplined children.

His mother offered a sympathetic look. "If you ask my opinion— and I know you didn't, but I'm offering it anyway—William and Jacob need a bit of separation from their friends at the orphanage. Not all the time, mind you, but occasionally. Promise me you'll pray about it. The Lord will guide you, I've no doubt."

Gene laced his fingers behind his head and leaned back, nearly ready to admit defeat. "I know they're a handful, but they're good boys at heart...in spite of their antics. It's only been two and a half years since Brenda and I took them into our home. They still consider those other children at the orphanage their real brothers and sisters. And now that they've lost the only mother they've ever known..."

"I know, son."

"At any rate, it's obvious we need help." Gene raked his fingers through his hair. "I've written to the head of the missions organiza- tion, in the hopes that he can send someone. If we have to shut down the orphanage, the children will be sent elsewhere. You know what that means—they'll *all* be separated. Brothers and sisters will be torn apart. Can you imagine what that will do to them?" The very idea made him feel ill.

"I don't think that will happen. I've taken the liberty of writing my best friend, Marla, in South Carolina. Do you remember her?"

"Of course."

"Her daughter, Janelle, is thirty-four and widowed. She has a young daughter about William's age. I think she would be the perfect choice."

Gene's spirits lifted at once. "Wait. Are you saying that she's agreed to take on the orphanage? We won't need someone from the missions society after all?" His heart felt lighter. *What wonderful news. This will solve everything.*

His mother shook her head. "She's not free to come until early May. Until then, we need a plan. A solid plan. Otherwise, I'm afraid the

1912

orphanage will come under the scrutiny of you-know-who." She waggled her brows.

Gene knew, all right. Mayor Albright had been intent on tearing down the orphanage from the beginning, garnering most of his information from Molly Harris. Gene wouldn't let that happen. Couldn't let that happen. He'd grown to love those children—every last rowdy one of them. And he'd be hanged before he saw them separated or farmed out to unwilling families.

In the meantime, it looked as if he had a lot of praying to do.

Chapter Two
....

Tips for Dealing with Unruly Young'uns—*Children need
to be loved and nurtured. They're looking for direction, of course,
and discipline. But most of all, they're longing for someone to
take an interest in them—to care about the things that matter to
them. They need someone who will kneel to their level and offer
encouragement, particularly when things get rough. We don't all
have the luxury of a great upbringing. Some children face unique
challenges. With those, we need to be more kindhearted than ever.
Most children are starving for affection. A little goes a long, long
way, especially with those who need it most.*

—Rena Jewel, of the Gulfport Mississippi Jewels

Gulfport, Mississippi, Jewel Villa

Rena pushed aside the feelings of jealousy that threatened to overtake her
as she eyed the vase of gerbera daisies on the foyer table. For a moment,
she contemplated snatching one of the brightly colored flowers and slipping up the stairs to her room. With her brother and sister-in-law out of
town, no one would be any the wiser.

Yes, she could bury the beautiful daisy between the pages of her half-written novel and pretend the handsome hero in her story had plucked it from the garden just for her. Better yet, she could imagine that she carried a whole cluster of daisies as she made her way up the aisle toward her husband-to-be. That would make for a lovely tale.

She began to sing, "'Daisy, Daisy, give me your answer, do'" and then smiled as her imagination carried her away to a happy place. After the possibility played itself out, she gave herself a good scolding. What purpose would it serve to steal one of her sister-in-law's flowers, anyway? Virginia might not know that a flower had disappeared from the bunch, but the Lord would. Besides, the daisy would soon wilt, then serving only as a limp reminder of all Rena did not have—all she would never have.

Yes, she might as well face the facts. Women with no prospects did not receive bouquets of freshly cut daisies from would-be beaus. They didn't get invited to dances, and they certainly didn't receive proposals of marriage. Instead, they created Adonis-like characters in books, giving them broad shoulders, winsome smiles, and elegant good looks. In other words, they lived in an imaginary world to soften the blows of the real one.

A familiar heaviness wrapped around Rena and she gave herself over to the blues. Moments later, she realized she was still staring at the colorful flowers and humming the same little melody. The song faded and she did her best to shake off her reverie, determined not to let discouragement get her down.

The housekeeper passed by on her way toward the stairs, her arms loaded with folded sheets. "Everything all right, Miss Rena?" Katy shifted her position to keep the pile from tumbling.

Rena managed a lame nod then pivoted on her heel, turning away from the daisies on the table. "Yes. Fine. Thank you." As she made her way through the villa's grand foyer, she tried to think of something she could do to occupy her time. She could always knit, of course. Reuben would approve of that idea, no doubt. Her older brother had been after her for weeks to finish up the hats and scarves for the Missions Society Christmas benefit, still months away. But with the temperatures outside blazing in the nineties this humid September afternoon, knitting seemed a bit ridiculous. Besides, she didn't feel like it. In fact, she didn't feel like doing much of anything these days.

Rena paused at the large mirror in the front hallway and fussed with her hair. Once again, the heat and humidity had wreaked havoc with it. Loose brown tendrils draped her neck, turning into moist curls. Not that she really minded. Who would notice, anyway? With Virginia and Reuben escorting their daughter off to college in New York, the ornate Gulfport mansion seemed hollow and empty. Glittering chandeliers hung over empty dining tables. Hallways once filled with the sound of laughter now held only framed photographs to capture the memories. Beautiful furnishings, most imported from Europe, sat empty.

Pushing aside the lump in her throat, she thought about her niece's departure to Vassar. Though Rena would miss her terribly, there was no point in crying about it. Sadie had the whole world in front of her, didn't she? And wasn't she the luckiest girl in all of Gulfport, to be accepted at Vassar? Everyone agreed. Yes, Rena should be celebrating her niece's good fortune, not mourning it.

She wandered into her brother's plush office in search of stationery. Composing a long, heartfelt letter to Sadie would do the trick. Yes, it would ease her mind and help her focus on the thing that really mattered—her niece's happiness.

Rena reached Reuben's ornate oak desk and opened the top right drawer. As she did, she managed to bump a tray of letters sitting on the top of the desk. They hit the wooden floor with a clatter. Katy quickly appeared in the doorway.

"Everything all right, miss?"

Rena looked her way, uneasiness setting in. "Just being my usual clumsy self." She knelt down and scooped up some of the pages, making a bigger mess than before.

Katy offered her a sympathetic smile. "Let me help you with those." She eased her ample frame to the floor beside Rena, and the two worked together to gather up the scattered pages.

Rena's gaze shifted to an empty envelope addressed to her brother. She held it up, double-checking to make sure it was truly empty. "Have you seen the letter that goes in here?"

"Where is it from?" Katy glanced her way. "I'll search through the ones I've collected."

"It's from…" Rena paused as she read the words SHERIFF WYATT. "Looks to be from a sheriff in Oklahoma."

"Something to do with that missions society of your brother's, no doubt." Katy went off talking about how Rena's brother gave entirely too much time and money to the organization.

Rena half listened to Katy's dissertation, stopping her only when she stumbled across the letter that matched the envelope. "Ooh, I found it." Her heart quickened as she read the passionate note written with large, sprawling strokes.

Dear Reverend Jewel,

Please allow me to introduce myself. My name is Gene Wyatt. I am the sheriff in the town of Daisy, Oklahoma. I'm writing to you today on behalf of our local Atoka County Orphanage, which your missions organization helped to establish approximately three years ago. The facility currently houses seventeen youngsters, primarily boys, from a variety of backgrounds. They have provided our tiny community with much joy and extemporaneous activity.

The director, a Mrs. Wabash, has recently informed us that she will be taking her leave. Perhaps she has already written to you about this matter. If she has, I would urge you to overlook any negative comments she might have made about the children. They are a feisty bunch, to be sure, but they are easy to love.

We will require someone to take Mrs. Wabash's place, preferably an older female—unmarried, of course. The job is best suited to one who has worked with children in the past and who understands the delicate art of negotiation.

Our situation here could be described as urgent. We must hear from you as soon as possible with a solution.

Thank you so much for your assistance in this matter.

With gratitude,

Sheriff Gene Wyatt,

Daisy, Oklahoma

Rena folded the pages, her hands now trembling.

"What is it?" Katy leaned over, a look of concern on her face. "Something important?"

"Oh, yes, well…" Rena shoved the letter back inside the envelope and set it atop the desk. "Something about orphans."

"In Oklahoma?" Katy erupted in laughter, and her ample midsection took to jiggling. "Can you imagine living with a bunch of waifs during a bleak Oklahoma midwinter?" She gave an exaggerated shiver. "Sounds like the worst possible punishment for one's sins."

Or the best possible way to escape a life of loneliness when there's nothing left to do with one's time but sulk about the dreams that haven't come true.

Rena dared not voice her thoughts aloud. Instead, she gave Katy a little shrug before making her way out of her brother's office, deep in thought. Why was Mrs. Wabash leaving the orphanage? Pressing family matters, likely. But how could she go away and leave seventeen children with no one to care for them? No one to prepare their meals or tuck them in at night? No one to kiss away their scrapes or offer comfort after a bad dream? What sort of woman abandoned precious children of God in their time of desperate need?

Rena's heels clicked on the marble floor as she made her way across the spacious foyer. She replayed the words of the letter in her mind: "*We will require someone to take Mrs. Wabash's place, preferably an older female—unmarried, of course.*" She paused in front of the buffet table, her gaze falling once again on Virginia's vase filled with flowers. The overhead glow from the chandelier brought out the daisies' lovely color, and they stirred her heart as never before. In that moment she felt a gentle nudge in her spirit.

Daisies.

Daisy, Oklahoma.

Surely this was no coincidence. The flowers were some sort of heavenly sign. They'd been sitting in this very spot for days, but she'd barely paid them any mind until today. Could it be…?

Oh, Lord, what are You saying? Would He really ask her to leave the comfort of home and family and travel to a place she'd never been, a place where she might actually make a difference in the lives of seventeen adorable children?

"'Daisy, Daisy, give me your answer, do…'" The words tripped over her tongue, and she couldn't help but giggle as the possibilities took root.

One more glance at the vase of flowers convinced her that she must take a leap of faith. With newfound determination, she spun on her heels and headed back to Reuben's office to locate the stationery. Looked like the only letter she would be writing today was a lengthy one to a certain sheriff in Daisy, Oklahoma.

Chapter Three
....

Tips for Dealing with Unruly Young'uns—*As a relatively new teacher, I don't have years of experience to offer. Still, I feel I've learned enough in my first year at the Daisy Primary School to comment on the topic of child-rearing. Children need discipline, naturally. I do my best to administer it when needed. But children also need to be praised for their good behavior. When my students act up, I take the time to offer a bit of extra attention. When their behavior is good, I brag on them in front of the others. Positive encouragement really does the trick. I've learned that we thrive on praise, even as adults.*

—Jenny Jamison, Teacher at the Daisy Primary School.

Gulfport, Mississippi, Mid-September

The next two weeks passed at a snail's pace. Rena could hardly stop thinking about the letter she'd sent to Daisy, Oklahoma. She also found herself fretting over what Reuben would say once he found out. Likely he would frown on the idea.

Then again, why should she care what her older brother thought? Shouldn't a thirty-eight-year-old woman be able to make her own decisions without consulting her brother?

The following Friday morning, Rena had the opportunity to find out, firsthand. She awoke a couple of hours before dawn to the sound of Reuben's and Virginia's voices outside her bedroom door. After rising and slipping on her robe, Rena headed to the hall to meet them.

"You're home!" She embraced her brother and then turned her attention to her sister-in-law, who leaned against the doorway. Virginia's normally perfect hair was a mess, and her eyes sagged with weariness.

"We just arrived." Reuben yawned. "And what a journey it was. We'll tell you all about it in a few hours. Right now we both need to sleep. We're exhausted."

"No doubt." Rena gave him a compassionate look. "How's Sadie?"

"Adjusting well, I think. She said to give you her love." He yawned once more. "Anyway, I'm headed off to bed. See you in a few hours."

A few hours might not seem like much to Reuben, but right now they felt like an eternity to Rena. Oh well. She'd waited this long to tell him her news. What were a few more hours, in the grand scheme of things? She passed them by making a list of all the things she would need to purchase from the local department store before leaving for Daisy. Her wardrobe would need some updating. From what she could gather, Oklahoma was colder than Mississippi was in the wintertime. And her favorite dresses might not be the best fit. Perhaps she would need a few simpler ones. And shoes. Definitely sturdy, comfortable shoes.

Oh, but how exciting this would be! If only Reuben would wake up so that she could tell him all about it.

He arose just after noon. True to form, he dressed in his usual conservative suit and bow tie and headed straight to his study, foregoing any food. From outside the door, Rena could hear him shuffling through the mail and talking to himself. After pacing the hallway for what seemed like an eternity, she finally worked up the courage to rap on his door.

"Come in." Reuben's voice sounded strained as he responded to her gentle knocking.

She eased the door open and stuck her head inside then forced a smile. "Reuben, could I speak with you for a moment?"

"Of course." He looked up from the stacks of opened mail on his desk. "Is everything all right?"

"Yes. Quite." She took a few steps inside the room and eased herself into a chair near the desk. For a moment she said nothing. She gazed at the rows and rows of bookcases and tried to summon the courage to speak.

"Something wonderful has happened," she said at last. "Well, I think it's wonderful, and I hope you agree. I've been waiting for you to return to tell you firsthand."

He gave her an inquisitive look. "I'm intrigued. Something to do with the missions society?"

"Yes. How did you know?"

He thumbed through several papers on the desk, not even looking her way. "Well, I left you in charge of the knitting for our Christmas event, so I would imagine you've had your hands full."

"Oh, that." She tried not to let her expression shift much. "No, actually it's something altogether different. I stumbled across a letter from a sheriff in Oklahoma. Now, mind you, I wasn't going through your mail. I'd accidentally knocked the tray of letters off the desk."

"I see." He glanced at her, tiny creases forming between his brows. "Oh, I remember the letter now. The headmistress at the orphanage is leaving, and they need someone to take her place."

"Yes, precisely." Rena smoothed her gray skirt with her palms, her anxiety growing. "Have you found someone yet?"

"No. I sent out a notice to various congregations but haven't heard back from anyone as of yet." His attention shifted to the papers on his desk. "Not sure what I'll tell the sheriff."

"Tell him you've located the perfect person." She sat up straighter in her chair. "Someone who would love nothing better than to care for children in an orphanage."

"The perfect person?" Now he gazed at her with intention, and she could read the concern written in his eyes. "Who do you mean?"

"Why, me, of course." She gave him a playful grin.

He looked stunned by this statement. "You?"

"Yes, brother. It's the perfect solution to their problem." *And mine.*

"Surely you can't be serious, Rena." With the wave of a hand he dismissed her idea. "You've not spent time with youngsters since Sadie was a child. And these are mostly boys. Troublemakers, I would imagine, based on the wording of the sheriff's letter. It's out of the question."

Rena's cheeks grew hot. How dare he answer for her? "It's not out of the question, and I'm perfectly capable of making up my mind, thank you."

"I'm only looking out for your best interests." Now he gave her his full attention. "I think perhaps the heat has gotten to you. This idea of yours is unrealistic at best."

If anything has gotten to me, it's the knitting, not the heat.

She rose and paced the office, pausing to gaze at the shelves filled with books. Though she had read dozens of them, the information seemed pointless now. What good was information if one could not act upon it?

"For years, you've been telling me to give of myself to the poor," she said.

"Well, of course. That's why I've given you so many opportunities to work with the indigent here in Gulfport. We are a team—all of us, working together."

"Reuben, I hope you won't find this irreverent, but I feel that much of my *doing* here is just busywork. I'm not changing lives for the better. Yes, I understand the concept. I'm well-read. I've studied the books you've given me. But I'm not making a difference."

DAISY
1912
OK

"Of course you are." He appeared to dismiss her concerns.

"I'll be forty in two years." Rena's hands trembled as the reality of her words settled in. "Forty."

"Rena, you just turned thirty-eight last month. You speak as if your days on earth are drawing to a close."

She paused before saying something she might regret. Truly, if she stayed here—if she remained captive in this overly spacious home in this well-to-do part of town—she might as well see her days come to an end. How could she state such a thing without hurting her brother's feelings? And what would he say once he heard that she'd already written to the sheriff, offering her services?

Her brother gave her a sympathetic smile, as if she were a small child in need of a lecture. "Your best days are ahead."

As Rena pondered his words, a gripping sensation took hold of her heart. Until this very moment, she'd never contemplated the fact that her best days might be in the future. More often than not, she found herself wondering if any of her tomorrows would be better than her yesterdays.

Suddenly her emotions got the better of her. "You have no idea what it feels like." As she turned away from him, Rena shifted her focus to a vase on the mantel of the fireplace and willed the tears not to come.

"What *what* feels like?" Reuben stood and took a couple of steps in her direction.

She refused to look his way; he would worry once he saw the moisture in her eyes. "Knowing that tomorrow will be exactly like today. And yesterday. And all the yesterdays before that." Her words came out sounding jagged. Cracked.

"Whatever do you mean?"

Rena pivoted on her heels and looked him squarely in the eyes, not caring whether he noticed her tears. "You will never understand what it feels like to know that people see you as superfluous."

"Superfluous?" He shook his head, clearly confused.

"Don't you see?" she whispered. "Isn't it obvious? I'm the old spinster aunt no one knows what to do with." Her tears came in earnest now.

"Spinster aunt?" He raked his fingers through his thinning salt-and-pepper hair and eased his way into his chair. "You speak as if your life is lacking in some way. You're family, Rena. We've never treated you as an outcast or in any way less because of your marital status."

"Of course not." She drew in a deep breath and fought to find the words. "The problem is all mine. I take both the credit and the shame. I've settled into my life here, and I've enjoyed most of it."

"Most of it?"

"Yes. Reuben, I can't help but feel…" She swallowed the lump in her throat. "I can't help but feel there's more for me out there." Her gaze shifted to the floor. "God has bigger plans for me."

"But you give of yourself on behalf of the needy right here in Gulfport. God is already at work in fulfilling His plan for your life. There's no greater cause than the poor and needy."

"Needy. Hmph." She did her best not to roll her eyes. "I darn socks for the folks at the missions house, yes. And I've knitted gloves and scarves for the homeless. Not that our winters are severe enough for them to see much use. What I'm trying to tell you is that I feel a tug on my heart to do more. And this orphanage…"

"What do you know of young children?"

"Did I not help you raise Sadie?"

"Of course. But she's an only child." Reuben rummaged through the mail, finally locating the letter, which he picked up. He traced a few lines with his index finger. "Sheriff Wyatt says that there are more than a dozen children at this orphanage. And you've no experience with children like this, from difficult environments. Likely some have deep wounds, heavy spiritual needs."

"Exactly." She squared her shoulders. "Which is precisely why I feel led to go."

"Did you read the entire letter? Why do you suppose an orphanage would require someone skilled in the art of negotiation? My guess is that it's because the children are problematic."

"They're in need of love, as all children are." She bit back the words that threatened to escape. Had she not shown Sadie love throughout the years, even when Reuben and Virginia were too busy doing good for others? Hadn't she negotiated Sadie's needs a time or two?

Her brother leaned back in his expensive leather chair, his brow so wrinkled that she almost called out to Katy to fetch an iron. Why, oh why, did Reuben always feel the need to tell her how to live, where to go, and what to do? This time he didn't speak a word. Apparently she had rendered him mute.

"There's one thing you should know," Rena said, finally breaking the silence. "I have already written to the sheriff and told him I will be there by early October. There's no point in waiting until November. Oklahoma is cold in the wintertime, you know."

"W–what?" His jaw dropped and he pushed back his chair. "Impossible."

"Not impossible. What I've said is true." She squared her shoulders. "This means I will be leaving in a week. So I would appreciate not just your letter of recommendation on my behalf, but also your blessing and your prayers."

Reuben shook his head and said nothing for a moment. When he finally spoke, his words surprised her. "Well, then, there's much to be done, isn't there? You will need Virginia's help, no doubt. I will put her on the task right away, as soon as she's rested up. And Katy too." He rose.

"You...you want to help me?" She gazed into her brother's eyes, suddenly energized. "Really?"

"You are my only sibling, Rena, and I want God's best for you. If you truly feel you are to go, then it would be wrong of me to keep you here. I've never known you to be impulsive or flighty, so I can only imagine you're following the prompting of the Lord."

"I am," she whispered. "Oh, I am."

The words came out sounding bold and confident. Inside, however, she quivered like a bowl of tapioca pudding. Soon enough her nerves would calm down. Right after she boarded the train. Right now...well, right now she had a lot of work to do.

Gene pulled off his hat as he made his way into Daisy's new schoolhouse to visit with Miss Jamison, his boys' teacher. She'd asked for a special meeting with him. He half-dreaded the meeting, but spending time with the green-eyed beauty couldn't be that bad, even if she did offer a bad report about the boys. He would gladly spend time with Jenny Jamison and hoped she felt the same.

It didn't take long to find out why she had requested his presence at the schoolhouse. Miss Jamison, with enough dramatic flair to earn her a spot on the stage, told him a story of how the boys had locked one of the female students—the mayor's daughter, no less—inside the water closet, keeping her there for a half hour during recess time.

"I feel sure that Calista's father will be along shortly to talk with us about it." Jenny took a lock of her long blond hair and wound it around her finger then glanced out the window. "And I can't imagine what I'll tell him. Mayor Albright is a rather intimidating fellow, you know."

"That he is."

"Poor Calista was both terrified and humiliated, as you might imagine."

"No doubt." Gene shifted his hat from one hand to another. So now the boys had taken to picking on girls? In vulnerable situations, no less? Why in the world had they chosen Mayor Albright's daughter, Calista? And what would they try next?

"I know they're wonderful boys, Sheriff," the teacher said. "Truly. And Lord knows I've worked extra hard to convince them of their value. I'm sure you have too. Why, I reinforce them with positive words as often as I can." She placed her hand on her heart. "Praising them for their good behavior—when it comes—is key to seeing even more of it. I believe that. Sincerely."

"Ah. I see. Well, actually, I…" His words drifted off. To be honest, he hadn't spent a lot of time in telling the boys how wonderful they were. Truth be told, he spent most of the time asking them to come down off the roof or to stop punching one another. Perhaps a bit of positive reinforcement *was* in order. The next time they did something right, he would give them a pat on the back. Of course, chances were pretty good that it would be some time before their behavior warranted such praise.

Though he didn't mean to do it aloud, Gene groaned.

Jenny offered him a bright, encouraging smile, her pretty green eyes capturing his attention. "I think, if we all work together, we can keep them walking the straight and narrow. I've already spoken to the reverend and he said—"

Gene started to attention. "Wait. You talked to the reverend about my boys?" Why the idea bothered him so much, he couldn't say. The reverend was a good man and not prone to overreacting. Well, unless you counted the time he'd made the boys repaint the church steeple. But that was only because they'd splattered it with eggs.

"Not just yours, but all the boys in town. The ones who, well, you know…act up."

"And what did the reverend say?"

"That prayer is the answer. That, surely, if David could take down the mighty Goliath with five smooth stones, I can handle a roomful of small boys."

"You're thinking of pummeling them with stones?"

At this, she began to giggle. "Sheriff, you're so funny. Truly. Besides, you know I don't believe in corporal punishment, so stoning is definitely not an option." Another giggle escaped. "To be honest, I'm relieved to see that you're taking this news so well. I thought perhaps my disciplinary action might offend you."

"Offend me? What do you mean? What disciplinary action have you taken? I've not heard."

Her smile shifted at once to a frown. "They left me no choice. I had to expel your boys from school for the next three days."

"They've been expelled?"

"Well, of course. You heard the part of the story where they locked Calista inside the water closet and wouldn't let her out. That is a direct violation of the code of conduct found in our student handbook. You received a copy at the beginning of the school year, did you not?"

"Oh. Well, yes, I suppose I did." *But I never read it.*

"I'm sure Mayor Albright will insist upon the disciplinary action. Besides, they've got to spend some time away to learn a lesson. This will be good for them…in the long run."

"Agreed. But I'm more concerned about the short run right now. I have to work. Where will they stay during the day?"

"I haven't got a clue, but I feel sure you'll figure something out. Perhaps your mother will care for them. It's only three days, after all."

Gene released a slow breath. "I don't think so. Not this time. She's…" How could he finish the sentence? His mother didn't have the stamina to spend all day with the boys. Nor did he. And if they kept up this sort of behavior, no one else in town would help him out either.

No, it looked as if his options were dwindling rapidly. And if he didn't do something soon, there would likely be no options left.

Chapter Four
....

TIPS FOR DEALING WITH UNRULY YOUNG'UNS—*Most folks take one look at my uniform and think I'm a tough guy. Truth be told, I'm softer than my mama's feather pillows where children are concerned. Maybe it's because I was such a ruffian myself, as a boy. My tip for keeping things under control with children is simple: stay calm. Just because they're out of control doesn't mean you have to be. If you need to blow off steam, do it in another place before confronting the child. That way you're not likely to scare anyone, yourself included. Even the rowdiest boys and girls settle down after a while. Usually. And if they don't, then divert their attention by playing "Cowboys and Indians" with them. Always works for me...and gives me the perfect excuse to rope 'em to a chair.*

—Charlie Lawson, Deputy Sheriff, Daisy, Oklahoma

Gene took a seat at his mother's dining-room table, his stomach rumbling as he took in the sight of his favorite foods—roast beef, mashed potatoes, and fried okra. After a hard day at work, he could hardly wait.

His mother busied herself, filling Jacob's and William's plates with food. Not that the boys seemed to be paying attention. No, they were far too busy punching each other's arms to notice.

He shushed the boys then made his announcement. "I've got some wonderful news."

"What's that, son?" His mother looked his way, still holding William's plate in her hand.

"I've received a letter from the missions board in Gulfport. They're sending someone to take Mrs. Wabash's place. She is on her way even now."

"Really?" His mother's eyes widened. "Did they... I mean, does this person know what she's walking into?"

Gene reached for a slab of roast beef, unwilling to answer the question just yet—at least the question his mother meant. The new director, whoever she was, certainly didn't have all the details. If she did, she'd likely run for the hills.

"I know the orphanage needs some work," Gene said instead. "It's in such a state of disrepair. The roof needs to be replaced, and the steps leading up to the front door are rickety. But don't worry. We'll get it done sooner or later."

His mother grunted. "The building needs work, to be sure. But I wasn't referring to that. I just wonder if this poor woman has any idea what sort of children await her."

Gene made up his mind not to demean the boys and girls, even if others struggled with them. "I feel sure she'll settle in nicely."

William and Jacob continued to squabble—William now frustrated with Jacob for having more food on his plate—and before long, they were out of their chairs and turning the corner of the dining room into a boxing ring. Jacob caught William's shirtsleeve and gave it a tug. A ripping sound followed. That, of course, only served to make William madder. He grabbed his brother's arm and twisted it behind his back.

In the scuffle, one of them managed to catch the hem of the table-cloth on the buffet and nearly pulled down the silver service.

Gene rose and moved their way, grabbing each by the shirtsleeve and gazing intently into their freckled faces. "Boys, this is not the time or place." He gave them each a little nudge toward their chairs and they sat, but not before scowling at each other and muttering a few words under their breath. Gene put the silver back in its place.

"You were saying?" Gene's mother folded her napkin and placed it on her lap. "She will settle in nicely, you think?"

Gene grunted then continued filling his plate. "I'm sure she will grow accustomed to the children with time."

"Time...and strong drink." His mother smirked before taking a bite of her mashed potatoes.

"Very funny. And just for the record, she doesn't drink. She made that plain in her letter. She appears to be temperate in every respect." He took a bite of the potatoes, grateful for the excuse it gave him to not say anything more on the subject.

"I was teasing, of course." His mother dabbed her lips with her napkin. "Though these children could drive a person to drink, no doubt about that."

As if to prove the fact, the boys took to fighting again, and their chairs shimmied across the floor. William knocked Jacob out of his chair with a loud smack to his cheek. Jacob responded with an exaggerated yelp.

"Ow!" Jacob rubbed his arm.

Gene glanced at the boys. "Tell him you're sorry, William."

"You're sorry," William said, before punching Jacob again.

Gene scooted his chair back. "I've had just about enough of this."

"Just about?" his mother said. "Or enough? There's a pretty big difference between the two."

He remained in his chair, frozen in place by her words. How did one go about filling in the gap between "just about" and "enough," anyway?

The boys dove into round three, and before long they'd landed in a heap on top of each other.

A familiar voice rang out from the front hallway. "Am I late for supper?"

Gene looked up to discover his deputy, Charlie, entering the dining room. With one swoop, Charlie reached down, gathered a boy in each arm, and plopped them into their seats. This move appeared to render the boys speechless. For a moment, anyway.

"For that, you get an extra-large helping of roast beef and two pieces of pie!" Gene's mother gestured for Charlie to sit, and she began to fill his empty plate.

"I can't wait." He rubbed his hands together, a crooked smile lighting his face.

Gene cleared his throat. "Charlie, I've got a job for you."

"Oh?" The young deputy glanced his way. "You need me to protect the town from harm? Or save females in distress?" He squared his shoulders and flexed a bicep, which made the boys laugh.

"No. I need you to make sure the children don't burn down the orphanage between now and when the new director arrives in a few days."

"Ah." Charlie took a bite of the roast beef and leaned back in his chair. "So, you've located someone gullible enough for the task, then? Do tell."

Gene cleared his throat and took a swig of milk to wash down the accusation in those words. "Yes, a new director is on her way," he managed. "But in the meantime, I need someone who's reliable to keep an eye on things. They're just children, after all. I'm not asking you to guard inmates."

"Hmph." Charlie rolled his eyes and raked his fingers through his disheveled blond waves. "Looking after the orphanage isn't exactly child's play. I think I'd rather wrestle thieves and robbers, if you don't mind."

"Look at it this way," Gene's mother said with a twinkle in her eye. "If you do agree to watch over the orphans, you'll be wrestling *potential* thieves and robbers." She filled his glass with milk. "That's got to count for something."

Gene groaned. As if he didn't have enough trouble with Molly. Now his mother too? Didn't she realize the boys were listening?

On the other hand, they didn't appear to be listening at all. Jacob had taken to kicking William under the table, and within seconds they were wrestling it out on the floor below. The whooping and hollering picked up and the table began to wriggle a few inches this way and that way as the boys took out their anger on each other.

Gene sighed, took another bite of his potatoes, and asked Charlie to pass the rolls.

Rena arrived at the crowded Gulfport train station early in the evening, ready to set off on her adventure. Behind her, Reuben droned on, giving her a lengthy list of dos and don'ts. She'd grown weary of it. Now that she had arrived—at the train station, anyway—it was time to get about the business of traveling. From this point on, she would be on her own. Well, not really on her own, exactly. The Lord would lead her every step of the way. And she would follow, no matter how difficult.

With Virginia's hand firmly linked in hers, they made their way through the noise, the smells, the people, toward the train. Reuben lugged her bags, his cheeks growing redder as they walked. A porter, a tall fellow in a black suit and cap, promised to see them delivered to her private car right away, and Reuben passed them off. Rena had fussed over the idea of a private car, but her brother had insisted. Now that she saw the crowd, she understood. Having a bit of privacy would be worth whatever price her brother had paid.

Her nostrils began to burn as the scent of burning coal filled the air. As she breathed it in, her throat burned too. And what a horrible, bitter taste! She reached for a handkerchief and pressed it to her face as a coughing fit began. Then her eyes started stinging, probably from the smoke. They filled with water, and she dabbed at them with the hankie as she struggled to catch her breath.

Reuben turned her way and waited until she regained her composure. "Now, Rena, I want you to mind who you speak to while you're on the train. You never know about people, particularly the men. And when you arrive in Daisy, please see to it that someone telephones us. I will be very concerned if I don't hear from you." He gestured to Virginia and added, "We will both be concerned, I mean."

"Yes, Reuben."

"And make sure you carry that letter to the sheriff. The one I gave you. It's filled with pertinent information about funding for the orphanage as well as a few other things he needs to know."

"Yes, Reuben."

A sudden shrill whistle filled the air, and she covered her ears for a moment. Pulling her hands back down, she found herself overwhelmed. The sound of voices with the roar of the engine and the constant flow of people kept her focus shifting all around.

Finally the moment arrived. Rena looked at the shimmer of tears in Virginia's eyes and gave her a tight hug.

"Have the time of your life," Virginia whispered. "Enjoy every moment. These adventures don't come along every day."

Rena nodded, her heart awakening at her sister-in-law's positive words.

"Be careful, and remember everything I've told you." Reuben's expression appeared stern, but Rena realized he was just anxious on her behalf. She gave him a hug then turned toward the train, ready to set off on her own.

DAISY
1912

She boarded it, leaving one world behind and facing another ahead. One final glimpse through the door offered the only temptation to turn around and go back to her former life. She saw the expression on Reuben's face…noticed the wrinkles between his brows. But instead of deterring her, she took them as a sign of release.

"No more worrying about me, brother," she whispered. "I'm a big girl. I can take care of myself."

Just as quickly, she bit back the words. She might not need her brother's care, but she would always need the Lord's. She would listen for the Almighty's voice and follow it to the best of her ability.

Rena glanced around, trying to figure out which way she needed to go. She held onto her purse as others boarded the train behind her. If only she could get to her private car quickly, then she could rest easy. One of the porters took her ticket and offered an abrupt nod.

"This way, ma'am." He led the way through the throng of people, weaving in and out. Rena found herself more than a little distracted as she sought to follow him, feeling as if her nerves could barely take much more.

Then a fellow with a cigar hanging from his lips tipped his hat at her and gave her a wink. Rena bit back a retort. Still another man paused to gaze at her, muttering something about how her blue eyes swayed him. *Honestly.* Just getting away from them might prove to be complicated. And why the sudden interest from men? In thirty-eight years, she'd scarcely had an offer to dinner, let alone anything more.

It's because you've been so wrapped up in fear.

Where the words came from, she had no idea. Sure, she'd been fearful—of life, of men, of relationships—but that was years ago. Nowadays she stayed plenty busy and conquered her fears at will. Take this trip, for instance.

This trip. Hmm. The idea of moving to a strange and unfamiliar place definitely unnerved her, even if she couldn't admit it to anyone but herself. Thank goodness she didn't have time to think about it. The porter stopped and opened the door to her private room, gesturing for her to enter. She stepped inside and was surprised at how lovely it looked. Ruffled blue-satin curtains hung in the open windows, and the ceiling was painted in a delicate scroll design.

Still, she couldn't seem to locate the bed. Before she could ask, the porter extended his hand to the wall. "When you're ready to sleep, just pull down on that latch, and it will release the bed."

"It's in the wall?" She could hardly believe such a thing.

The porter chuckled. "Yes. Let me show you." He proceeded to demonstrate, and seconds later a bed emerged from the wall, just as he'd said. He then lifted it back into place and it disappeared from view. "Will you require my assistance in unpacking your bags?"

She quickly declined his offer, convinced she needed no such help, especially from a perfect stranger. The very idea of someone seeing her garments—especially the underclothes—made her uneasy.

He took a few steps toward the door. "Well, then, is there anything I can bring you, miss? Something from the dining car, perhaps?"

When she shook her head, he paused in the doorway. Rena quickly came to her senses, fumbled through her purse, and came up with a coin to tip the fellow. He nodded and then left, closing the door behind him.

The next few minutes were spent familiarizing herself with her car and peering through the window. She couldn't get over the beautiful red, velvet-covered cushioned benches and other fineries. Yes, this would be just fine. Perhaps the journey wouldn't be as nerve-racking as she'd secretly feared.

Feared. There was that word again.

For whatever reason, she thought of Reuben. From this side of the train, she could no longer see him. Perhaps he and Virginia had already returned home.

No, knowing her brother, they would stay until the train was out of sight. He would be praying all the while—and probably hoping she would change her mind and return home where she belonged.

Home. Strange, that Gulfport would no longer be her home. From the age of fourteen, it had been the only home she'd known.

Through the open window, ash and cinders swirled about in the air, creating a dizzying haze. Rena closed the window and the dust soon settled. She sat in one of the cushioned chairs and looked down at her once-white gloves. They were smudged with soot. By the time she arrived in Daisy, they would be absolutely ruined.

Oh well. No bother. She could always buy another pair. Surely Daisy had an adequately stocked department store. And a dressmaker.

Rena turned her attention to the menu on the side table. Her stomach grumbled as she read over it. "Mmm. Steak…grilled lamb chops… and asparagus with hollandaise sauce?" She hadn't expected such a fine menu.

Rena's mouth began to water—until she thought about those people in the regular cars with their bag lunches. All those mothers and their children she had passed by on her way to her private car wouldn't be eating steak or lamb chops, would they? Suddenly Rena didn't feel so hungry.

Moments later, another shrill whistle rang out and the train jolted. Rena watched as thick black smoke and white steam filled the air on the other side of the window. The train lurched forward, and she very nearly toppled off the bench. She managed to hold on tight, but the high collar on her gray dress very nearly choked the life out of her in the process.

Why, oh, why, had she worn this particular dress? The heavy fabric bound her. Still, as one who wanted to present herself as both polished and chaste, she'd chosen what felt right in the moment. Right now she would gladly trade this constrictive dress for one of Sadie's flowing gowns.

A loud clack-clacking began, slowly at first, then faster, faster,

faster.... Rena closed her eyes and held on as the car jerked and swayed back and forth from side to side. Nausea kicked in, so she took a few deep breaths. Hopefully she wouldn't meet with fiasco this near the beginning of her trip.

When the nausea passed, she eased her eyes open. Through the window, the crowded train station disappeared from view. Leaning back, she decided to rest for a few minutes. Before long, her eyes grew heavy and she drifted off to sleep.

Chapter Five
....

TIPS FOR DEALING WITH UNRULY YOUNG'UNS—*From the day my son adopted two of the most challenging boys at the Atoka County Children's Home, I knew I had my work cut out for me. William and Jacob are a handful, to say the least. That said, I'm up to the challenge. After all, I did a fine job in raising their father. Of course, my hair went completely gray when he reached his teen years, but that's another story. And speaking of gray hairs, I've figured out why the good Lord gives children to the young. He knows that we older folks would rather give in than take the time to discipline. When my grandsons act up, I simply refer them to their father. After loading them up on homemade cookies and candy, of course.*

—Carolina Wyatt, Daisy's Favorite Grandma

Rena rested a few minutes and then began the journey to the dining car. As she made her way through the other cars, she observed her fellow passengers. All around her, people laughed and talked—whole families enjoying each other's company. Children wrestled and played together while mothers appeased them with sack lunches. Fathers read newspapers while little boys vied for their attention. And all this happened to the ever-present clack-clacking as the train rolled ever northward toward Oklahoma.

For a moment, a pang of homesickness gripped her. But just as quickly, it faded. Gulfport wasn't her home anymore. No, she must focus on her destination, not the roads leading her to this point.

She shivered in spite of her wrap, noticing that the air had cooled a bit. Of course, the farther north the train went, the colder it would be. October in Oklahoma would be a sure sight cooler than in Gulfport.

"One for dinner, miss?" a waiter in a black suit asked.

"Yes, thank you."

He disappeared for a moment and then returned. "I'm afraid we don't have a table for one. Would you mind joining a party of ladies who happen to have an extra space? They've assured me you will be welcomed, and one of them told me to promise you that they don't bite."

For a moment Rena thought about rejecting his offer. Then her empty stomach growled. "I suppose that would be fine."

She followed behind him to a table of rambunctious and somewhat rotund older women, who explained that they were on their way home to Tulsa after a wondrous adventure along the Gulf Coast. The ladies introduced themselves as Amy, Jamie, and Mamie—sisters, and very much alike in every respect, particularly when it came to their colorful attire and lavish hats.

Rena found herself caught up in their chatter, particularly when they began to share the stories behind the peculiar hats they were wearing. Only when Mamie asked about her destination did she feel comfortable chiming in.

"I'm headed to Daisy, Oklahoma, to work with children." She shared the story of finding the sheriff's letter, her enthusiasm growing as she went along. Mamie appeared to listen in rapt awe. The peacock feathers atop her large round hat moved back and forth as she fanned herself.

"Oh, you sweet girl." Amy, the sister with the black feathered straw hat, rested her hand on Rena's. "What you're doing is so admirable. Giving of yourself like that to those poor babies—what a sacrifice. I'm honored to know such a giving person."

"I don't really consider it a sacrifice," Rena said, a little startled by the woman's words of praise. "I'm sure it will be pure delight, in fact."

"Well, perhaps." Jamie, the sister with the bright red hat, looked flabbergasted at this proclamation. "But orphans? And most of them boys? You couldn't pay me enough!" She chuckled. "What a life that would be." Jamie speculated about the possibilities, and before long all the women were laughing.

Rena found herself affected by their what-if stories. "It will be quite different from what I'm used to," she said after a moment's reflection. "But I feel sure it will be an adventure."

"That it will," Mamie said. "I've no doubt about it."

Yes, indeed, it would be an adventure. But from the looks of things, the adventure had already begun. Settling in, Rena decided to enjoy every moment.

Gene glanced down at his sons, who had both fallen asleep on his mother's sofa. "Thanks again for helping with the boys today."

His mother reached for her cup of tea. "You know I love those boys to pieces, don't you? They're a handful, but I love 'em. Wouldn't trade 'em for anything in the world." She took a sip of the tea then put the delicate rose-painted cup back on its saucer.

He paused to think through what she'd said before responding. Thank goodness the boys were sleeping, so he could speak openly. Still, he lowered his voice to a whisper, just in case. "I know it was Brenda's idea to adopt them, and I went along with her." He sank into the chair across from his mother's. "If we'd had any idea how things were going to turn out…" He stopped himself before saying anything else.

How could they have known that an innocent trip to visit her ailing mother in Atoka would end in tragedy and that he would be left alone to care for the boys she'd loved so dearly?

Gene reached for his coffee cup, took a swig, then put it back down. "I'll tell you one thing that's hard to swallow."

"What's that?" his mother asked.

"If Brenda were still here, she could have fixed everything—the situation with the children at the orphanage, the behavior of William and Jacob, the problems with the mayor…all of it."

"Gene." His mother's eyes narrowed. "Brenda was a wonderful woman. Probably the best woman I've ever known. But even she didn't have that kind of power. She was human, like the rest of us."

"I'm just saying she had a way about her. She knew how to get people to go along with her. I think it's because she loved so deeply. She could get folks to do the impossible."

"You're right about that. She did have a way about her. She could charm a snake out of his venom. But, ultimately, you have to admit that even she couldn't fix things. Not really." His mother folded her hands in her lap. "Only the Lord can do that. And we have to trust Him. It might not be in our time or our way, but He hasn't forgotten these children. There are dozens of Scriptures on orphans to prove that. He's a father to the fatherless, remember?"

"I remember." How many times had he heard that since his father's death? A hundred, likely. Still, it hadn't taken root. Not really.

He thought about his mother's words on the drive to his house. After getting the boys into their beds, Gene retreated to the front porch, where he listened to the sound of the crickets in their nighttime chorus. Out here, underneath the heavy, dark skies, he finally found himself free to think, really think.

Off in the distance, he caught a glimpse of the moon covered by a thin layer of hazy clouds. Somehow, staring at the night sky reminded him of a particular night just two and a half years ago, when he and Brenda had sat under a full moon and talked about the possibility of adopting William and Jacob, two little rascally boys she'd fallen in love with. Boys who'd won her heart with both their antics and their need for parental love. How excited she had been…and how happy he had been to go along with her plan. Together, they would raise the boys to be fine young men everyone would be proud of.

Only, Brenda hadn't lived to see them grow up, and that fact nearly drove him mad at times. What sort of God would take a mother from her children? And not just any children, but orphans who'd finally found a home? It was unthinkable. And how could an all-knowing God possibly think that Gene was capable of raising these boys on his own? Did the Lord not see his shortcomings, his inability to discipline properly?

The wind whistled through the trees, sending a chill down his spine. He still couldn't feel the touch of a breeze without thinking of the tornado that had taken his wife. One strong wind had changed everything—for her, for him, and for their boys.

He rose and walked across the front yard, his gaze still focused on the stars overhead. After a few deep breaths, he finally managed to spout out a few words to the sky, arguing things out with the Almighty. On and on the words flowed. He walked and talked until he'd emptied himself of the day's anxieties. Then, as always, he begged God to forgive him for being so wishy-washy. Surely a better man could handle a couple of boys without losing his faith.

He reached into his pocket and came out with the letter from Gulfport. Miss Rena Jewel was on her way to town to take Mrs. Wabash's place. Once she arrived, all his troubles would be behind him. His faith would be restored and the children at the orphanage would be well cared for.

Until then…well, until then he would go on shouting to the sky.

Chapter Six

....

Tips for Dealing with Unruly Young'uns—*I've never been one for children. A-course, my ma tells me I used to be one. But putting up with those rascals from the orphanage—especially the boys—has worn my patience to a thread. I overlooked the time they busted out the window at the front of my barbershop, and I turned the other cheek when they lathered up my barber pole. But I refused to turn a blind eye when they used my best razor to carve their initials into my front door. My tip for dealing with unruly young'uns? Stay as far away as you can. Keep 'em at arm's length. And for Pete's sake, lock your doors. That way they can't do too much damage.*

—Joe Braswell, Daisy's Finest (and Only) Barber

Gene spent the last Wednesday afternoon in October reclining in the barber's chair at Joe's barbershop—the most popular spot in town for the menfolk. He listened to the men seated to his right and left ramble on about the weather and finally managed to get a word in edgewise. His question was meant for the barber. "Joe, can you go a little faster?"

"What's yer hurry?" Joe swiped the edge of the razor on his white jacket then returned to shaving Gene, the razor swishing this way and that across the sheriff's stubbly chin. "House on fire or sumpthin?"

Old Man Tucker laughed, his thinning wisps of hair bobbing up and down on his head. "With those boys of his, I wouldn't doubt it." He shoved his hands into the pockets of his overalls and snorted.

"Nah." Joe stopped shaving and wiped the blade once again. "A fire would be small potatoes for his boys. They're into bigger mischief these days, haven't you heard?"

Gene did his best not to groan aloud. "That's enough of that. Besides, the only fire is on my face. You using a different kind of shaving lotion or something?"

"Nope. Same old, same old." Joe scrutinized him. "If I didn't know any better, I'd say you're looking a mite frazzled today. Everything okay?"

Gene drew in a deep breath, determined to give a calm answer. "Yeah. You almost done?"

Joe nodded, flashed a smile, then gave a final swipe of the blade before setting it aside. "Hold still. I need to clean you up. Don't want you to make a bad impression."

"Bad impression?"

"Well, sure." Joe chuckled. "You think I don't know that yer meetin' a woman up at the station? Yer mama told me all about it when she stopped by earlier this morning. I think it's a fine thing she's doing, this woman. She must be a brave soul to take on those children. If she lives through it, we'll have to give her a plaque...or maybe name the town after her."

"Town already has a girly name," Tucker said, turning to look in the mirror. "Named after Daisy Beck."

"What's this new gal's name, anyway?" Joe asked. He wiped the lotion from Gene's face then covered his cheeks with a hot towel. "Yer mama didn't mention a name. Not that this gal will be stickin' around long enough to get to know it. Or her."

Gene counted to ten silently under the towel and then muttered, "Rena."

"Rena." All the men echoed the name in unison.

Pulling off the towel, Gene sat up in the chair. "Yep."

"Guess we won't be changing the name of the town after all," Tucker said. "I was hopin' she'd have a name like *Centerville* or something like that." He slapped his knee and erupted into laughter. When he finally calmed down, the men began a discussion about what Miss Jewel would look like. Old Man Tucker had his bets on a redhead. Rudy Williams insisted that she would be an older woman with white hair and arthritic joints. A couple of the other fellas figured she'd be middle-aged and plain, a spinster with no prospects.

Gene didn't want to speculate. Frankly, he didn't care what she looked like, as long as she stuck around. He'd initially taken a liking to Mrs. Wabash, after all. Before she showed how she truly felt about the children. And the director before that had seemed to be fine at first. As had the one before that. But every one had abandoned him— er, the children—in short order. Likely this one would do the same, white-headed or not.

He wouldn't allow himself to befriend the orphanage's new director, even if she did happen to be easy on the eyes...which he doubted. No, he would keep things on a business level, as always.

Off in the distance the church bells rang out the hour. Three o'clock in the afternoon. Yikes. The train would arrive shortly. He needed to meet Miss Jewel and then take her to the orphanage to introduce her to the children. Hopefully she wouldn't run for the hills at that point.

"You still with us, Gene?" The barber gave him a brusque pat on the shoulder and Gene jerked to attention. "Looked like we lost you there for a minute."

"No. Just thinking."

"No doubt thinking about that pretty gal who's about to step off the train. Well, remember, there are plenty of fine single men in town if she's not what you had in mind. All right?"

Gene groaned. When would these fellas learn that he wasn't interested? They'd be better served by talking about the weather.

Thank goodness, the conversation shifted back to just that. And before long, Old Man Tucker began talking about some sort of problem the children at the orphanage had caused in town. Just one more reason to celebrate Miss Jewel's arrival. She would be the calming factor. Yes, before long the chaos would die down and life would return to normal. Whatever that looked like.

A squeal of brakes sounded and the train jolted with such force that Rena almost toppled out of the chair where she'd been reading a book. Through the window, she saw bits of soot and ash floating in the air. They must've arrived in Daisy. She hoped so, anyway. After three days of stops and starts, she was ready to step off this train and find her legs again. And her stomach, for that matter.

She rose and did the best she could to make herself look presentable. One look in the mirror showed her that the task might be hopeless. Her hair needed a good washing, and her puffy eyes carried the weight of three days' travel.

Still, she gave it her best try, washing her face and pulling her hair up loosely. She put on a sensible, sturdy dress and buttoned her shoes before giving her cheeks a pinch to add some color. "There. Not too bad, not too bad."

A rap on the door roused her from her ponderings. "We've arrived in Daisy, miss," the porter's voice rang out. "I'll be back shortly to fetch your bags."

She spent the next few minutes organizing and packing. By the time the porter returned, she'd managed to get everything into place. She swung wide the door, offered him a smile, and gestured to the bags. Inside, she felt like mush, but on the outside she maintained a level of decorum and composure.

"All ready, I see." He nodded and took hold of the bags. "Follow me, then." He led the way through a train car still loaded with people. Most of these folk—like the trio of sisters she'd grown so fond of—were going on to Tulsa, not getting off in Daisy. In fact, hardly anyone appeared to be exiting the train. Was she the only one? Was Daisy really that small?

The three sisters approached and each took her turn wrapping Rena in her arms and offering advice.

"We're going to stay in touch, sweet girl." Mamie gave her a final squeeze. "And that's a promise."

"I'm counting on it." Rena flashed what she hoped looked like a brave smile.

As the porter took her hand to help her down from the train, she noticed he was whistling a familiar little tune. She began to hum along in unison as the melody took hold. "'Daisy, Daisy, give me your answer, do....'" She could hear the ladies singing along inside the train at the top of their lungs.

Rena couldn't help but smile...for a moment, anyway. Then the smoke cleared and she could see the town in all its glory.

What there was of it.

Turned out there was little to this place. A tiny general store with a broken sign out front. A jailhouse. An even smaller milliner's shop. A hay-and-feed store, the largest of the four. Was there even a post office? However would she mail letters to Sadie? Ah, yes, she could see the sign now. The post office was inside the general store.

She shivered and pulled her wrap tightly over her shoulders. *Yes, Reuben, you were right. It's cooler here in October.* Determined to stay positive about the situation, she took another glance about.

Off in the distance a man pushed a wooden cart loaded with goods, which he hawked to anyone willing to listen. Nearby, a handful of boys dressed in ragged overalls hovered over a game of marbles. A dog, matted and dirty, rested nearby.

"Daisy, Oklahoma, miss." The porter tipped his hat, set her bags on a bench, and extended his hand. She fumbled inside her purse for a coin, which she delivered with a half smile.

"Enjoy your stay." The porter tipped his hat once more then scurried aboard the train.

For a moment, she thought about joining him. She glanced back and noticed the three sisters in the window, who were waving like mad. Perhaps it wasn't too late to turn back. Yes, now that she'd caught a glimpse of Daisy, Gulfport was looking more appealing than ever. Or maybe she could go on to Tulsa with Amy, Jamie, and Mamie—to spend a few weeks with her new friends before heading back to Gulfport, where Reuben would give her an "I told you so" speech.

"Miss Jewel?"

Her thoughts were interrupted by a man's deep voice and she turned, her gaze falling on a fellow so rugged and handsome that he nearly took her breath away. She'd seen pictures of cowboys, of course, but none of those quite compared to this dashing fellow with the dark, wavy hair and dimpled smile.

Rena noticed the Stetson right away. And the blue jeans, starched and pressed. He wore a silver badge, pinned to his brown button-up shirt. What drew her eyes the most, however, were the broad shoulders. And the boyish smile. And those bright blue eyes. Why, this fellow would be the perfect candidate to grace the cover of her novel, should it ever be published. And with that gun strapped to his side, he was ideal "hero material" for the story inside, no doubt about it.

Heavens. Suddenly she felt a little warmer than before.

"Miss Jewel?" he said again.

Rena came to her senses. "Oh, yes. I'm Rena Jewel. And you are…?"

"Sheriff Gene Wyatt." He tipped his hat. "I'm so glad you've come. You're a godsend."

Rena managed her rehearsed speech, hoping to make a good impression. "I do hope I can be of service to the children and the community. It's my fondest wish." She offered a smile. Perhaps, if she managed to keep her head about her, he wouldn't realize just how inadequate she suddenly felt.

He gazed at her, his deep blue eyes offering a penetrating gaze. She found herself enraptured. If she were to paint them, she would choose a sky blue. No, perhaps midnight blue would be best. On the other hand, midnight blue might be a tad bit dark. His eyes were really more bright than dark, weren't they?

"Are you ready to meet the children?"

Rena jolted to attention and nodded. She secretly wished she could bathe and put on a pressed gown before meeting her young charges. In fact, she rather wished she'd had the opportunity to do that before meeting this handsome stranger. Still, what else could she do? Some things couldn't be avoided.

Rena managed a quick yes and watched as the sheriff gathered up her bags and led the way to a vehicle. He opened the passenger-side door and she climbed inside, suddenly feeling quite adventurous. As he cranked the car, she peered through the window. Off in the distance, a boy in tattered brown dungarees rolled a hoop down the road. A mangy-looking dog ran alongside him, yapping all the way. Behind them, an older man gave chase, hollering something indistinguishable.

"Gracious." She smoothed her skirt with gloved hands and sighed as he climbed into the driver's seat. "Is it always like this?"

"Nah." He shook his head and she noticed a hint of a smile. "Sometimes it's worse."

"Hmm." Perhaps the sights in Daisy were a bit different than Gulfport, but wasn't that the idea? Hadn't she come looking for new experiences? Yes, if one wanted something new and different, this was certainly the place. Now, to get this adventure underway.

Gene tried not to stare, but the woman seated next to him left him more curious than he'd imagined. She wore her light brown hair pulled back in a loose style he'd rarely seen. The dress was store-bought, no doubt about that. And it showed off her trim figure. She'd paid a pretty penny for it, to be sure. Still, he couldn't help but think it made her look a bit stiff. She didn't exactly look matronly…more cautious. Likely the children would give her even more reason to be cautious.

He did his best to make light conversation but wondered all the while just how much he should tell her. Should he warn her about her young charges—let her know what she'd be walking into? Should he mention Mrs. Wabash's reasons for her sudden departure, or just let nature take its course?

He glanced at Miss Jewel once more, noticing for the first time her delicate features, lace-trimmed gloves, and pristine movements as she brushed a loose hair from her face.

Hmm. No. No point in giving away the problem just yet. He would let the chips fall where they may. No doubt they would fall sooner rather than later.

Chapter Seven

· · · · · · · · · · · · · · · · · · · ·

Tips for Dealing with Unruly Young'uns—*As the former director of the Atoka County Children's Home, I have much to add to the discussion on child-rearing, particularly when it comes to boys. Unfortunately, much of what I would have to say could not be committed to the written page, for fear that it would be used against me as I seek employment in other faraway states. Suffice it to say, I will no longer be serving the children of Daisy, Oklahoma, as director. My wounds—physical and emotional—will heal in time, but I will not return even if they plead. The Wednesday afternoon train has carried me to a far safer place, one where the children can do me no harm. My words of wisdom for the new director? Run as fast and as furiously as you can in the opposite direction. You can thank me later for warning you.*

—Mrs. Wabash, a Reformed Lover of Small Children

As they made the drive to the orphanage, Rena tried to keep her wits about her. She found Daisy smaller than she had expected and somewhat behind the times, though she would never say so. Very few vehicles graced the main street. Folks still moved about in wagons and on horseback. That would be intimidating enough, but the clothing! She'd hardly ever seen people in such worn attire. The men, for the most part, wore overalls and graying white shirts. In spite of the cool weather, children ran about in bare feet. The women wore sensible cotton dresses much plainer than the ones she'd brought with her, and many of their dresses had faded to unrecognizable shades. Would folks find her uppity if she wore her store-bought dresses from home?

Home.

The word flitted through her mind and a pang of homesickness gripped her. She couldn't help but wonder if she'd made a mistake. But just as quickly, she scolded herself. Just because people in Daisy dressed differently didn't mean anything. Who was she to judge folks based on appearance?

Rena made up her mind to give the town a second chance. Through the window she caught a glimpse of a large ramshackle house off in the distance next to an overgrown lot high with weeds. She held her breath as he pulled up in front of it.

"Welcome to the Atoka County Children's Home." Sheriff Wyatt turned off the car and got out. He came around to her side and opened the door. Though hesitant, she stepped out, her gaze shifting to the house before her.

Rena took in the dilapidated brown building—the sagging roof, the rotted porch, the woodwork in need of painting—and immediately felt her throat constrict. She knew that tears would shortly follow. She'd pictured a great many things, but not this. Never in her born days had she seen a home so broken down, so in need of repair. "This…this is it?" she managed at last.

"It is." The sheriff opened the half-broken front gate and ushered her inside. "I know it's not much to look at. But it's a fine old building." His brow wrinkled as he turned back to face her. "Please give it a try?"

DAISY
1912

"Yes, of course." Rena's years at the Villa in Gulfport had done little to prepare her for such a home, but to snub it because of its age would be wrong. Perhaps the outside appearance was deceiving. Surely the inside would be better. She would not panic, regardless. Perhaps this was one reason the Lord had brought her here, to shine a light on the problem. Surely the missions society would help once they learned of the home's poor condition. She hoped so, anyway.

"Can I meet the children now?" she asked, more determined than ever.

"You sure you're ready?" The sheriff quirked a brow, and for a moment she thought she saw a hint of a nervous smile on that handsome face. Was he teasing her, perhaps? If so, she wouldn't allow him to deter her from the path she was meant to follow.

"Why, of course. I wouldn't come all this way, otherwise. I've been ready for days. I've thought of little else." Squaring her shoulders, she offered up a silent prayer that the Lord would go before her and make her path straight. She also added a quick *And give me courage, Lord!* addendum to stop her knees from shaking.

He cleared his throat. "Fine, then. Our former director, Mrs. Wabash, left just this afternoon, so my mother has been watching the children in her stead. They're inside, waiting. I know they're very excited to meet you."

He swung wide the door and gestured for her to step inside the empty foyer. Rena had no sooner taken the first step than an avalanche of water soaked her from above. Shaken, she glanced up and noticed the tipped bucket suspended from the door. She shivered and tried to gather her thoughts, but it was no use. Water dripped from her new skirt into puddles on the floor below. In desperation, she looked at the sheriff, hoping he would help her make sense of this.

Instead, he hollered out, nearly deafening her: "William and Jacob, you get your tails out here at once before I knock you into tomorrow."

Two sandy-haired, freckle-faced little boys appeared from the next room with sheepish grins on their faces. The one with the milk moustache looked to be seven or eight. He took one look at her soggy attire and erupted into laughter. Seconds later, the other one—probably nine or ten—joined in. Rena did her best not to cry, though tears willed themselves to come. She drew a deep breath and did her best to stop shaking.

The sheriff grabbed the boys by the ears and pressed them in her direction. "Miss Jewel, meet my two boys, William and Jacob. They've got a dozen or more friends nearby, I've no doubt." He paused and looked around. "Might as well c'mon out. Miss Jewel will likely forgive you for the impromptu baptism if you ask nice and proper, but I wouldn't hold to her sticking around very long if you don't."

From around every corner they came. Scraggly-looking boys, mostly, but three girls too. A ragtag lot of them, wearing clothing in sizes that made no sense to their bodies. The girls, pretty as they were, needed someone to tend to their matted hair. And whatever did they do for shoes? One of the girls—the one with the long, blond hair—wore a little locket around her neck, which she fingered as she gazed Rena's way.

The children put Rena in mind of street urchins, though she never would have voiced that sentiment aloud. She took them in with a gaze—every last one of them—and the water incident slowly faded from her mind. All that mattered now were these precious children. Their darling faces shone with excitement. At least it looked like excitement. A couple of them, both girls, muttered something that sounded like an apology. The boys stood back, their arms crossed at their chests, and glowered.

"You think you're ready for this?" The sheriff turned her way, a hint of panic in his eyes.

She nodded, reaching down and squeezing the excess water out of her dress. It dribbled onto the floor. "I'm as ready as I'll ever be."

An older woman in a flowered blue dress appeared in the opening leading to the hallway. She rushed Rena's way, her hands clasped together over her chest. "Oh, you poor, sweet girl. Whatever have these little monsters done now?" She took one look at Rena's wet attire and began to cluck her tongue at the children. They responded with more giggles.

"I'm Carolina, honey. Gene's mother." The woman brushed back the loose gray hair around her face. "I do hope you'll forgive the way I look. I had to make a quick dash to my place for some butter. I was only gone a few minutes." She looked Rena over and shook her head. "I can see now that they just wanted to get me out of here to accomplish this dastardly deed. How they managed to get that bucket hung in such a short amount of time is nothing short of miraculous. We could fault their actions, certainly, but I've got to admit, they're very efficient. They know how to get things done in a hurry."

Rena hardly knew what to say. Apparently a great deal of effort had gone into her welcome. The children must be delighted with themselves. Should she counter their move with quick, strong discipline, or turn a blind eye?

The youngest of the girls smiled, and Rena's heart melted like butter left out in the afternoon sun. She would turn a blind eye, at least for now.

"Well, c'mon in, hon," Carolina added. "I'm going to have the girls draw you a bath while I finish making your supper. You look exhausted. No point in feeding you until you're clean and dry. Sound good?"

"Sounds wonderful. I'm long overdue for a good soak."

Carolina sent the three little girls upstairs with Rena's bags in hand. They were given specific instructions to draw her bath as well. Rena began to relax, finally letting her guard down. She gave the parlor another quick glance but then wished she hadn't. Nothing about the place held any appeal, from the worn curtains to the torn paper on the walls to the uneven floors.

"Gene, why don't you give Miss Jewel the grand tour and then point her in the direction of her room? Her bath should be ready in a few minutes." Carolina retied her apron and turned back toward the kitchen. "All this nonsense will wash away with a good hot bath, Miss Jewel. I promise you, you'll feel better once you're clean and dry."

Rena nodded, realizing how good that sounded.

"I'd be happy to show her around first," Gene said, giving his mother a nod. Then he turned to Rena. "You ready for a quick look-see?"

"I guess." She followed along behind the sheriff as he showed off the various areas of the old home. The downstairs areas were in great need of updating, especially the furniture. The sofa had broken springs, the wingback chair was barely standing, and the end table looked as if someone had taken a knife to it. Were those initials in the arms? There were no pictures on the walls and no flowers or any other decor in sight. Everything was stark and broken-down. Well, all but the sheriff. He appeared to be in great shape. Her cheeks grew warm as the thought flitted through her mind. Heavens. Who knew she noticed such things?

Gene led her up the stairs and into the children's areas. The section that housed the girls didn't look too bad. It was small but cozy. She'd never seen so many beds pressed into one room, however, and the place was rather stark. Metal bed frames, white sheets, brown blankets... nothing at all like the bedrooms back home.

"Has anyone ever given thought to painting in here?" she asked. "I do think a nice coating of soft pink paint would make it feel girlier."

Judging from the smile, he appeared to find great humor in the idea. "Don't suppose anyone would mind."

The boys' area left Rena reeling. For one thing, none of the beds had been made. The paint was cracking, the ceiling was leaking, and the floor was creaking. And those beds! Broken-down. Rusty. Missing pieces. Talk about hideous. How the boys could sleep on something so primitive was beyond her. She would have to arrange for new beds to be sent as soon as possible. A good night's sleep would do wonders for the children and help them with their studies as well.

Gene continued showing her around, focusing on the remaining downstairs rooms at the front of the house. The parlor was far too small for social gatherings. Where did the children play? Was there no space to gather with friends and share in an afternoon's activities?

"Where do the children socialize?" she asked after seeing the entire home.

"Beg pardon?" He gave her a funny look.

"Play. Where do they play?"

"Ah." He shrugged. "I guess you could say the town is their playground."

"But there's no area here for them to just be children?" she asked. "No rope swings? No parklike areas to run freely and get the necessary exercise? However do you expect them to stay healthy if they can't go outdoors to burn off energy and be in the sunshine?"

He still looked perplexed. "There's a small yard out back. They make do. But, as I said, they have the whole town."

"Surely you don't mean that they roam about the town on their own."

"Oh, I…" He paused. "Well, I guess that'll have to change. We've always just sorta expected it. They show up all sorts of places in town. Mrs. Wabash tried to curtail some of their extracurricular activities, but they were left to their own devices much of the time."

Rena shook her head, unable to fathom such a thing. If the children ventured into town, who watched over them to make sure they weren't up to mischief? "I can assure you that will not be the case now that I'm here. I firmly believe in spending time with the children. Roaming about the town is not my idea of child's play."

A little girl tugged on her arm and Rena glanced down, taken in by the welcoming smile. The youngster had a beautiful face, but seeing it through the unruly dark hair was not easy. "Miss Jewel, I'm Callie."

"Nice to meet you, Callie. And you can call me Miss Rena."

"Miss Rena, your bath is drawn."

"Yes, do go up and relax," Carolina said, appearing from the kitchen. "You will feel so much better afterward."

Rena took a couple of steps away then turned back as she heard the sheriff's voice. "I hope you will forgive the boys for getting you wet earlier. I feel sure it was just a prank to welcome you to the fold. It won't happen again."

Rena nodded and turned to face him. "Guess I'd better go on up. Will I see you at supper?"

"I'll be the one roping the boys to their chairs."

She had to look twice to see the twinkle in his eyes.

"We put your bags on your bed, Miss Rena." The girl with the blond hair offered a sweet smile.

"And put lots and lots of bubbles in your bath," the littlest girl added. "Hope you like 'em."

"Oh, I adore bubble baths." She offered the children a smile of thanks. "And I'm in need of a hot soak. That train trip wore me out."

"Well, take your time, honey," Carolina added. "When you're done, c'mon down for supper. I've prepared a meal fit for a king."

"Smells heavenly. I can't wait."

Rena followed behind the girls, who led her up the stairs. With each step, her hands quivered and her knees grew wobblier. Probably exhaustion. Either that, or fear had suddenly locked her in its grip.

"This is your room, Miss Rena," the younger girl said. "Ain't it purty?"

"It's lovely," Rena said. She took in the room, somewhat surprised to find it in good condition, right down to the four-poster bed and chenille spread. Likely Mrs. Wabash had left it this way for her benefit. Rena would have to remember to send her a note of thanks.

"Yer bath is just past that door." As Callie pointed, the dirt under her fingernails came into full view. Rena would have to do something about that. Tomorrow.

In the meantime, she just needed to bathe, eat, and collapse onto the bed. Rena nodded and thanked the girls as they left her alone.

A yawn threatened to escape as she made her way into the bathroom and saw the large claw-footed tub overflowing with bubbles. The girls had outdone themselves. Double-checking the door to make sure it was locked, she slipped out of her clothes, readying herself for a good, long soak.

She stepped into the tub then eased her way into the water. As she attempted to sit, something sharp jabbed her in the backside—and not just in one spot, but several.

Rena let out a holler then came shooting up out of the water, rubbing her bare backside. "What in the world?" She reached down into the bubbly water, coming up with several large pinecones. And pebbles. Dozens and dozens of pebbles.

"Those children!" She wrapped herself in a towel, leaned over the tub, and fished out every last offending object Then, convinced it was safe, she climbed into the tub once again.

Unfortunately, she'd somehow missed the biggest threat of all: a large, unhappy lizard.

From the floor above, Gene heard Miss Jewel let out a yelp. At once he turned to look at the children. Lilly, the youngest of the girls, giggled. The other two girls turned red in the face. A couple of the boys began to cough, and William and Jacob snorted with laughter.

"Okay, 'fess up. What have you done to her this time?"

Lilly paled. "What do you mean?"

"You know perfectly well. That was a holler I just heard, and it was coming from—" He never had time to say "Miss Jewel," because she let out another cry from above. He sprinted up several stairs then stopped cold, realizing he couldn't interrupt her bath to rescue her. "Mother!" He aimed his voice in the direction of the kitchen. "Mother, I need you."

She appeared in the hallway, wiping her hands on her apron. "What is it, Gene? I'm trying to make supper for this crew."

"Something's wrong with Miss Jewel. Didn't you hear her cry out?"

"No, I couldn't hear anything from the kitchen. Are you sure she—" Another piercing cry sent a shiver through the room. At this point, the three girls looked at each other, unable to hide their mischievous grins.

Gene's mother sprinted up the stairs and disappeared into the corridor. A couple of minutes later she reappeared, shaking her fist in the direction of the children. "You've done it this time, haven't you? Don't think you're going to get away with this one. Putting pinecones and pebbles into her bubble bath isn't a very nice how-do-you-do, now, is it?"

Gene turned to face the girls, flabbergasted. "You put pinecones in the tub?"

"That's not all," his mother added, easing her way down the stairs. She held out her hand and a wet lizard slithered off, dropping to the floor and disappearing lickety-split into the dining room.

Gene's mother ran after the lizard, and he turned his attention to the children. "I cannot believe you would do this to her, her first night here. Shame on you."

"It was William's idea," Lilly said, her eyes now brimming with trears. "He told me to."

"And I suppose if he told you to jump off of a bridge, you would do that too?"

Lilly's eyes widened and she shook her head. "No, sir."

Gene dropped onto the sofa in the living room, closed his eyes, and wondered if Miss Jewel would last the night, let alone till May.

Chapter Eight

. . . .

Tips for Dealing with Unruly Young'uns—*I've only been a father for two and a half years, and I have to confess, my situation is different from most because of my wife's passing. Still, I can't help but think that some folks just get too riled up where children are concerned. They make mountains out of molehills. My suggestion? When your children are naughty, don't overreact, and don't take their bad behavior personally. If you're doing the best job you can as a parent, you can't allow others to bring you down, even if the children thrive on disgracing you. Remember, all children act up. Even the best child has a rough day. It's not the parent's fault. Well, most of the time it's not. Just do your best to build trust and establish authority, and the children will eventually outgrow their poor behavior. I hope.*

> —Gene Wyatt, Local Sheriff and Father to William and Jacob

In spite of the startling face-to-face encounter with the soggy lizard, Rena managed to calm down after Carolina carried him off to the great unknown. She somehow talked herself into climbing back into the tub, where she took the fastest bath ever. So much for relaxing. As she bathed, a thousand thoughts rolled through her mind. How would she ever manage with children such as these? Clearly, they were as far removed from Sadie as one could imagine. Add to that the fact that they seemed intent on bringing her down…

A shiver wriggled down her spine. In all of her thirty-eight years she'd never encountered such opposition, and in such a short period of time too.

"Reuben, you were right," she whispered. "I wasn't prepared for this."

Still, what could she do? There were choices to be made, and she was the only one to make them. After a few moments of silent prayer, she rose from the tub, dried off, and dressed for dinner in her most practical, clean, brown dress. No point in putting on airs when those around her were doing without.

Staring at her reflection in the mirror, Rena felt herself emboldened with courage. "I can either let them win or beat them at their own game," she said.

Yes, she would face these children without flinching. She would show them…all of them.

Rena did her best to pull her damp hair into a sensible style, gave herself another glance in the mirror, then headed downstairs for dinner.

As she entered the dining room, the sheriff took one look at her and sighed. "I hardly know what to say in response to what they've done to you this time. 'I'm sorry' hardly seems adequate."

With a wave of her hand, she attempted to dismiss his concerns. There was no point in letting him think she was weak. "Think nothing of it."

"Nevertheless, the children have something to say to you."

He gathered them together, and Rena gazed down at their faces, innocent and sweet. Clearly a facade.

"Go ahead." The sheriff nudged the blond girl after introducing her as Josephine.

The youngster shifted her gaze to the floor. "I'm sorry…," she muttered, adding, "…we got caught" under her breath.

Rena pursed her lips. After a second's thought, she knelt beside the girl. "I'm not sorry you got caught. I always think it's better to get things out in the open, don't you?"

Josephine shrugged.

"Getting things out is for the best." Rena gazed into the youngster's eyes. "Sometimes we do things for reasons we don't even recognize at the moment. Surely you didn't realize your little prank would startle me so."

"Oh yes she did!" the littlest girl piped up. "We all did! We've been planning it for days. Henry showed us how to weigh the pinecones down with rocks. We even did a practice run on Mrs. Wabash."

The sheriff groaned and leaned against the wall, his slumped posture a sure sign that he'd given up on these children. Rena couldn't really blame him. No doubt he'd seen many more of these types of shenanigans and had grown weary of it all.

"Hmm." Rena rose and looked over the group. "Well, you've had your fun. And I have to admit, you got me." She offered a smile. "But it will be the last time. Have I made myself clear?"

The boys and girls nodded.

Carolina appeared, looking a bit winded. "Got that rascally lizard and showed him the back door. He won't be back anytime soon." A more relaxed smile took over. "Everyone ready for supper?"

Rena wasn't sure how they'd transitioned from "lizard" to "supper" but did find herself hungry. Hopefully the children hadn't poisoned the food. The very thought made her sick to her stomach.

She followed the crowd into the dining room. Gracious, however would they fit so many in such a small space? Why, this room was

scarcely big enough for two tables, let alone one, two, three, four...
twenty chairs.

"Please be our guest." Carolina gestured to the seat at the head of the table. "We want to welcome you in style."

"Pretty sure we already did that," the sheriff muttered as he took a seat beside her.

Thankfully, the meal passed with little incident. Carolina's pot roast was every bit as good as Virginia's, if not better. As they ate, Rena was peppered with questions about her life in Gulfport. She did her best to answer them, though she grew wearier as the meal passed. Thinking of Gulfport reminded her that she needed to telephone Reuben, to let him know she had arrived safely. Surely there would be time for that tomorrow.

By the time they reached dessert—a lovely strawberry shortcake— she could barely keep her eyes open. Still, she had no choice. The director of an orphanage must be alert, especially with children such as these. And she did want to make a good impression on the sheriff. No point in having him doubt her abilities, at least not yet. There would likely be plenty of opportunity for that later.

When the meal ended, Carolina dismissed the boys and girls, sending them off to brush their teeth and change into their nightclothes. The sheriff—God bless him—began to clear the table. Rena would have to remember to thank him later. He disappeared into the kitchen with an armful of dirty dishes.

"Let's sit and chat for a spell," Carolina said. "I'm sure you have a lot of questions for me."

She nodded. Above her head, the ceiling began to quiver and shake. She could hear the children running and shouting upstairs. A couple of the boys hollered out obscenities. Just about the time she started to rise to deal with it, Carolina headed for the stairs. Seconds later, the buffalo stomping ended.

When she returned, Carolina gestured for Rena to relax. "Now, back to those questions. What can I do to help make your transition here smoother?"

As Rena looked around at the mess the children had made, several questions ran through her mind. In all the years she had lived with her brother and his wife, there had always been housekeepers to keep things tidy. Who cared for such things here? Would that fall to her? And what about the cooking? Who would manage the meals?

Fear swept over her. Why hadn't she thought this through? Would she have to prepare meals for seventeen children, morning, noon, and night? Rena found herself in a panic at the very idea. Still, she couldn't let her anxiety show.

Take a deep breath.

She turned to look at Carolina, knowing she must voice her questions aloud. Steadying her voice, she said, "Well, I do have a question about housework and such."

"What is that, dear?"

"The last director—she did everything for the children? Besides caregiving, I mean. Was she responsible for the upkeep of the house?"

"Well, the children are responsible for making their own beds and tidying up after themselves." Carolina pointed at the messy tables, the overturned chairs, and the messy floor underneath it all. "Though you can see how well that's working out. I'm sure you saw the boys' area upstairs."

"Yes." Rena bit her lip. "There's work to be done in convincing them, I see. I, well, I do have to wonder about something else. What about food? Who does the cooking?"

"Ah." Carolina nodded. "Mrs. Wabash was a wonderful cook. One of the best in the county, actually. The children were a bit spoiled in that regard."

"I see." Should Rena mention that she usually burned the toast and overcooked the eggs? Should she add that the cook in Gulfport had forbidden her from helping in the kitchen for fear that she would burn the house down? Why, oh, why hadn't she thought about this in advance? Her confidence faded more with each passing moment.

The sheriff reentered the room and reached for several more plates. She stood to help him, but he gestured for her to sit. "No, please. It's the least I can do."

Rena nodded and sat once more.

Carolina reached over and patted her hand. "Don't fret over the cooking just yet, honey. I've put together a list of ladies from the church. They'll come by to help you over the first couple weeks until you learn your way around the kitchen. And Jenny Jamison, our teacher, will help, too. She's a peach. I just know you're going to love her. Besides, I had a feeling you would need time to adjust."

Rena was struck with an idea. "Do you suppose you could spend a little time helping me with the meals the children love most? I'd like to cook the things they enjoy, but I'll need a bit of assistance."

"Of course. Happy to do it. I'm at home in the kitchen, as are most of the women in town."

A wave of relief washed over Rena. "Thank you so much. And what about the laundry? Do I...I mean, am I responsible for..." The words sounded ridiculous even to her own ears. Still, she'd barely laundered her own clothes, let alone the clothes of others.

"Mr. Kovach, the laundry man, comes around on Saturdays to pick up the week's laundry. He sends a bill every month, but the missions society covers it. The children know to put their laundry in the bin on Saturday mornings. You can do the same with your personal items, but be advised that Mr. Kovach often loses things, so hand-wash anything you might be attached to."

"I will do that." Rena leaned back in her chair, feeling a mixture of exhaustion and relief. She wouldn't have to handle all this on her own, at least not yet.

"Just relax, Rena," Carolina said. "Your primary task here is to make sure that the children are cared for. I think it would also be a lovely idea to train the little girls to be ladies, if such a thing is possible." She paused. "And the boys…they need attention, lots of attention. Most of all, they need your love, as you will quickly learn."

"That, I can give them." Rena smiled, feeling more hopeful than she had since her arrival. "I've plenty of love to give."

"I've sensed that about you," Carolina said with a reassuring smile. "You strike me as someone who has a full heart, spilling over. You must be well versed in the Scriptures, to have such a sweet countenance."

Unaccustomed to such flattery, Rena felt heat rise to her cheeks. "I've had plenty of time on my hands, since I've not had a family of my own to raise. So, yes, I've spent a great deal of time studying the Scriptures. My brother is a reverend, and so was my father." A lump rose in her throat as she mentioned her father. "We have a great love for the Bible and for those less fortunate."

"Then surely you know the verse about tending to the widows and orphans." Carolina put her hand on Rena's arm. "What you're doing—sacrificing your time, your plans, your own personal life— is admirable. It's also biblical. If you ever feel like running for the hills, remember that caring for the orphans has always been something God smiles upon."

Rena nodded, suddenly feeling better about her situation. If, indeed, God was smiling on her situation, then surely He would give her the wherewithal to see it through. Another yawn escaped.

"Sweet girl, I can tell you're exhausted." Carolina rose and gestured for her to do the same.

The sheriff appeared just in time to help Rena with her chair. She gave him a shy smile, and he responded with a crooked grin. She couldn't have sketched a finer portrait for the cover of her novel.

Not that he would ever know she penned stories. Oh no. She would hide that fact from everyone in town, just as she'd done back home.

Home.

There was that word again.

Oh well. No time like the present to start thinking of Daisy as her home away from home. What else could she do, really?

Gene noticed the shy smile from Miss Jewel and responded with a grin. Her gaze lingered on him for a moment longer than he expected, and he found himself feeling a bit unnerved. Was she working up the courage to quit already? Would he end up hauling her bags back to the train station before morning?

With his mother leading the way, the ladies walked into the front hall. Gene lagged behind in the dining room, knowing that he should finish clearing the tables. Still, there was one thing he needed to do first.

"Miss Jewel?" He called her name and she turned his way.

"I want you to know that we've heard from another interested party—someone who is willing to come in May to take over the orphanage full-time."

"Ah."

Not much of a response, really, but he could read the relief in her eyes.

"Yes." He nodded. "I would've written to tell you, but I've only just learned myself."

His mother took Miss Jewel's hand and gave it a squeeze. "It will be your choice, of course, dear. We just wanted to give you the choice to go, should you decide to."

A hopeful shimmer lit her eyes, which gave Gene the courage to continue. "No doubt your family back home would be thrilled to have you back before summer."

"No doubt." A look of sadness swept over her briefly, and he wondered if she was already battling homesickness. "Oh, and speaking of my family, I wonder if you could tell me how to go about telephoning my brother to let him know I've arrived."

"There's a phone at the jail. I'd be happy to make the call tomorrow."

"I would be grateful." Her shoulders slumped forward, and he thought for a moment that she might fall asleep standing up. Instead, she offered him a weak smile. "And thank you for doing the dishes, by the way. I'm sure things will settle down before long."

She'd no sooner spoken the words than the herd of buffalo above took to stomping and screaming again. A couple of the boys—likely his—had taken to fighting at the top of the stairs.

Gene bounded up the stairs once more, took William and Jacob by the collars, and led them back down downstairs. "Sit in the dining room until we're ready to leave," he said. "I don't want to hear a peep out of either of you."

"But, Pa, he called me a sissy." William scowled and crossed his arms over his chest.

"I've told you a thousand times to treat each other as you would want to be treated."

"That's the Bible's way," Rena added. "'Do unto others—'"

"*Before* they do unto you." Jacob punched his brother again. "I always do things the Bible's way."

Rena looked stunned by their behavior. "Doing what's right isn't easy," she said. "But we're to do unto others as we would have them do unto us. That means we treat them kindly if we want to be treated kindly."

William muttered, "He don't want to be treated kindly, trust me," before slugging his brother back.

Jacob doubled up his fists and put them in the air, but Gene pressed them down. "Enough. Go. Sit."

The boys retreated to the dining room, and he glanced at Miss Jewel. The weariness in her eyes spoke volumes. She wouldn't last long. Just like Mrs. Wabash. And the director before her. And the one before her.

"Well, I guess I'd better tuck in the children then head to bed myself." She stifled a yawn. "These last couple of days have been exhausting."

"Just one thing before you go up," he said, reaching out and touching her arm.

She gazed at him, her brow wrinkled. "Yes?"

"Thank you. From the bottom of my heart, thank you."

It took the better part of an hour to get the children settled down. Rena had enough trouble keeping all their names straight: Lilly, Josephine, Wesley, David, Oliver, Callie, and at least a dozen more. However would she remember them all?

No time to worry about that now. She went about settling disputes, one on top of another. She then picked up at least a dozen articles of clothing from the floor in the boys' room. From the top of the stairs she offered an exhausted good-bye to the sheriff and his mother, who headed home with the sheriff's two boys in tow.

By the time she retreated to her bedroom, Rena could scarcely think straight. She felt the sting of tears but pushed them away, determined not to give in to the emotions. Instead, she dressed for bed, spent a few minutes unpinning her hair, and stared at her exhausted reflection in the mirror.

"Ugh." No woman thirty-eight years of age should have bags under her eyes.

Still, she'd earned them, hadn't she?

She walked over to the dresser, wondering if she should take the time to unpack her clothes and put them away. Determined to get the job done before settling into bed, she pulled the handle on the top drawer. It fell off in her hand. She reached for the handle on the second drawer. Same thing. The third worked, but as soon as she pulled the drawer open, its contents fell out all over the floor with a loud clatter.

"What in the world?"

Someone had put the drawer in upside down. She knelt on the floor to have a look at what had fallen and nearly lost her breath when she found several marbles, which rolled across the uneven floor and under her bed. She scrambled to fetch them, but it was no use. Though they were out of sight, she could still hear them rolling.

From outside her door, Rena heard giggling and realized that the perpetrators were nearby.

"Get back in bed," she called out. "I mean it."

A scuffle of feet against the wooden floor convinced her they'd headed down the hall. Still, she could hardly compose herself. Now, seated on the floor, she began to cry. Her tears fell—slowly at first and then with abandon. So much for thinking she would unpack tonight. After a few deep, cleansing breaths, she willed herself to settle down. And after a few moments, she found herself wrapped in a quiet calm. Finally.

Reaching into her bag, she came up with a carefully wrapped teacup and saucer. She unwrapped the layers of dish towels surrounding the pieces and then put the precious items on the dresser. Willing the tears not to return, she fingered the hand-painted saucer. Silly, she knew, to care so deeply about a teacup and saucer. But they had belonged to her mother. Oh, how she missed her.

Rena stuck her hand into her bag and came out with the china doll, one her mother had given her as a youngster. It, like the cup and saucer, had survived the house fire that had taken her parents from her. A lump rose in her throat as she clutched the doll to her chest. The tears started again.

Not tonight, Rena. You have enough on your mind without going there.

Composing herself and settling into the four-poster bed, Rena's thoughts began to tumble. The sheriff's words replayed themselves in her mind: *"We've heard from another interested party—someone who is willing to come in May to take over the orphanage full-time."* Could she possibly manage until then?

"It's only for seven months," she whispered, before rolling over in the bed. "It's only for seven months."

Chapter Nine

....

TIPS FOR DEALING WITH UNRULY YOUNG'UNS—*When it comes to child-rearin', the Bible is filled with pertinent advice. We're taught to train up our children in the way they should go and when they're old they will not depart from it (Proverbs 22:6). We're instructed to diligently teach our children, talking about God's precepts as we come and go (Deuteronomy 6:7). We're told to not provoke our children, lest they become discouraged, and we're instructed to bring them up in the nurture and admonition of the Lord (Ephesians 6:4). Most of all, we are to love them as we want to be loved. This is, perhaps, the hardest commandment of all, particularly in the town of Daisy.*

—Reverend Thomas Harding, Pastor of
Daisy Community Church

Rena spent the first few days in Daisy acquainting herself with the children. In spite of their previous antics, most were adorable, on the outside. Deceptively adorable. What was it the Bible said about wolves in sheep's clothing? Oh well. She would conquer her fear of wolves soon enough. What these youngsters needed was a good old-fashioned church service to get them walking the straight and narrow. Though she couldn't imagine getting seventeen children dressed and ready for a Sunday morning walk to church, she would give it her best shot.

On Saturday morning she arose and dressed then went to wake the boys. They fought one another to get to the water closet just outside their room. Next Rena headed to the girls' room. The little darlings had somehow managed to sleep through all the noise coming from the rowdy boys next door. As she gazed down at Lilly, her heart began to flutter. The child—just a wisp of a thing—was so innocent. When sleeping, anyway.

Rena wrinkled her nose as a pungent odor greeted her. The room had a—what was that? musty? moldy?—smell. Everything would need a thorough cleaning, and the sooner the better.

She called Lilly by name and then rested her hand on the little girl's shoulder.

Lilly awoke abruptly, let out a cry, and pulled the covers over her head as soon as she saw Rena. Then she began to cry.

"What is it, honey?" Rena asked.

Callie yawned and stretched in the next bed. The youngster's eyes grew wide as Rena started to sit on the edge of Lilly's bed. "No, Miss Rena, don't sit down!"

"Why?" Rena rose to a standing position.

"Because." Callie lowered her voice to a whisper as she scrambled out from under the covers. "Lilly, um…she probably wet the bed again."

"Ah." Rena took a little step back. She gestured toward the hall and Callie followed her.

"Has this been going on long?" Rena whispered.

Callie nodded and continued to speak in a lowered voice. "She don't want anyone to know, but she pees the bed most every night. Sometimes I wake her up really early and take her to the water closet, but sometimes even then…" Her words faded.

"Ah." Rena pursed her lips and thought through her response.

"She takes her nightgown and wads it up under the bed, but it smells real bad," Callie said. "And her sheets stink too." An innocent shrug followed. "We got used to it after a while. Hardly even notice it anymore."

"Still…" Rena paused and tried to think of what to do. She didn't want to humiliate Lilly, but how could she handle it otherwise? She thought for a moment longer. "I'll tell you what," she said at last. "This will be our little secret. If you're willing to pull off the wet sheets whenever Lilly has an accident, you can put them under the bed with the wet nightie. I'll come along and fetch all the wet things after you children go to school, and I'll make over the bed with clean linens. In the meantime, I'll switch out the mattress with a spare one from the extra bed and figure out some way to protect it underneath the sheets."

Callie smiled and reached out to squeeze Rena's hand. "Thank you for not yelling at her."

"Yelling at her?"

"Yes." Tears brimmed the youngster's lashes. "When Mrs. Wabash would catch her, she would say horrible things to Lilly. She called her a pee-pot and made her cry. It was awful…for all of us."

Rena shook her head. "I never understood such behavior from adults. To demean a child is…" She shook her head, unwilling to finish her thoughts aloud. "At any rate, please tell Lilly that she needn't worry, should an accident occur again. But also please tell her not to drink water just before bed. That will help a lot."

"Yes, ma'am." Callie gave her a wink. "It's our little secret."

"And we will think of what else we can do to get this under control," Rena said, still deep in thought about the situation. "Perhaps a visit to the doctor is in order to make sure she is in good health."

"Lilly don't like Doc Moseley," Callie said. "The last time Mrs. Wabash took her, she bit him right on the arm."

"Not a pleasant scenario for patient or doctor, then." Rena paused. "Well, go on back in your room and help Lilly. Make sure Josephine wakes up too. She's still sleeping. We have a lot of work to do around here today."

"Josephine is spoiled rotten." Callie rolled her eyes. "She ain't never had to get up early or work or nuthin'. Says her mama made the servants do all the work."

"Ah." Rena hardly knew what to say in response. Still, her heart went out to Josephine. Living in an orphanage would be quite a shock to a youngster from a well-to-do family.

The rest of the morning was spent in getting the laundry situation under control. Mr. Kovach arrived promptly at eight that morning to take away the dirties and leave them with the clean clothes from the week prior. Sorting through everything almost proved to be Rena's undoing. Thank goodness Carolina arrived just in time to help. Together, they managed to get the job done.

The schoolteacher, a pretty young woman named Jenny Jamison, stopped by with the noon meal. She'd prepared sandwiches, lemonade, and potato salad. Somehow she managed to keep the children from fighting while they ate—not a minor feat. She promised to come by again later in the week to check on everyone. Rena had a feeling Jenny would be a great friend.

Late that afternoon, the reverend stopped by. He was kind enough, even offering to tutor her in what the Bible had to say about child-rearing. She found herself growing uncomfortable with the length, width, and breadth of his dissertation and prayed that tomorrow morning's sermon wouldn't be quite as dull as this speech.

His words were cut short by an act of fate—or, rather, the act of a small boy throwing a rock at the dining room window and shattering it into tiny shards all over the room. This was, thank goodness, enough to send the reverend packing. The incident left Rena shaken, however. As she swept up the glass, she thought about her own fragile emotions. They weren't in much better shape right now than this window, were they? If only someone would sweep in and piece her shattered thoughts and emotions together again. Then, perhaps, she could handle everything.

By the time the day wound down, Rena was exhausted. She was also extremely confused about the children's names. Determined to find a solution to that dilemma, she pulled out her notebook and made a list:

Lilly: The youngest girl. Six? Seven? Black hair. Precious smile. Speaks with a lisp. Shows a lot of emotion, both good and bad. Cries, kisses, and hugs a lot. Wets the bed. Like so many of the children, was left homeless after a tornado swept through Atoka County two years ago.

Callie: Lilly's older sister. Maybe nine or so? Matted dark brown hair. Not as precocious. Stares at her reflection in the mirror a lot but doesn't appear to like what she sees. Very protective of her younger sister.

Josephine: Blond. Approximately eleven years old. Comes from money and doesn't seem to be adjusting well to having none. According to Carolina, both parents died in a house fire last year. No living relatives.

Rena's thought shifted to the boys. What a handful they were! Why hadn't the sheriff warned her in his letter that the new director would be walking into the equivalent of a barroom brawl, only with younger participants?

She paused to think about each boy and then began writing.

Wesley: Stringy blond hair. Needs a haircut. Ten years old. Likes to talk about his grandfather, who was a (supposed) hero in the War between the States.

Oliver: Light brown hair, a bit too long. About eight years old. Repeats everything everyone says. Will have to figure out a way to stop this annoying habit. Another parentless victim of the tornado.

Mochni: Atoka boy. Beautiful dark skin. Claims to be a distant relative of Choctaw warrior Captain Atoka. His name means "Talking Bird." That would account for the nonstop chatter.

Kenny and Kieren: Twin boys from Ireland. Came by ship with their mother, who died en route to Tulsa two and a half years ago. The boys talk at length about the big ship that brought them here, and both hope to be captains. Or pirates. I'm not sure which.

Mikey, Bubba, and Tree: Three sandy-haired boys with dirty faces who all hail from the same family. Ages range from six to ten. Maybe. Tree, the little one, could be a bit younger. (Note: I have no idea why any well-meaning parent would name a child Tree. A nickname, perhaps?) Parents dropped off the boys at the orphanage after the tornado destroyed their home because they couldn't afford to feed them. Promised to be back in a few weeks to pick them up but moved on to another state and never returned.

Henry: Oldest of the pack. Maybe fourteen or fifteen. Threatens to run away. Disgruntled. Says the last director worked him like a slave. I'm inclined to believe him. He's strong and aggressive and plays the role of instigator with ease. No one is quite sure how he came to be orphaned. Rumor has it that his father is still alive.

Several other faces came into view, but Rena couldn't remember the boys' names. Hopefully she would keep them all straight before too long. In the meantime, she needed her rest. Tomorrow would be a busy day.

She fell into a fitful sleep, the list at her side. Her dreams were complicated and filled with fearful images of children, ragged and thin. When she awoke the next morning, Rena could hardly collect her thoughts. She had no choice, however. The boys and girls needed supervision…and from the sound of things, sooner, rather than later. As she dressed, several of the names she'd forgotten came to mind: David, Timmy, Joseph, Nate, and Evan. She would have to remember to add them to her list. When things settled down, of course.

She made her way downstairs, helped Carolina prepare breakfast, then rang the bell. The children arrived at the table, dressed and raring to go. She could hardly believe her luck. Every last one of them was clean, pressed, and smiling.

Lilly wore a heavy coat over her clothes. For that matter, all the boys and girls wore sweaters or coats.

"Are you cold?" she asked.

Callie gave a little shiver. "Yes, ma'am. I'm always cold in the mornings. I'll be fine in my sweater, though."

"It's chilly out this morning," Henry said. "If'n we're gonna walk to church, we need to stay warm."

"Well, this oatmeal will warm you up." Carolina appeared from the kitchen. "So take a seat, all of you. Eat up."

Rena joined the children at the table for a quick breakfast. About halfway into the meal, Oliver rose to grab the sugar bowl, only to discover that one of the boys—likely Henry, judging from the laughter—had tied his shoelaces to the table leg. Oliver appeared to take it in stride but spent the rest of the meal repeating every word Henry spoke.

After breakfast, Rena instructed the children to make their beds. Out of the corners of her eyes, she gave Callie a "remember what we talked about yesterday?" look, and the little girl nodded. There would be wet sheets waiting for her under Lilly's bed, no doubt.

The children scurried around the house more obediently than usual. Afterward, Rena gathered them together, gave a few instructions, and—with her heart in her throat—led them down the road to the church. She had to wonder about two things: how the children would behave in church, and why they were all suspiciously good this morning.

They arrived at the church and the children scurried off to their classroom. She followed behind them, introduced herself to their teacher, a Mrs. O'Shea, and then headed to the sanctuary to locate Jenny Jamison, who had offered to sit with her.

As she rounded the corner, she ran headfirst into Gene Wyatt, dressed in his Sunday best.

"Oh, I'm sorry. I…" She felt her cheeks grow warm as she glanced up into his handsome face. Then she took in his attire. If he'd looked good in his work clothes, he impressed her even more in the striped jacket and cuffed trousers he wore. The white dress shirt with its winged collar was impressive too, as well as the dark tie. *My goodness, if he doesn't clean up nice.…* Why, he could give any of the fellows back in Gulfport a run for their money, no doubt about it.

"No problem." His blue eyes twinkled with a hint of mischief. "Good to see you again, Miss Jewel."

"Rena." She couldn't help the smile that nearly gave away her embarrassment at being so close to him. "Please call me Rena."

He gave her a little nod. "Rena it is. You settling in all right?"

"As well as can be expected."

He placed his hand on her arm, the look on his face growing more serious. "If you're ever *not* fine, please let me know. I know you'll have questions and concerns, and we're here for you. You don't have to handle the children on your own, I promise."

"That helps a lot," she whispered.

The reverend walked by and glanced over at them, and Gene removed his hand from her arm. Rena's cheeks heated up right away. She muttered a few words and then slipped into the back of the little chapel to search for Jenny Jamison. She'd just settled into the pew next to her when the children's Sunday school teacher appeared, looking frazzled.

"Miss Jewel, could you come with me?"

Oh no. Not so soon. We just got here. Rena followed behind her to the classroom. Once inside, she glanced at the children. They all sat in their chairs, still and silent. Why in the world had their teacher found the need to fetch her?

On second glance, something about the children seemed…off. Amiss.

Rena gave them another look. "For heaven's sake." Lilly's dress was inside out. For that matter, so were Oliver's slacks. And his shirt. And Callie's dress. Rena scanned the group, stunned to find that every single one of them had shown up with clothing inside out.

The snickers filled the room, and before long all the children in the place erupted into laughter. In fact, they made so much noise that Rena wondered if the folks in church could hear them.

She gestured for the girls to join her. Lilly, Callie, and Josephine followed on her heels. Rena located a small water closet and instructed the girls to go inside and dress properly. Once they were situated back inside the classroom, she went in search of the sheriff. Hopefully he could help her with the boys.

She found that he'd taken her seat next to Miss Jamison and was all smiles as the two engaged in conversation. Just as an elderly woman took her seat at the piano up front, Rena managed a quick, "Sheriff, I need you."

Perhaps not the best choice of words. And maybe she shouldn't have raised her voice, but to be heard over the piano-playing was nearly impossible.

"I mean, the children need you," she said. "There's a problem with the boys."

Several of the women turned to look her way then began to whisper among themselves. Chief among them was a petite older woman with soft white curls. She appeared to be glaring at Rena.

"What else is new?" the woman said, rolling her eyes.

Rena turned to face her as the sheriff slipped out of the pew and headed off toward the Sunday school classroom, muttering, "I'll handle it, whatever it is."

The older woman with the sour expression marched Rena's way. She was small in stature but came across as intimidating nonetheless. Just as the piano music began a rousing chorus of "We Shall Not Be Moved," the woman crossed her arms and commenced with what sounded like a rehearsed speech. "You're the new director over at that orphanage?"

"I…I am." Rena felt the eyes of several parishioners on her. Up front, the pianist was really going to town on the song.

"I have a few things I'd like to say to you." The woman's volume increased as the song continued. "But I guess most of it'll have to wait till after service. That's fine. It'll give me plenty of time to gather my thoughts."

"Gather your thoughts?" Rena asked.

"Yes." The woman gestured for Rena to lean down to her level, which she did. "But I'll give you a little how-do-you-do to get you started, so you know where I stand." She paused and her gaze narrowed. "I've been against the idea of this orphanage from the time I first heard about it. This town was respectable before those hooligans came along. Just last week I started a campaign to rid the town of their nonsense. If you haven't heard about it yet, you will. So don't get any big ideas about staying long. If I get my way, the whole lot of you will be gone soon enough. I've already passed around a petition stating as much. I've got over a dozen signatures too. As soon as the mayor signs on, we will shut that place down. Mark my words."

With a huff, the woman marched up the aisle toward the front of the church. Her sour countenance changed long enough for her to shake the reverend's hand, but as she settled into the first pew, she turned and gave Rena a look that was clearly meant to send her packing. The music began to slow, but Rena's heartbeat did not.

Jenny Jamison gave her a sympathetic look. "Pay her no attention," she said in an exaggerated whisper. "Just sit down and go on with the service as if that never happened."

Half relieved and half frozen with fear, Rena slipped into the pew next to Jenny. "I...I..." She shook her head, unable to speak.

"Molly Harris often renders folks speechless," Jenny said with a smile. "But don't let her get to you, promise? She's poisonous at times, but there are plenty of other kind folks to counteract that sting."

"Bu–but..." Rena still couldn't speak.

Of course, with "Hallelujah, What a Savior" now being played in full force, she didn't need to be speaking, anyway. The choir director rose and called the congregation to join him, and they all began to sing at the top of their lungs.

Gene took one look at the boys with their inside out clothes and laughed. "So, this is what I've been sent to fix? I'd rather leave you this way so folks can have a field day over it."

"They're a distraction, Sheriff," Mrs. O'Shea whispered. "The other boys and girls can't concentrate on the Bible story if they're all laughing at this. You understand. So please take them and do with them as you will."

She sighed, and Gene got the point. Still, he could hardly punish the children for being clever, now could he? No, he'd rather give them an *E* for effort. At least his own two weren't involved this time. He gave William and Jacob a warning look, hoping they wouldn't further aggravate the situation with any antics of their own.

"Come with me, boys." He led them down the hallway to the water closet, where he sent them inside, two at a time. Wesley went first, his blond hair a bit of a distraction as he barreled past, rambling on about his grandfather. The kid needed a haircut. Oliver, ever the clown, followed suit, mimicking Wesley's every word. Next came David, followed by Timmy, Nate, Joseph, and Evan, the four quietest in the bunch. The twins took their turn next, filling his ears with stories too, but he couldn't make much sense of them, with their brogue so thick and all. After that came Henry, who looked as sour as always. Mochni followed Henry, chattering all the way.

"You gonna keep up that talking?" Gene asked the last boy.

"Yep." He offered a toothless grin. "I'm Mochni. Talking Bird."

"That would explain the inability to keep quiet," Gene said. "Now get in there and turn your clothes right-side-out."

The infamous trio of brothers—Mikey, Bubba, and Tree—went last. They smelled as if they'd not bathed in weeks. Several of the other boys were in similar conditions.

Finally convinced they'd all been taken care of, Gene led the way back to the classroom. Doing his best to hide a smile, he gestured for the boys to go inside.

"Now, don't make me come back here," he said. "This is Sunday. I'd like to rest, if you don't mind. Even the Lord got one day off."

The boys settled back into their chairs and Mrs. O'Shea carried on with her lesson. Convinced that one problem had been alleviated, Gene walked back toward the sanctuary. Miss Jewel's interruption couldn't have come at a worse time. He'd finally worked up the courage to sit next to Jenny Jamison during church. Oh well. Maybe he could still slip into that spot without too much notice from the other parishioners.

Making his way into the small sanctuary, Gene caught a glimpse of the beautiful Jenny Jamison. He took a couple of steps in her direction but discovered that someone else had taken the coveted spot at her side: Miss Jewel.

From a few rows up, his mother turned around and gave him a little wave. With a sigh, he decided to take his usual spot—beside Mama.

Chapter Ten

....

TIPS FOR DEALING WITH UNRULY YOUNG'UNS—*Most folk 'round these parts know me as a newspaperman, but I see myself more as one who exposes problems and offers solutions. I shine a journalistic light on situations and invite my readers to join in the quest for making things better. When it comes to the children of Daisy, I can see both sides of the story. As a reformed rapscallion myself, I see those youngsters through hopeful eyes. Perhaps they will one day transform their world, as I seek to do with the pieces I write. One can hope, anyway. In the meantime, I plan to do what I can to turn the hearts of the grown-ups toward the children. It's the least I can do.*

—Jonathan Brewer, Journalist for the
Atoka County Register

Rena managed to make it through the first fifteen minutes of the reverend's sermon on patience when a tap on her shoulder caught her attention. She turned to see Lilly standing beside her.

"Mrs. O'Shea says you need to come and get the boys." The child spoke in an exaggerated whisper. "She can't take it anymore."

Rena closed her Bible and brushed the wrinkles out of her skirt before standing. A quick glance up the aisle clued her in to the fact that the elderly woman who'd confronted her had turned and was glaring at Lilly.

"Want me to come and help?" Jenny whispered.

Rena nodded and mouthed the word "Please."

Together they slipped out of the pew and tiptoed down the aisle. Minutes later, Rena found herself getting an earful from a very unhappy Mrs. O'Shea. Rena sighed then lined up the boys—all fourteen of them—in the hallway for a little chat. She paced in front of them and they stared at her as if they were facing a firing squad. Well, maybe they were. With her temper rising, it was all she could do not to come out swinging.

Deep breath, Rena. Give them a chance to explain their poor behavior before trying to correct it.

"Is it true?" she asked Henry. "Did you really shoot spit wads at the teacher?"

"She's boring," he said. "Had to do something to stay awake."

"I see." Rena turned to Wesley. "And you glued her papers to the desk?"

He smirked. "Pretty clever, huh?"

"Pretty clever, huh?" Oliver mocked.

Rena took him by the shoulders. "Oliver, Mrs. O'Shea tells me that you brought a spider into the classroom. Where is it now?"

"Where is it now?" he echoed.

Rena resisted the urge to turn the youngster over her knee and give him a spanking. Instead, she dove into a lengthy speech about their behavior, honing in on Scriptures that she hoped would prove helpful.

Off in the distance, the piano playing began once more, and the congregation began to sing "It Is Well with My Soul." Ironic, since she'd never felt more ill at ease.

Rena continued her lecture on behaving, and the boys stood in silence, listening. A couple of times Henry tried to interrupt or offer excuses, but she would have none of it. By the time she finished, the congregation had wrapped up the hymn and the whole place fell silent. For a moment, anyway.

"Gee-willikers, Miss Rena, you sermonize better than the reverend," Wesley said with a look of admiration in his eyes. "You should ask to take the pulpit next Sunday." He brushed a loose string of hair out of his face and offered a delightful grin.

"He's got a point," a deep male voice rang out. "I found your message quite convicting."

She turned to find a man about her age. He looked polished and refined in his Sunday-go-to-meeting suit, very much like most of the men from back home.

Home. There was that word again.

"Jonathan Brewer," the handsome fellow said, extending a hand. "I've been meaning to stop by to meet you. I live in town, just off Main. Work for the paper."

"John writes for the *Atoka County Register.*" Jenny's eyes shone with delight as she gazed up at him somewhat starry-eyed. "His stories are read all over the county."

Rena shook his outstretched hand. "Nice to meet you, Jonathan."

"Jonathan, this is Miss Rena Jewel, the new director of the orphanage," Jenny said. "She only just arrived three days ago."

"Miss Rena Jewel." Jonathan gave her hand a squeeze. Gazing into her eyes, he said, "Well, now, I heard a rumor that we had a rare jewel in town. I've been dying to see if you were a Ruby or a Pearl. Looks like you're a Rena." He gave her a little wink, and her heart began to flutter. His hand lingered in hers for a bit longer than necessary. When he finally withdrew it, he raked his fingers through his dark brown hair. "I must confess, I made a point of meeting you this morning because I want to discuss a topic of great importance with you."

The strains of a rousing closing hymn played, and before long the people began to stream out of the chapel, anxious to fetch their children from the Sunday school classrooms.

Rena started to respond to Jonathan when the boys began to squirm.

"Miss Rena, can't we go now?" Oliver asked.

"Yeah, Mrs. Wabash always let us play outside fer a spell after church," Henry added.

"If'n we behaved ourselves," Callie said as she walked by. "And you boys did not behave yourselves."

"Not even close," Josephine added, her nose tilted upward.

The girls giggled and took off with Lilly on their heels.

Rena looked at the boys. "You've already endured one 'sermon' from me, as you called it. If I hear of any more trouble from you boys, there will be far worse than a sermon to contend with. Have I made myself clear?"

"Yes'm." Henry gave her a nod.

"Go on with you, then." She waved her hand to dismiss the group. "Try not to burn anything down."

"We'll try!" Wesley's voice rang out, followed by a burst of laughter.

"Cain't make any promises!" Henry added.

"Cain't make any promises!" Oliver echoed.

Mikey, Bubba, and Tree led the way outside with the twins on their tail, who were carrying on about the big ship that had brought them to America years ago. The rest of the boys—including David, Nate, Timmy, and a couple of the others—tagged along behind with smiles on their faces.

"You know, they're really not bad kids." Jonathan looked after them as they took off at a fast pace. "In fact, a couple of them remind me of myself as a boy." A wistful look came over his face for a moment. "I grew up in the Texas Panhandle. What about you?"

Jenny slipped her arm through Rena's. "Rena comes to us all the way from Gulfport, Mississippi."

"Gulfport!" His eyes lit with apparent delight. "Why, I have family in Gulfport. Do you know a Mildred Brewer, perhaps? Or a Mary-Lou?"

"I knew a Mary-Lou Brewer years ago in high school."

"My cousin." Jonathan crossed his arms and smiled. "Well, it's a small world, now, isn't it?"

"It is. But I didn't really grow up in Gulfport. I moved there when I turned fourteen because..." She paused, unsure of how much to share.

Thank goodness, she didn't have to finish the story. A swarm of people passed by. Many gave Rena curious looks. She couldn't be sure if they were suspicious or upset at her for some reason. At any rate, few paused to give her more than a polite nod.

"I guess this isn't the best time or place to talk," Jonathan said. "But I wanted you to know that I plan to run a piece in the paper about the children's home. That was the matter of importance I mentioned earlier."

"Oh?"

"Yes. There's so much scuttlebutt from some of the folks in town.... They don't give the boys and girls half a chance before they crucify them. I think it's about time someone spoke up for them."

"What a wonderful idea."

"Yes. Well, I'm trying to come up with a plan of action to put the children in a favorable light."

"Good luck with that," Mrs. O'Shea said in passing. She muttered something about how even God Himself couldn't accomplish such a feat.

"Anyway, I would love to meet with you sometime this week to talk through my ideas." Jonathan gave Rena a thoughtful look. "I believe this story needs to run in the paper. Think of the good it will do those children. Why, some of them might find good homes if we do this. You want that, don't you?"

"Of course." The very idea of finding good adoptive homes for the boys and girls sent a rush of excitement through her. What greater goal could there be? And, certainly, she'd met no kinder man than Jonathan Brewer since her arrival. Yes, she could surely trust this fellow to do right by the children.

"Well, then…" Jonathan flashed a smile so broad it warmed her heart. She noticed a shimmer of something—was that interest?—in his eyes. "I'll be in touch. We can set up a visit. With the two of us on the same team, perhaps we can keep Molly Harris and Mayor Albright at bay."

"Molly Harris?" Rena asked, puzzled. The name sounded familiar, but she couldn't be sure why.

"That little spitfire who gave you a piece of her mind before service started," Jenny said.

"Ah." Rena paused. "And the mayor too? He's not partial to the children?"

"Not partial?" Jenny snorted. "That's putting it mildly. He and Molly are two peas in a pod where the children are concerned. They would like nothing more than to shut down the orphanage."

"Children's home." Jonathan's brow wrinkled. "Let's call it a children's home, not an orphanage. Imagine how the boys and girls must feel when they hear the word *orphanage*."

"Children's home…" Rena repeated the words. Yes, it made perfect sense.

The only thing that didn't make sense about Jonathan Brewer was his apparent interest in the children. Perhaps—she looked into Jenny's smiling face—yes, perhaps he was doing all this to impress a certain woman. Hmm. That would certainly explain his efforts on the children's behalf.

Well, regardless, Rena would take his kindness any day over the ranting of one Molly Harris. Just thinking about the elderly woman sent a shiver down her spine and a stab of pain through her heart.

"It was great to meet you, Miss Jewel." Jonathan's voice interrupted her thoughts. He reached for her hand once again and lifted it to his lips. "Glad to see that the children have someone in their court for a change."

"Y–yes." She nodded, feeling a bit discombobulated by the touch of his hand.

Goodness. Had someone turned up the heat? Suddenly she could scarcely wait to get outside to cool down.

Gene watched from a distance as Jonathan Brewer moved into the spot next to Rena. She seemed oblivious to his tactics. Still, the flirtatious behavior coming from Jonathan did not escape Gene's notice.

"We might need to keep an eye on that." His mother's voice sounded from behind him.

"What do you mean?" He turned to face her.

"He's playing that new director like a fiddle. But it seems to be a tune she enjoys. I'm pretty sure she was spellbound by his flirtations."

"Hmm." Gene wasn't sure what to say.

"Not that I blame her. That Jonathan Brewer is one mighty fine specimen of a man." His mother began to fan herself with her hand.

"Mother!"

"I'm old, but I'm not blind. And don't think it's gone unnoticed by the single women in town that he's not yet found a wife." Her voice lowered to a whisper. "Though I have it on good authority that Jenny Jamison is more than a little interested in acquiring that position."

Gene decided he'd had just about enough of this conversation. Time to turn things around. "I'm not saying Miss Jewel is naive"—he lowered his voice, so as not to be overheard—"but I do have to wonder. She doesn't seem to be as knowledgeable of children as I'd expected. At the very least, we can say that she's not as familiar with boys."

"All this you've gleaned from only three days of knowing her?"

"Well, it's more my intuition at work. I'm not saying she's the wrong person for the job. She's certainly…" He turned back to watch as she continued her chat with Jonathan Brewer. *Pretty?* No, that wasn't the word he meant to say. Then again, she was pretty, in her own way. Not like Jenny, of course. No, seeing the two side by side, it was easy to see who held the upper hand in the beauty department. Still, Rena had a certain sense about her, a city-like sophistication.

"Son, did I lose you?" His mother's voice brought him back to the present.

"Oh, no, I…" He paused. "I do hope we've done the right thing by bringing her all the way from Mississippi. I just want everything to be perfect—for her *and* the children."

"Things around here are a long way from perfect." His mother paused. "Speaking of imperfections, have you heard the latest on Molly?"

He shook his head.

"She's started some sort of campaign."

"Campaign?" That certainly got his attention. "What do you mean?"

"She's calling it the 'Fresh as a Daisy' campaign. Honestly, I think the mayor put her up to it."

"'Fresh as a Daisy'?" Gene shook his head. "What do you make of it?"

"It's something about the town starting fresh—a new beginning. I'm pretty sure they mean *without* the children. She's been circulating a petition, trying to get local business owners to sign it."

"Have you seen the petition?"

"No. But I can guess what it says. Maybe a certain number of names and they take the issue before the county representatives or perhaps approach the missions board. I'm not sure. I just know that I've been hearing folks talk about it all morning. She's called some sort of meeting at the church a couple weeks from now."

"I think I'd better keep an eye on things, then." Gene turned his attention away from Jonathan Brewer and Miss Jewel and headed down the hallway in the opposite direction. His mission? To find Molly Harris.

He made his way past the reverend on the church steps, muttering something kind about the sermon on patience as his two boys raced by, hollering at each other. Truth be told, however, his patience with Molly was wearing so thin that he could practically see through it.

He found her making her way across the church lawn with some sort of paper in her hand. He watched as she moved from person to person, starting with the mayor and then moving to Mrs. O'Shea.

"What are you up to now, Molly Harris?" he whispered.

"No good, most likely." A familiar voice sounded from behind him.

Gene turned to see Jonathan standing there with Miss Jewel at his side. They were soon joined by Joe, the barber, and Mr. Whitener, the postman.

"Have you all seen the petition she's passing around?" Jonathan asked.

"Nope." Gene shook his head. "Not sure I want to, to be honest."

"Well, you might want to have a look. She just started the fool thing this morning, but from what I hear, it's already been signed by a handful of businessmen."

Joe looked a bit unnerved by the conversation and took a couple of steps away from the group.

"Got something you want to tell us, Joe?" Jonathan asked.

"Tell you?" Joe looked perplexed by this question.

"Don't tell me you signed it." Gene gave him a pointed look.

"Aw, shoot." Joe kicked the dirt with the toe of his boot. "Molly got to me. You know how persuasive she can be. Besides, those boys cost me a lot of money with their shenanigans awhile back. Don't want to go through that again."

"Yes, but do you really think that sending them to another town to live is the answer?" Gene could hardly believe it. "What would be the point in it?"

"Peace of mind?" Joe offered. "Shucks, I don't know. I just know that something's got to change. I can't take much more."

"Well, then, you're a prime candidate to hear my idea." Jonathan's expression brightened. "Let Molly have her campaign. We're going to have one of our own—one designed to renovate the orphanage and help folks take a positive interest in the children."

"A campaign of our own?" Joe looked boggled by this idea.

"I'm of the firm belief that people are afraid of what they don't understand," Jonathan said. "Many of the older townspeople have forgotten what it's like to be a child, so they don't understand when the boys and girls act up. Others don't appreciate the various ethnicities of the children. There are some hidden—and not so hidden—prejudices against those of a different race."

"Never really thought of that, but I suppose you're right." Gene paused to think about it. *Well, sure. That last thing alone must surely be at the root of the problem for some.* Though they wouldn't speak of their prejudices aloud, many held them in their hearts. No doubt about that.

"Leave it to me," Jonathan said. "I'm going to come up with a solution to draw attention to the plight of the children's home, and it's going to be far-reaching. People all across Atoka County will want to pitch in. Maybe even people across the state—or in other states. The whole country."

"You think?" Joe appeared to be mesmerized by this idea.

Jonathan crossed his arms over his chest. "I *know*. Watch and see."

Gene wasn't sure if the newspaperman exuded confidence or cockiness. Still, he could hardly fault the fellow, when the sole intent was to spare the children more grief. Out of the corners of his eyes he caught a glimpse of Miss Jewel, whose eyes were fixed on Jonathan Brewer. Why this bothered Gene, he couldn't say. What did it matter if the new director of the orphanage hung onto the reporter's every word?

As his thoughts drifted toward Rena, he paid less attention to Jonathan's speech. Then, off in the distance, a little girl's cries rang out. Gene turned to see little Josephine fighting—literally fighting—with the mayor's daughter, Calista.

He ran toward them alongside Rena. They approached the girls just as Josephine shouted.

"I do so too have a mother!" Josephine shoved Calista, knocking her to the ground. "She's in heaven!" Josephine's blond braids flew into the air as she took another swing at the girl.

Calista rose, brushed the dirt off her frilly Sunday dress, and stuck out her tongue at Josephine. "You just wait and see, you stupid orphan. At least I can talk to my mama. You can't." She straightened the bow in her hair and brushed the dirt from her dress. "So there."

At this, Josephine gave her another push, which sent Calista sprawling. This time her dress didn't fare as well. When she rose, a large rip in the beautiful blue skirt was obvious. And the dirt smudges might be a problem as well.

Calista took one look at her dress and erupted in tears. "Just you wait!" She shook her fist in Josephine's face then went crying to her mama. No doubt this would only stir up trouble even more.

Gene looked Rena's way. "Better get while the gettin's good."

"Beg your pardon?" Fine wrinkles appeared between her eyes.

"Take the children and run. Trust me on this. You haven't met the mayor yet, right?"

"No, but I'd like to. I think, perhaps, I could persuade him to—" She never got to finish her sentence. Gene took her by the shoulders, turned her around, and said, "You need to go. Now. Take the children home. I'll be by later to check on you."

Rena found herself so incensed by the sheriff's insistence that she leave that she could barely speak. She couldn't remember ever being so angry.

"Who does he think he is?"

"He's the one trying to save your life," Jonathan suddenly said beside her. "We don't have time to explain right now, because you really do need to take the kids and run for home."

Josephine swiped at her dirty face and took Rena by the hand. "Miss Rena, I'm sorry I hit that prissy Calista. I really am. But we've gotta get going. C'mon. She's gone to fetch her papa."

Rena nodded but refused to be swayed by Josephine's nudging. "That's what the sheriff said. But I still don't understand why we need to run. Let's just face him, and you can make the proper apologies."

She shook her head. "You don't understand, do you?"

"No."

"C'mon!" The boys all appeared at once, Henry leading the pack. "Hurry up, everyone."

Rena tried to gather her wits about her but felt a little out of sorts. One thing was apparent—she needed to get out of here quickly. Everyone seemed to be in agreement about that.

"Come on, boys and girls," she called out. "We're headed back to the house now."

The boys gathered around her like flies to honey. With Henry leading the way, they fell into a line and started the march—actually, it felt more like a sprint—toward home. Rena did her best to count heads but found it nearly impossible.

About a half block away from the church, Callie ran up to her with tears streaming down her face. "Miss Rena, I can't find Lilly anywhere."

"No!" Rena stopped then turned and looked in every direction. Off in the distance she saw one of the boys up a tree. A second glance revealed the truth. "That's not a boy. That's Lilly."

Callie ran off to fetch her little sister, and before long the group was nearly home.

"Whew, that was a close one." Wesley drew near and took her hand as they approached the house.

"Why do you say that?"

"You haven't met the mayor yet, have ya?" He squinted up at her.

"No. I hope to very soon, though, especially now that Josephine owes his daughter an apology. Though, I must say, I can see her side in this too. That little girl had no call to say such ugly things to her."

"Calista always says ugly things. But she's not the one you need to be afraid of." Wesley gave a visible shiver then released his hold on her hand. "You'll see, Miss Rena. One of these days...you'll see."

"One of these days you'll see!" Oliver echoed, his eyes wide.

She slowed her pace as they entered the house, her mind still awhirl from everything that had happened this morning. The incidents of the morning—the inside-out clothes, the run-in with Molly Harris, the reverend's sermon on patience, the lecture she'd given the boys, the conversation with the newspaperman, the news about Molly's campaign against the children's home, and Josephine's fight with the mayor's daughter—all these things had worn her out, and it was barely noon.

What else could the day possibly hold?

Chapter Eleven
....

TIPS FOR DEALING WITH UNRULY YOUNG'UNS—*It's the mayor's job to lead the people and offer advice when necessary. That's why I can no longer hold back my opinion regarding the little devils who've taken over our fair town of Daisy. Never in all my fifty-three years have I seen youngsters so intent on bringing destruction to a place. Oh, I know, some well-meaning locals insist that the hooligans from the orphanage can be reformed. My opinion? That's a pie-in-the-sky concept. Personally, I'd like to drive them all out of town on a rail so that I can focus on what's really important—my upcoming reelection campaign.*

> —Mayor Albright
> ("A Vote for Albright Is a Vote That's All Right!")

On Monday morning during breakfast, Rena led the children in morning devotions and prayer. Just about the time she bowed her head to pray for their upcoming school day, loud knocks on the front door interrupted her. She tried to keep praying, but the persistent pounding forced her to stop.

"Who would stop by at this time of the morning?" she asked as she took a couple of steps toward the window to peek outside.

Several of the children rose from their chairs and joined her.

"Oh no!" Josephine paled and dove under the table. "It's him!"

"Him? Him, who?" Rena asked.

Callie turned away from the window, her eyes wide. "The...the mayor!" She dropped to her knees and crawled under the table to join Josephine.

At this point, even the boys looked nervous. Oliver's eyes widened, the twins raced for the kitchen, Wesley and even Henry shot out of the room and up the stairs. Tree began to babble nonsensically and Mochni joined him, going on and on in an unfamiliar language.

Rena wondered at their inordinate fear of the man. Was he really such an intimidating fellow? She peered through the window once more but couldn't see him from her angle. And still the knocking at the door continued. Rena took a few steps toward the foyer.

Carolina joined her, wiping her hands on her apron. "Three of the boys just bounded into the kitchen and told me to get out of the house while the gettin's good. What's happening out here?"

"The mayor's come calling."

Carolina paled and wiped her hands on her apron. "Are you sure?"

"Well, I've never met the man personally, but I'm quite sure it's the mayor based on description alone. And from the children's reactions, of course."

"Well, in that case..." Carolina turned around and hightailed it to the kitchen.

"Whatever are they so worried about?" Rena muttered.

She eased the door a crack, ready to do business with the man once and for all. *Might as well get it over with.* Peering through the small space she'd created, Rena took in the stern-faced man in front of her. Short. Rotund. Tiny tufts of gray hair so thin, she could see right through them down to his scalp. His plump cheeks seemed to swallow up his marble-sized eyes. Still, she felt their penetrating gaze, and there was no denying the anger in his expression. He wore a gentleman's suit—expensive but ill-fitting around his expanded midsection. His collar looked tight against the folds of skin in his neck. Maybe that would account for the red face she saw.

"Miss Jewel?" He offered a brusque nod. She half expected a smile to follow. No such luck.

"Y–yes?" she managed.

"Mayor Albright. I've stopped by for an unavoidable conversation."

"O–oh?" Though everything inside her fought against it, she opened the door a bit wider. "Well, do come in, then."

"I believe I will. Do you have any coffee made?"

"Coffee?" She shook her head. "I'm a tea drinker, myself. But I could—"

"Black. No sugar or cream. Largest mug you've got. Can't very well have this conversation without stiffening my backbone. Get to it, woman." He marched into the parlor and took a seat, drumming his fingers on the chair arm.

Ugh. No doubt he'd come to talk about the run-in between Josephine and his daughter. Well, she would win him over with her coffee. If she could figure out how to make it.

Thank goodness she didn't have to. A quick trip to the kitchen showed her that Carolina had already set the coffee to brewing. "Knew it would be the first thing he'd ask for," Carolina said. "Always is. Sometimes I think the man has coffee running through his veins instead of blood."

"Then one can hope it will calm him down," Rena said.

"Agitate him is more like it," Carolina said. "Doesn't take much to get him going. But you're about to find that out firsthand."

A few minutes later he took a sip from the cup she offered him then wrinkled his brow. "This stuff's not fit to clean out the sewer system."

"Oh, I'm sorry, I—"

His eyes narrowed into slits and he gazed at her in such an intense way that she felt shivers run through her. "Miss Jewel, I won't waste your time. I've just come by to speak with you about the incident at church yesterday. I'm sure you know what I'm talking about."

"I do." She nodded and offered what she hoped would look like a compassionate smile. "And I'm so awfully sorry about what happened between the girls."

"Well, that would make two of us. Three, if you count my dear wife. She took to her bed over this." He pursed his lips for a moment. "She suffers with nerves."

"I see." Rena bit her lip. "Well, how is Calista this morning?"

"Her ego is bruised, but her backside is worse, according to my wife. If I'd been there, I would have taken a switch to that Josephine at once. She deserves a solid beating for what she's done to my girl. This is not the first time the two have scuffled, but it will certainly be the last, if I have anything to do with it."

Rena bristled. "I can offer my assurances that Josephine was disciplined for her hasty and somewhat careless actions. But you might as well know that Calista started the fight by calling Josephine a rather ugly name and saying awful things about her mother. I heard it myself and was stunned, to say the least. I do hope you will encourage her not to instigate trouble again."

The mayor leaned forward, his jaw tightening. She could almost see the steam coming from his ears and wondered if he might blow like a teakettle.

His next words were sharp. Crisp. Defined.

"Listen. Up. And. Listen. Good. We're. Going. To. Have. An. Understanding. You. And. Me." At this point, his pace picked up and he spoke with a terrifying intensity. "There will never—and I repeat, never—be an instance where I will lend my support to one of these orphans, so get that idea right out of your head. They've brought nothing but grief to our fair town and to my little girl." His volume rose and the veins in his neck throbbed. "I won't have it, you hear me?"

Rena heard the scuffling of feet in the dining room. The children were stirring. No doubt his words had sent terror through the whole lot of them. Not that she blamed them for being scared. The man was intimidating, just as she'd been warned. Still, even the hottest-tempered soul could be reasoned with. Right?

She'd just opened her mouth to interject a few thoughts when he went off on another rant. "These children are determined to destroy this town, lock, stock, and barrel."

"Destroy the town?" She stifled a laugh as she realized just how absurd his words sounded. "Well, sure, they're a handful. I've witnessed it firsthand. But honestly, Mayor, they're just being children. I'm sure that after a bit of time and discipline you will see a marked improvement in their behavior."

"Say what you like, do what you like; it will make no difference. Trust me. I watched Mrs. Wabash try, that poor, gullible, old soul. She did everything a woman could do, but they trampled right over her. I have no doubt they will do the same to you, if you let them." He leaned forward, his elbows on his knees, and gave her a look that could only be defined as a warning. "So don't let them. You've got to be stern. Lay down the law. Speaking of the law, you've met our sheriff?"

"Well, yes."

"He was a fine fellow until he and his wife adopted those two boys. Now I wouldn't give a nickel for any of them."

"Well, that's hardly fair. His mother told me that he's been raising those boys by himself since his wife's death. I'm sure he's doing the best he can. From what I can tell, the children in Daisy adore him. He's like a father figure to them all."

"He's a fine sheriff but a terrible excuse for a father." The mayor squared his shoulders. "Those boys of his are the worst of the lot. He goes way too easy on them. Feels sorry for them, from what I've been told. So I must insist that you keep the orphans away from the sheriff's youngsters. When they all get together, the potential for danger is everywhere."

Rena couldn't think of anything kind to say, so she kept her mouth shut. Oh, but she wanted to give this man a piece of her mind. What a cruel fellow he must be, to judge the sheriff so. Why, anyone who was paying attention could see that Sheriff Wyatt was struggling to care for his boys without his wife. Some compassion was called for here, not judgment.

The mayor rose and took his hat in hand. Fingering the brim, he said, "Brace yourself for hardship, Miss Jewel. These boys and girls are liable to make your life a living—"

"Please, sir!" Rena put her hand up. "For pity's sake, don't say it. You have made your point, and you've made it well. There is no need to continue."

He slapped his hat on his balding head, marched to the door, and flung it open. "Until next time, then."

She gave the door a shove—perhaps a bit too hard—and it slammed shut, almost catching him in the rear. Wishing it had actually done so was probably sinful, but she couldn't help herself.

The children streamed from the dining room and the upstairs, all of them talking at once. The cacophony of the children's voices was nearly deafening.

"Miss Rena, you told him!" Henry gave her an admiring look.

"No one ever talks to the mayor like that," Wesley added. "You're a hero, just like my grandpa." He started talking about his grandfather, the war hero, once again.

Carolina entered the room and untied her apron. "I was listening from the kitchen. Thought he was going to take you down a notch or two, but you got him in the end. Good for you."

"Yes, good for you!" Josephine echoed.

Rena knelt in front of the youngster and took her hand. "Josephine, you realize that much of this trouble came about because you chose to fight with Calista, don't you?"

"I didn't want to fight with her, but she said mean things." Josephine's eyes brimmed with tears. "I used to have a mama and a papa just like her. And I lived in a big, fine house too. So she's got no right to say those ugly things to me."

Rena's heart twisted. "Honey, even if you never lived in a fine house… even if you never knew your mama or papa…she still had no right to say ugly things to you. Ugly words are painful. The Bible says we are to guard our tongues." Here Rena paused and gave Josephine's hand a squeeze. "But the Bible also says that we're to guard our temper. I want you to keep that in mind the next time she hurts your feelings. When she says something mean, you should turn the other cheek."

"Calista's the one who needs to turn the other cheek," Henry said. "So Josephine can smack her on that side too!"

At this, several of the boys began to laugh. Wesley let out a snort, which tickled the girls. Before long, their giggles filled the room. At this point, Rena finally let down her guard and laughed with them. It felt good. Very good.

When the laughter died down, Oliver tugged on her sleeve. "Don't let that old grouch get you down, Miss Rena. He was a kid once too, ya know."

"Can't imagine what sort of child he was," Rena said.

"I can." Carolina gave her a knowing look. "He was a bully just like Calista. A know-it-all bully who thrived on making others feel like the dirt under his heel."

"Hmm." Rena stared at Carolina as the realization hit. "You're speaking from experience? You knew him as a child?"

"Knew him?" Carolina's eyes widened. "I was terrified of him. All the boys and girls at the school were. And he only got worse as he aged."

"Then however did he get elected mayor if folks were so scared of him?"

Carolina shrugged. "You know how it is. Folks vote for him because they're scared not to. He's been the mayor 'round here for as long as I can remember, and I daresay he'll go on being the mayor until the Lord returns to sweep us all away."

"I wish He'd sweep Mayor Albright away," Henry said, rolling his eyes.

Rena sobered at these words. "Henry, we can't talk like that. The mayor—crusty or not—is still one of God's children, just as you are. And he's probably got a story of his own."

"What do you mean?" Wesley wiped his nose with his sleeve.

"I mean, his bullying ways are probably linked to something that happened when he was a boy." Rena paused to think about her words. She would take what she had learned and use it as she disciplined Henry, Oliver, and the other boys. She didn't want them to grow up to be mean-spirited or hateful like the mayor, even if they seemed a little devilish now.

Really, there was only one word that came to mind as she considered the outcome of the boys standing before her now: love. She would love the devil right out of them. And, by gum, she might just love it out of the mayor too.

Gene sat in the barber's chair, a captive audience to Joe's chatter.

Joe swished the blade this way and that across Gene's cheeks before wiping off the shaving cream. "You saw what that newspaper fellow's done now, didn't you?"

"What's that?" Gene asked.

"Happened just this morning." Joe took a warm cloth and laid it across Gene's face. "He posted an article in the *Atoka County Register* about child-rearin'."

"I read it too," his deputy, Charlie, added from the chair next to

Gene's. "He said that if we work together, we can get the situation with the children under control."

"Interesting." Gene spoke from underneath the cloth on his face.

"As if anyone could get those unruly children under control." Old Man Tucker snorted.

"You'll love this part," Joe added. "He encouraged citizens to write to the paper and offer suggestions for how to handle unruly young'uns. Said if we came up with workable ideas, he would post them, one a day. What do you think of that?"

This certainly piqued Gene's attention. He pulled off the cloth and sat up. "I think I'm ready to read that article. Do you have a copy of the paper on hand?"

"I do." Joe reached behind the counter and pulled out the newspaper, which he passed to Gene.

"First page, far right column," Charlie said.

Gene skimmed the page until he found the article in question. He folded back the page and read the piece quickly. Sure enough, Jonathan Brewer had come out swinging for the orphanage. He'd crafted a well-written article in defense of the children and encouraged residents of Daisy and nearby towns to link arms to make the situation better.

"Listen to this." Gene read aloud, "'If the residents of Daisy work together, if we're all on the same team, we can turn around this situation. But we have to link arms. If even one person won't join in, this won't work. The children need to see a solid front. We can give it to them, if we try.'" Gene looked up from the paper and nodded. "Well, this is great. I knew he was talking about some sort of plan to counteract Molly's 'Fresh as a Daisy' campaign. Guess this is it."

"Yes, but child-rearing tips?" Old Man Tucker asked. "We're supposed to turn it around by offering up tips for raising children? How will that fix anything?"

"I suppose if we're focused on what we can do to help the children, we won't have time left over to be angry at them," Charlie said. "Guess that's the idea."

"I guess." Joe grew silent as he cleaned out Gene's shaving mug. When he finished, he looked Gene's way with a sheepish expression on his face. "Look, Gene…you know I'm not really angry with the children, right? I just got a little riled up when they damaged my property. Truth is…" He removed his hat and raked his fingers through his hair. "Truth is, I just don't know how to stop Molly when she comes around ranting and raving about the children. She's one determined woman."

"That she is," Gene said. "No question about that."

"She's a fireball. And even though I've tried to throw water on her, she still keeps blazing."

"I've thrown a few buckets of water that way myself," Gene said. "But she's hotter than an egg frying on the sidewalk in August."

"Why do you suppose she's so bent on closing down the orphanage?"

"Not sure," Gene said. "I've often wondered."

"I knew her as a girl," Old Man Tucker said. "She was a right nice little thing till her ma and pa adopted that baby sister of hers. I always figured she was jealous of the attention little Prudence got. Probably didn't help that Prudence was really pretty. Molly was always a bit on the plain side, ya know."

Gene didn't know, but it all made sense. It would appear that Molly carried a grudge, one going all the way back to her childhood. That explained a lot.

Old Man Tucker kept on talking about what a looker Prudence had turned out to be, but Gene's thoughts shifted to the article in the paper. He skimmed the words once again and a renewed sense of hope kicked in. With everyone working together, maybe they really could turn things around for the town of Daisy. One could hope, anyway.

He said his good-byes and headed back to the jail, anxious to get to work. He'd no sooner stepped inside than his mother appeared, all smiles.

"How's your day going, son?"

"Fine. Yours?"

"Wonderful. Guess you've heard what's stirring with Jonathan Brewer."

"Yes."

"He's a peach, isn't he?"

"Well, I don't know that I would call him that."

"I do believe he's got his eye on Rena. Should be interesting to watch. Oh, and speaking of Miss Jewel, she's invited us to Thanksgiving dinner. We're to bring the cranberry dressing and a couple of pies. I told her that you like to bake."

"I like to bake?"

"Well, now, don't fret." His mother gave him a wink. "I'll teach you. You've always liked my pecan pie. It's about time you learned how to make one yourself."

"Wait." He shook his head and tried to make sense of things. "In the last two minutes you've informed me that Jonathan has his eye on Miss Jewel, we're having Thanksgiving dinner at the children's home, and I'm baking a pie. And somehow the common denominator in all these stories is Rena Jewel. Is that right?"

"You've hit the nail on the head, son. She is, indeed, the common denominator." His mother winked. "Couldn't have put it any better myself." She paused. "So, what do you say?"

"To the dinner or the pie?"

"Both."

"Yes to the dinner, no to the pie." He released a breath and thought it through. "Or, rather, a maybe to the pie. But I still don't know why I'm making it and not you. I have my hands full with the boys."

"They can help you." She snapped her fingers. "Oh, there's a lovely idea! The boys can help you. That way you can all tell Rena that you made it together. She will see how much your boys look up to you."

"Why should I care how she perceives my relationship with the boys?"

His mother gave him a sheepish look then cast her gaze to the floor. "Oh, I…well, I was just thinking it would be inspirational to her, now that she's caring for so many youngsters herself."

"Mm-hmm." He shook his head then took his mother by the shoulders, gazing directly into her eyes. "Mother, no matchmaking."

"Matchmaking?" She feigned innocence. "You offend me at the deepest level. I would never stoop to—"

"And another thing." He crossed his arms over his chest. "I've never been any good at baking. Remember that cake you helped me with when I was a kid? I almost burned the kitchen down."

"Well, yes. But that was years ago. Surely you have improved. Most things do get better with time, you know." She gave him a wink. "Look at me. I'm turning sixty-seven this spring and I feel like I'm in my prime."

He reached over and gave her a kiss on the cheek. "You don't look a day over forty."

"Forty?" She smirked. "You meant thirty, didn't you?"

He laughed. "Yes, Mama. Thirty. And yes to the pie. I'll bake whatever you like, but I can't do it by myself."

"Son, there are a great many things menfolk could learn from women. But I have a feeling you're a ready learner. Stick close and you'll learn a thing or two from this wise old sage."

He gave her a curious look, wondering what she had up her sleeve. They weren't talking about pies anymore, were they? No, judging from the crooked grin on his mother's face, she'd shifted the conversation entirely. Where she was headed with it, he could not say.

Chapter Twelve

....

TIPS FOR DEALING WITH UNRULY YOUNG'UNS—*Miss Rena said I should write this here note to the fella at the paper, so here goes. My name is Tree but folks 'round here call me by all sorts of other names, some I can't say out loud fer fear Miss Rena'll stick a bar of soap in my mouth to teach me a lesson. I don't really mind so much. Me 'n the boys like to pull a few pranks, sure. That's what we're known for. I don't reckon I've got any tips for raisin' young'uns, 'cept if yer a parent, it's better to stick around instead of droppin' yer kids off at an orphanage and tellin' 'em you'll be back to fetch 'em shortly...'specially if you never plan to come back at all.*

—Tree

Over the next three weeks, Rena did everything in her power to keep the peace, both inside the walls of the children's home and out. She skillfully avoided both the mayor and Molly Harris, though the children's antics nearly drew their interest on more than one occasion. A handful of folks in town rallied around the children. Many turned in child-rearing tips to Jonathan, who posted them, along with several positive articles about famous grown-ups who'd once been intolerable children. He seemed to have won over Joe, the barber, who was now more approachable.

And speaking of winning folks over, she'd spent plenty of time with the sheriff. In spite of the mayor's warnings, she found him to be a fun-loving man and a good father. Sure, he still had a lot to learn, but so did she. Perhaps—she often smiled as she thought about it—they could learn together.

Her days were filled with caring for children, but during the late evening hours, after the children were tucked away in their beds, she pulled out her notebook and began to add scenes to her novel. She added a cowboy, of course. One with broad shoulders and a happy laugh. She named him Gerald…and made him a Texas Ranger. That way no one would ever suspect the real object of her affections.

Hmm. She would have to keep an eye on that. No point in letting herself think for a moment that her blossoming friendship with Gene Wyatt—or Jonathan Brewer, for that matter—might turn into something more. She'd long since stopped imagining such a thing possible.

Still, Gene's dimples held her spellbound at times. How could she possibly control the fluttering in her heart when he looked at her that way? Another thing captivated her as well: his boyish grin. And so did his eyes—which she'd now determined to be cornflower blue, not midnight blue—along with his broad shoulders. All these things served as ongoing distractions and the perfect fodder for her novel.

Besides, no one would ever read her story, anyway. She kept it hidden away under her pillow. The words were meant for her eyes only.

As Thanksgiving approached, her spirits lifted. She had one goal in mind—to make this the best holiday the children in her care had ever experienced. With that in mind, she put them to work carving pumpkins and creating a holiday display out of crisp red, gold, and brown fall leaves. They also baked gingerbread cookies together. The cookies hadn't exactly

turned out as she'd planned and the kitchen suffered terribly in the process of trying, but what a great time they'd all had. Well, until the boys
got into a fistfight and started throwing dough at one another. Everything
unraveled at that point. Still, she had bright hopes for the big day.

On the morning of Thanksgiving, Rena awoke with renewed zeal.
Carolina would arrive soon to help with the meal. Jenny Jamison, who
had offered to cook a few of the side dishes, would come at nine o'clock.
And Jonathan Brewer, who claimed he needed more information for
future articles, had invited himself to lunch, as well. Not that Jenny
seemed to mind this news. Oh no. Her face lit with joy the moment Rena
told her.

The only person who didn't seem terribly excited about the prospect
was Gene. He'd fallen silent at the news that Jonathan would be joining
them for the holiday meal. Did he have something against the man, perhaps? Rena couldn't be sure, but she had her suspicions. On more than
one occasion she'd noticed Gene looking at Jenny with a gleam in his
eyes. Who could blame him? Jenny was an enviable beauty, after all. Her
perfect blond hair always seemed to stay in place. Her cute-as-a-button
nose wrinkled every time one of the men told a joke, and her sparkling
green eyes seemed to hold Gene captive.

Still, it wasn't exactly the story Rena would've written. Not that any
of her stories had ever actually come true, but one could hope that a
handsome fellow would look her way every now and again instead of
being sidetracked by a woman of real beauty.

As she came fully awake that morning, Rena offered up a prayer of
thanks for all that the Lord had done in her life over the past few weeks.
Sure, there were still problems. And she missed her family terribly. But
overall, things were going well. She rose from the bed, determined to
make this the best Thanksgiving ever.

After rushing to get the turkey into the oven, she headed back upstairs, opened the wardrobe door, and stared at the dresses inside. Under ordinary circumstances, she would have chosen a practical one. Still, the idea of celebrating Thanksgiving Day in a boring dress held no appeal. She reached for a soft white blouse, one Virginia had purchased for her. Fingering the imported lace on the collar, Rena smiled. Wearing something so delicate and soft didn't make a lot of sense. Not with all the work she had to do. Still, the idea of cooking all morning in a drab brown dress seemed less appealing.

She reached for the blouse and took a few steps toward the large oval mirror. Holding the blouse in place, she smiled. Yes, this was exactly what she needed. And she would wear that pretty blue skirt to go with it, the one Virginia had brought back from New York.

Suddenly an idea took hold, one Rena could not ignore. She sprinted toward her wardrobe and pulled open the door. Her eyes shifted from dress to dress, skirt to skirt. So many things. So many, many things.

She grabbed hold of a dress and pressed it close, looking at her reflection in the mirror. Why hadn't she thought of this earlier? Why, with all the clothes she'd brought, many items would never get worn. She could take the excess dresses and skirts—ones with solid, practical fabrics—and use them to create new clothes for the girls for Christmas. Yes, what a marvelous idea. And why not shop for bits of lace and trim from the general store? Why, the girls would probably jump for joy if she added a bit of finery to the dresses.

Still in the holiday spirit, she tiptoed into the girls' bedroom to wake them up after she dressed. She had to laugh when she found them already up and dressed. Rena gazed at them in their tattered pinafores and tried to imagine what they would look like on Christmas morning, all decked out in the dresses she would present to them.

A delicious thought flitted through her mind as she pictured Lilly, Callie, and Josephine all dressed up for Christmas in their Sunday finest.

Wouldn't Calista be surprised? And jealous, likely. Yes, the girls could give her a run for her money in the clothing department.

Just as quickly, Rena asked for forgiveness for thinking such a thing. If she made new dresses for the girls, it would only be to make them feel better about themselves and let them know that someone cared enough to craft something of beauty for them.

And as for Calista, well…in her heart of hearts, Rena longed for all the little girls in town to become playmates to her girls.

Her girls.

Rena smiled, realizing that they were finally becoming her children. It would take some doing to feel the same affection for some of the boys, but perhaps with time they could be one big family.

Lilly's voice interrupted her thoughts. "Oh, Miss Rena!" She wrapped her arms around Rena's waist. "You are the most beautiful person ever!"

It took a moment for Rena to figure out what had brought about such excitement. Then she remembered her blue skirt and frilly blouse.

"You look like a lady from a picture book," Callie added, her eyes wide.

"Ooh, my mama had a blue skirt like this." Josephine's eyes filled with tears. She ran her fingers over the fabric of Rena's skirt and sighed.

Rena knelt down and wrapped the little girl in her arms, her heart so full she could hardly stand it. This one had certainly won her affections, no doubt about it. "I'll bet your mama made Thanksgiving really special," Rena whispered, running her hand across Josephine's blond hair.

"She did." Josephine's little smile counteracted her tears. The youngster fingered the lace on Rena's collar. "And she had a blouse like this too. She always said that one day I would grow up and wear pretty things." After a pause, she whispered, "I guess that's not gonna happen now."

Suddenly feeling very motherly, Rena turned the girl around to face the mirror on the wall. "Josephine, you are beautiful on the inside and on the outside. You don't need adornment to prove it. But your mama was right—one day you will grow up, and I'm sure you'll have lovely things. In the meantime, we'll give thanks for the things we do have."

"I'm thankful for you, Miss Rena!" Josephine flung herself into Rena's arms and planted little kisses on her cheeks.

Before long, they were all giggles. Rena felt sure they'd awakened the boys with their laughter, but it was not so. She found them sleeping soundly. They sprang to life the moment she reminded them of the turkey and dressing they would eat later in the day.

By the time she arrived downstairs, Carolina was knocking at the front door. She'd brought William and Jacob with her, but Gene was nowhere to be seen. The boys were dressed in their Sunday clothes but didn't seem happy about it. With freckles scrubbed clean and sandy-colored hair slicked back, they looked like young gentlemen. Except for the scowls, of course.

"Gene will be along shortly," Carolina said, brushing through the door, her arms loaded with food. "He had to tend to an inmate at the jail." She gestured to the pecan pie in William's hands. It looked a bit lumpy and sort of strange. "Gene made the pie himself. Wish he could've delivered it."

Rena wasn't sure which surprised her more—the fact that he'd baked a pie or the idea that he was currently at the jailhouse guarding an inmate.

"He's got a prisoner?" she asked.

"Yes." Carolina gestured for William and Jacob to go to the kitchen then lowered her voice. "Don't want to scare the children. From what I hear, a couple of men got liquored up and robbed the bank over in Tushka. Gene and Charlie have been on the lookout for them ever since they got word that the bank robbers were in this area."

"And he caught both of them?"

"No, just one. Still has his eyes open for the other one."

"How frightening." Rena shivered, realizing that a bank robber could be roaming the streets, even now.

"Anyway, I went by the jail this morning to drop off food. Thought a hearty breakfast was in order. Gene and Charlie were up all night." She paused a moment then snapped her fingers. "Oh, speaking of the jail, there's something I want to talk to you about."

"Oh?"

"Just an idea I had." Carolina smiled.

"You had an idea about the jail and it somehow involves me?" This made Rena very curious. Still, Carolina didn't seem ready to talk about it just yet. She disappeared into the kitchen humming a happy tune, and before long the clanging of pots and pans took over.

Rena busied the children, who agreed to set the table. She gave them instructions, which she hoped they would follow. They were to use the tablecloths from Carolina, along with the centerpiece they'd made. And to top the whole thing off, they could spread the fall leaves around on the table.

Before long, Jenny arrived. Within minutes, she, Rena, and Carolina were up to their elbows in holiday foods. They talked at length while cooking up a storm. In the other room, Rena could hear the children laughing and playing. She prayed they were doing as they'd been instructed. Before long, the smell of the turkey baking permeated the building. Rena's lips watered, but she had to be patient. There was so much work left to do, so many dishes yet to prepare.

The noon hour arrived all too quickly. Rena could hardly believe it. Still, with Jenny and Carolina's help, the meal really was coming together.

She paused from her labors to wipe the perspiration from her brow then looked at the other ladies. "Isn't Gene coming?" she asked. "I'd hoped he would carve the turkey for us." Back home in Gulfport, Reuben had always done the honor. It just seemed a fitting job for a man.

Carolina looked up from the pumpkin pie she'd just fetched from the oven. "What time is it?"

"Twelve-ten," Jenny said, as she finished whipping up the mashed potatoes.

"Something must've gone wrong at the jail," Carolina said. "I'll telephone him and tell him he's about to miss out on the best meal ever if he doesn't hightail it over here."

Rena wasn't sure why, but the idea of carrying on without him just seemed…wrong. She didn't have long to think about it, however. A knock at the door signaled their first guest—Jonathan Brewer. She ushered him inside, her eyes widening with delight when she noticed his fashionable gray suit and tie.

Jenny seemed tongue-tied in his presence, but not Carolina. She swept in, offered to take his hat, and then began to cluck her tongue.

"My, if you don't look nice." She let out a whistle.

His cheeks turned the cutest shade of pink. "Why, thank you, ma'am." He gave a formal bow. "My mama always taught me to dress up for special occasions. Hope that's all right."

"Oh, it's all right." Jenny continued to stare, bug-eyed. "Glad you could make it, Jonathan." Jenny gave him an admiring glance. "You look like a million bucks."

"If I look like a million bucks, then Rena must look like ten million. What a beautiful skirt and blouse you're wearing today." He reached for Rena's hand and gave it a kiss. As always, she felt a fluttering sensation in her stomach. This fellow really knew how to get to a woman, didn't he?

Out of the corners of her eyes she caught a glimpse of Jenny, who didn't look happy at all. "Well, thank you. And don't you think Jenny is the belle of the ball in this new white blouse?"

"Beautiful, as always." He kissed Jenny's hand and her cheeks turned pink.

"Well, enough about how beautiful we all are. Let's go into the dining room, shall we?" Carolina led the way, chattering about the meal they'd cooked. Jenny and the children followed along behind her with Rena and Jonathan lagging in the rear.

Rena gasped as she saw the large oak tables adorned with the hand-tatted ivory tablecloths Carolina had brought over. The colorful fall centerpieces the children had worked so hard to prepare were just the right accompaniment, especially the cornucopias, which spilled over with vibrant autumn vegetables. Recently polished silver forks, knives, and spoons glistened at each place setting and had been carefully placed on delicate lace napkins, another loan from Carolina.

Perfect. Truly, there was no other word to describe the scene before her.

Now, if only the sheriff would get here. Then they could all take their seats and begin this special meal.

Gene had spent all morning at the jail, processing his latest criminal. What a night, trying to catch the guy! But now the fella was safely locked behind bars and awaiting his turn before the judge at the county seat.

Sometime around noon, the telephone rang. Gene assumed Charlie would pick it up, but from the look of things, his deputy had fallen asleep at his desk. Who could blame him?

Gene stifled a yawn and answered on the fourth ring. "Hello?"

"It's time to give thanks!" His mother's cheerful voice rang out on the other end of the line. "We're about to put the food on the table. Hope you're hungry."

"Starved," he said. As if to prove it, his stomach rumbled.

"Well, c'mon over, then. Charlie coming with you?" she asked.

"Nope. He's gonna stay here and guard our prisoner while I eat. Then I'll come back so he can rest."

"We'll send food back with you when you go," she said. "But in the meantime, I hope you'll hurry up. We're ready to get the children seated and dive in."

"Are William and Jacob behaving themselves?"

"They're being themselves." A chuckle followed. "But so far no bones broken, and that includes the wishbone on the turkey we're itching to eat. So, hurry up, son. We're starving over here."

"All right. I'll be right there."

Gene checked on their prisoner, who still looked pretty inebriated from all the whiskey he'd consumed the night before. According to the sheriff in Tushka, there was still one more outlaw on the loose. Gene would celebrate with the others, but he would keep his eyes open for anything suspicious along the way.

He rattled the jail keys, which woke Charlie up at once.

"Leaving?" Charlie yawned.

"Mm-hmm. I'll bring back some food when we're done."

"Sounds great." The young deputy rose and stretched then gave Gene a scrutinizing look. "You're going to Thanksgiving dinner looking like that?" He pointed at Gene's shirt and trousers, but his gaze lingered on the muddy boots.

"Don't really have time to go home and change. They're waiting dinner on me. Do I really look that bad?" For once, he wished for a mirror in the jail so he could see for himself.

"Well, if you're headed to the field to work, you don't look half bad." Charlie chuckled. "But if you've got your heart set on impressing a woman, I'd say you'll have the opposite effect. You've got rips in your jeans, and your boots are caked with mud."

"Nothing I can do about that. Don't have any other boots to change into."

"You definitely don't want to know what your hair looks like."

Gene ran his fingers through his wavy hair and sighed. "Probably like I've been out running in the woods all night, tracking a bank robber."

"Exactly." Charlie laughed. "One thing's for sure—no one can accuse you of not working hard. You might not show up at the dinner table looking like a dandy, but at least you've got a good reason. And I'm pretty sure the smell of the pumpkin pie will drown out the odor from not bathing."

Gene groaned. "That bad?"

Charlie wrinkled his nose. "Maybe the smell's coming from the boots. You were wading in the swamp, right?"

"Had no choice. That's where I caught up with him." Gene gave the raggedy-looking fellow in the jail cell another glance. The man had caused more than enough grief last night.

"Guess I'd better git." Gene offered Charlie a quick good-bye and headed off in his car to the children's home.

He pulled up to the front of the house and gave it a long look. Though Rena had done her best to clean up the place, it still needed a coat of fresh paint. And new boards to replace the busted front steps. And a new roof.

Perhaps he and Charlie could put together a team of men to help with all of that. Surely they could get Jonathan to help. He seemed more than a little interested in the orphans these days. Or maybe his real interest wasn't with the children at all. Maybe he had his eye on someone else entirely. Rena, perhaps? Or Jenny?

Why this idea bothered him so much, Gene couldn't be sure. Jonathan was a great guy. Maybe a little too great.

Gene glanced at the dining-room window and sighed. Likely Brewer would be waiting inside, dressed to the nines and cooing over Jenny's every word. Well, he would give the man a run for his money today. If only he'd had time to bathe and change into a decent suit. Oh well.

When he stepped out of the car, a scream came from the house. He recognized the voice at once. "Rena!"

Her bloodcurdling wails pierced the air. At once he feared the worst. Had the missing bank robber shown up here? With his mother and boys inside?

Gene drew his pistol and rushed the door, kicking it open. Another scream sent a shiver down his spine. It was followed by the sound of multiple squeals coming from the dining room, including a definitive one from Jacob. Gene pointed the gun in front of him as he eased his way down the hallway, closer and closer. The screams continued, which only agitated him further.

He found Rena standing on a chair in the dining room, pumpkin pie in hand, the children gathered around her. He expected to find them in tears, so the laughter from the children confused him. The goofy grins on William's and Jacob's faces alerted him to the fact that mischief was at work.

"What in the world?" He slipped his pistol back in its holster and took a few cautious steps into the room. "What's happening here?"

"It's a m–m–mouse!" Rena gripped the pie tin with one hand and pointed to the floor with the other. "Fool thing's going to ruin a perfectly good Thanksgiving!"

He glanced down and saw what appeared to be a large white mouse scampering under the table. After a couple of seconds, something about the little critter seemed a bit odd. "Wait a minute."

He knelt down and reached for the mouse, finding it to be a hand-carved bit of wood, cleverly painted with mouselike features. The so-called mouse began to move under his fingers and he started...until he realized that the string attached to it was being pulled by one of the boys on the far end of the table.

"Henry, you drop that string this instant."

At once, the mouse ceased to move. Several of the boys—including his own—erupted in laughter. Even Timmy and Nate, usually the quietest of the bunch, doubled over in raucous chuckles.

"W–what?" Rena looked stunned. She shifted the pie from one hand to the other, nearly dropping it in the process.

"You've been duped, Miss Jewel." Gene held it up, and the boys snickered. Well, all but Henry, who doubled over in laughter.

"You mean to tell me I almost sacrificed this pumpkin pie on account of a wooden mouse?" Rena placed the pie on the table, reached for a napkin, and began to fan herself.

"That would have been a tragic loss, Miss Jewel," Jonathan said with a sad look. "I hear your pumpkin pie is the best in town."

This seemed to calm her a bit, but Gene felt like rolling his eyes at Brewer's compliment. For one thing, the man hadn't even tasted her pie yet. How did he know it was the best in town? For another, why did that scoundrel have to show up dressed in such finery for a simple Thanksgiving dinner?

Rena turned to Jonathan and batted her lashes. "Actually, it's the first pumpkin pie I've ever made. And after you taste it, I'm pretty sure you're going to wish I'd dropped it on the ground."

"Doubtful." Jonathan reached for her hand and gave it a squeeze, which seemed to render her speechless.

"Well, all's well that ends well," Carolina said. "Let's pray, folks. I'm hungry."

"Just a moment, Mother." Gene put up his hand. "Before we do that, I believe the boys need a bit of comeuppance about the prank they just played on Miss Jewel."

"Right now?" Rena asked. "We're just about to sit down to dinner."

"Right now." He gave his boys a warning look and then pointed to Henry. "You. Come with mc."

Henry followed him out of the room and received a brief but effective tongue-lashing. By the time they walked back into the dining room, Gene was starving. Apparently, so were all the boys. At this point the children began to talk above each other, their high-pitched voices overlapping. The twins were already scuffling to see who could reach the mashed potatoes first. One of them—Kenny, maybe?—flung his body across the table, now face-to-face with his brother on the opposite side.

"Yes, let's all sit down, shall we?" Rena plopped down in her chair at the end of the larger table. When she landed, the strangest sound erupted. She glanced down, her eyes growing wide, and the boys took to laughing all over again. Her face turned bright red, and she started to fan herself with her napkin once more. "Oh my!"

"Stand up, Miss Jewel." Gene gestured to the seat.

She eased her way up and he reached down and lifted up the poo-poo cushion.

"Merciful heavens." She shook her head and closed her eyes.

"It would appear you've been had once again." Gene offered her a smile, which he hoped would be encouraging.

"I suppose I have." Her nose wrinkled, and he realized the swamp smell must have gotten to her. Oh well. Surely she would understand. He hoped.

"Did someone just kill a skunk in here, or am I imagining things?" his mother asked. She pinched her nose.

Gene groaned. "It's my boots, Mother. They got wet when I… aw, never mind." He walked to the door, pulled off the boots and the wet socks, and tossed them out onto the front porch.

He walked back inside the dining room just in time to see Jonathan playing the role of host, carving the turkey. Gene groaned inwardly, realizing that the dapper fellow had stolen the attention and admiration of both young women. Well, surely Rena wouldn't pay him too much mind.

Rena?

Jenny, of course. Surely *Jenny* wouldn't pay him too much mind.

Gene turned to look at the two women seated beside each other. Jenny's beautiful face caught his eyes at once, but it was Rena's laughter that filled the room. For a moment, he looked back and forth between them, torn. His gaze finally rested on Rena.

Gene paused to think about the changes that had taken place in the orphanage since her arrival. Sure, her attempts to teach the children manners were admirable, though the results—or lack thereof—were laughable. Still, there was something about those beautiful eyes. Something about her gentle, loving spirit that he suddenly found himself drawn to.

"White meat or dark?" Jonathan asked as he looked Gene's way.

Gene attempted to refocus his thoughts. "Oh, dark, please. I'm a leg man myself. Always have been."

This proclamation started the laughter all over again, especially from the boys. Gene fought the instinct to slap himself in the head and took a seat, instead, at the opposite end of the table from Rena, just next to Oliver. Great. Now he would have to go through the whole meal hearing his sentences repeated.

Sure enough, the youngster looked his way and echoed, "I'm a leg man. I'm a leg man!"

"You're about to be a whupped man if you don't stop that," Gene whispered, then offered a forced smile.

Oliver's eyes widened and he nodded before taking the plate given him. Gene settled back in his chair, overwhelmed by the odor now coming from his bare feet, and made up his mind to give thanks whether he felt like it or not.

Chapter Thirteen

. . . .

Tips for Dealing with Unruly Young'uns—*My pa says I should do as I'm told. He don't know how hard I try! When Jacob smacks me upside my head, I count to ten every time before smacking him back. And I tried turnin' the other cheek once, but he hit that one too. Honest and true, I wish Pa would take me fishin' so we could talk. He says he's too busy sheriff'n and such, but I think he could lasso the bad guys with a pole in his hand. Might be fun to watch him try, anyhow.*

—William Wyatt, Age Eight

The Thanksgiving meal moved along at a happy pace until William and Jacob got into a fight over the cranberry relish. Jacob began a kicking fit, which caused the large oak table to vibrate. Gene had just started to speak up when Rena rose and walked their way.

"Boys, we love having you here, but we don't tolerate fighting. Our fighting days are behind us now."

Jacob shoved William so hard that he fell out of his chair and landed on the floor. Before long, they were really going to town, the smacking and punching louder than ever.

Gene watched with a smile as Rena tried her psychological approach once more. Her words fell on deaf ears as the boys continued to tussle. By now, the other boys were standing on their chairs, some rooting for William, others for Jacob.

Seconds later his two were up again. Jacob ran down the side of the table, knocking into one of the chairs and nearly toppling it. Lilly let out a cry, and Callie smacked Jacob upside the head.

"Be a gentleman," she hollered.

This, of course, served to get the youngster madder than a hornet. He doubled up his fist and prepared to take her down a notch or two. Rena looked like she was just about to cry out a warning when Gene rose, took Jacob's upraised hand into his own, and counted to ten. Slowly. By the time he'd finished, the boy had relaxed.

"There now. Apologize to Lilly and take your seat."

He refused. Instead, he started punching William again, this time giving his brother's right eye a real shiner.

"That'll show you!" Jacob hollered from the floor, where he'd pinned William.

Gene grabbed Jacob by one foot, lifted him—upside down—and left him hanging.

"Anything you want to say to your brother?" Gene asked.

"Yeah. He's a snot-nosed, rabbit-eared thief who was gonna take my helping of cranberry relish. And that ain't all. He's a—"

Gene righted Jacob and slipped a hand over the boy's mouth before he said something they'd all be sorry for. William sat on the floor, nursing his swollen eye and muttering under his breath.

Gene's mother rose and walked to the kitchen. She returned a minute later with a raw beefsteak in hand, which she passed to William. "You know what to do with it," she said with a nod.

The unhappy boy placed it over his eye and took his seat once more.

Using his free hand, he scooped a large serving of cranberry relish, taking the last of it. A crooked smile lit his face.

From the end of the table Rena sighed then took a bite of her roll.

They somehow settled back into their meal. Gene kept a watchful eye on Jenny, who kept a watchful eye on Jonathan, who appeared to be keeping a watchful eye on Rena. This couldn't have gone any better if he'd planned it. Maybe Jonathan wasn't interested in Jenny at all.

Not that Jenny looked his way. No, the only one paying him much attention today was Oliver, who repeated his every word—a parrot in dungarees.

Finally Gene could take it no more.

"Can't you think of anything original to say?" he asked.

"Can't you think of anything original to say?" Oliver echoed.

Gene sighed and turned his attention to Rena. "Best meal I've eaten in ages. Now, where's that pumpkin pie I rescued when I first arrived?"

"Where's that pumpkin pie I—" Oliver didn't get to finish because Gene clamped a hand over his mouth.

"This one gets no pie unless he's quiet."

Thank goodness, that shut the youngster up once and for all. Rena and the other ladies sliced pieces of pie—pumpkin, pecan, and cherry— and before long, the children were smacking their lips and offering up contented sighs. Gene took a cautious bite of his pecan pie. Turned out, it wasn't half bad.

By the time the meal ended, he was stuffed full. He rubbed his belly and looked around at the messy table. Jenny rose and began to clear the dishes, so he decided to help her. Perhaps this would put the two of them alone in the kitchen.

No such luck. After just a few minutes, Jenny headed off to the parlor to play board games with his mother, Jonathan, and the children, while he and Rena worked side by side in the kitchen.

"You wash, I'll dry?" she asked.

He nodded. "Yep. Sounds good to me."

He was elbow-deep in soapy water as she chattered on and on about how wonderful the day had been.

"Were we at the same table?" he asked. "Because my memories of the event are a little different from yours."

She flashed a smile so sweet that it stopped him in his tracks. "Oh, but don't you see? We were all together. In one place. Together, to celebrate God's goodness. Sure, the boys were a handful, but at least they were safe and happy and well-fed."

He wasn't sure how to respond to that. Gene stopped his work and scrutinized her. She seemed more relaxed today, almost like a different person. But how did one go about saying such a thing without causing offense? And there was something about her physical appearance too. She looked...extra pretty. He shifted his gaze to the dishes and started scrubbing once again, now deep in thought.

Perhaps the change in appearance had something to do with her statement about God's goodness. Yes, she certainly seemed content. Thank goodness for that. Perhaps she wouldn't run off before the new director arrived in May. That would certainly ease his mind on many levels.

"What?" she asked after a moment. "What is it?"

He paused, lifted a soapy finger, and pointed to her light brown hair, which hung loose around her shoulders. "I *knew* there was something different about you today."

"Different?"

"Yes." He pointed again and then pulled his hand back, remembering his mother's words about pointing being impolite. "I know what it is. You're wearing your hair down. You never do that. It's always up."

Her eyes widened, and she reached up to touch the length of her hair. "Oh my. I meant to put it up after we finished cooking. And then, of course, the children distracted me. You heard what they did, didn't you?"

He sighed. "It might be easier to tell me what they didn't do. I'm sure the list of evil deeds is growing as we speak."

"Let's just say they're rowdy and leave it at that."

The overhead light happened to pick up the various shades of her hair at that very moment, distracting him.

"Sheriff?" She gave him a curious look. "Is everything all right?"

"Oh, yes. Of course." *If only you hadn't worn your hair down. I might've stood a chance at paying attention to what you're saying.* "What were we talking about again?"

"I was about to explain why the boys had me so distracted. You're probably not going to believe this…."

"Try me."

"Well, it's the strangest thing. They—"

"You're wearing lace." Had he interrupted her again? From the look on her face, yes, he had. But, still, he would be remiss in not pointing it out. The woman never wore lace. Nothing frilly. Only sensible brown or gray dresses. Nothing like this soft white blouse she wore today.

He pointed to her blouse. "Don't think I've ever seen you in lace before. And that blue skirt. You don't usually wear blue."

"Oh, that." Her cheeks turned the prettiest rosy-pink. "You're right. I've been trying to wear more practical clothes because of the heavy work involved, but this is a holiday, a day to celebrate."

"Well, then, you should celebrate every day."

"O–oh?"

Gene felt the strangest sense of wonder pass over him as she smiled. He didn't get to revel in the feeling for long, though, because the boys and girls ran through the kitchen to the back door, jarring him back to his senses.

"Whoa, Nellie!" Gene dropped the dishes into the sink and blocked the door. From the ends of his fingers, soap bubbles dripped onto the floor. "Where are you going?" he asked.

"Miss Jenny said we could play in the piles of leaves in the backyard," Callie said.

"Aw, she just wants an excuse to be alone with Mr. Brewer," Henry threw in, rolling his eyes.

Gene fought to keep from responding to that comment. His mother entered the kitchen and glanced his way. "Don't pay them any mind. They're prone to exaggeration."

"No doubt." Gene wasn't sure what to say.

"You're making a mess, son." His mother gestured to his soapy hands. "Almost as big a mess as you made in putting together that pecan pie."

He groaned.

"Better get back to work. I'll go out back with the children." She looked between Gene and Rena. "If you two can handle the work in here, I mean."

"We're doing just fine," Rena's happy-go-lucky voice sounded. "Have fun out there."

The children disappeared through the door and Gene returned to his labors at the sink. He and Rena worked side by side, occasionally pausing to gaze out the kitchen window at the piles of leaves and the children who danced through them.

"I've always loved Thanksgiving Day because of the changing of the leaves," Rena said. "We had some beautiful magnolia trees in our front yard in Gulfport. I used to love them so."

"Why do you say *had*? Did a hurricane blow them away or something?"

"Actually, yes." Her expression shifted, and he could read the sadness in her eyes.

"Ah. Sorry. Didn't really think you'd say yes. We don't see hurricanes up this way. Just tornadoes." The moment he spoke the word, visions of Brenda arose. He did his best to shove them back down.

"Actually, I'm pretty sure I just saw a tornado whip through right here." She drew so near they were practically touching, as she pointed at Callie through the window. "See? She's stirring up the leaves like the wind."

"Um, yes." Gene paused, wondering if the delightful smell of perfume Rena was wearing had somehow affected him. He couldn't seem to think straight today.

Rena's eyelashes fluttered a bit and then she went back to work, drying the large turkey platter. "I've been waiting for this day ever since I got here. The children deserve a special day like this, don't you think? I know they're a handful, but they're so precious."

Precious wasn't exactly the word he would've chosen, and he did have to wonder if Rena was being sensible in her approach to the children. Did she not realize how easily they could turn on her? Perhaps someone needed to fill her in before the boys and girls took advantage of her generous nature once more.

"Couple things you should know." Gene pointed to Josephine. "That one right there…she's a snitch."

"Meaning she tells on the others?"

"Yep." He nodded. "Thrives on it, in fact. She doesn't always get her stories straight, but she's happy to tell you who committed the offense."

"Oh, but she's such a darling little thing. And she's been through so much. She lost her parents in a house fire, you know. If you really take the time to get to know her, you will see a scared little girl in need of a mother. That's all she's crying out for—the attention every child deserves."

"Hmm."

"Getting to know the children is key." A dreamy-eyed expression settled onto Rena's face. "For instance, I've been getting to know Lilly and Callie. You might be surprised to hear that Callie writes letters to her mother, though her memories are fading. Don't you find that endearing?"

"I had no idea. Mrs. Wabash never told me."

"It's true." Rena gazed at Callie. "Poor little thing has a whole drawer full of them. I found them when I was putting clothes away." Rena's eyes misted over. "I want so desperately to make a difference in their lives, Gene. I hope I can." She dried a plate and set it on the counter.

"You already are." Should he tell her that she was the only director thus far who'd actually fallen in love with the children? That they seemed to be responding to her in a way he'd never seen before? That her kindness and gentle nature had taken everyone by surprise…even him?

Gene had just opened his mouth to share these thoughts when Rena gestured toward the twins. "They're the cutest little things, aren't they? That red hair and all those freckles." Her nose wrinkled. "But I have a hard time understanding them. The brogue is thick, but the curls are thicker. They're long overdue for a haircut, but Joe refuses to touch them. I did my best with Wesley's hair, but he's not happy with the outcome. Not sure I am, either."

"Certainly looks better than before."

"Thank you. I'm still learning, of course."

"Of course."

"I'll tell you someone else who's overdue for a haircut, and that's Oliver."

Gene fought the temptation to repeat, "And that's Oliver." Instead, he chuckled. "Good luck in getting him to sit still long enough to cut his hair. He's slipperier than a worm avoiding the hook."

Rena chuckled. "You have such a quaint way with words." She finished drying another plate and added it to the stack.

He felt his smile fading. "I'm not a city fella, if that's what you mean. Just a good old country boy from Oklahoma, and right proud of it."

Her cheeks turned pink, and he could read the concern in her eyes. "Oh, I wasn't poking fun. I...well, I think your way of speaking is..." She paused. "Cute."

"Cute, eh?" He found himself smiling again. "Ain't been called 'cute' since I was a boy. But I can't say as I mind, as long as you smile like that when you say it."

Her eyelashes fluttered a bit, but the smile never diminished. Yes, indeed. She could call him anything she liked.

An odd silence grew between them. Gene needed to figure out a way to break it. "What are you planning for Christmas?" he asked after a moment.

"For the children, you mean?" She seemed to come alive once more. "They've absconded with the Sears, Roebuck and Co. catalogue and have nearly worn it out. I plan to contact my brother with a list. Perhaps our friends and church members in Gulfport can meet the need for Christmas gifts. I'm sure they would like the opportunity to try. And anything they don't come up with, well..." Her words drifted off.

"Well, what?" he asked.

She reached for a dishcloth and started drying a drinking glass. "I don't mean to sound presumptuous, but I have some money put away. I wouldn't be opposed to the idea of providing Christmas for the children. It would be my honor, in fact. The more I get to know them, the more I see the particular needs, especially for clothing and shoes. It's just a matter of listing the right sizes. My brother and sister-in-law can take care of the rest. And if they can't, I can." She put the glass down and reached for another.

"Still, I hate to see you spend your own money on them."

"What else is it good for?" She began drying a large kettle.

"True." He released a slow breath, contemplating her words. He and Brenda had never had more than a couple of nickels to rub together, so he truly could not relate to Rena's financial status. Still, she didn't seem to mind spending it on the children, a trait he found admirable.

"I'm going to make new dresses for the girls for Christmas, but I'll need to order clothing for the boys. I could use your help with that."

"Of course." He paused and gave her another look. "You're a very kind woman. Has anyone ever told you that?"

She smiled. "Well, some of the folks I worked with at the missions society said something similar once. I've always loved tending to the needs of others."

"It suits you."

"I had little else to do back in Gulfport, to be honest. I spent most of my days rather bored." She chuckled. "Those days are behind me."

"They sure are." He paused. "Before you arrived, I wondered what sort of life you would be leaving to come here."

"Did you now?" A slow smile tipped up the corners of her lips. "What did you imagine, based on my letter?"

Gene took a moment to think about his answer. "I don't suppose I saw you as a socialite. I rather envisioned a woman more…" He hesitated. "Tough?"

"I'm tough."

He tried not to laugh. "Maybe, but…"

"And I was no socialite. That's not to say I didn't taste of that world, but my heart was never in it. I was only there because…" Her gaze shifted downward. "Well, because there was nowhere else for a single young woman to live. I found myself in a rather awkward predicament after my parents died, but I was too young to do anything about it."

"I'm sorry." He took her hand, realizing too late that the soap bubbles might be less than desirable. "I'm not trying to make this uncomfortable for you. I'm just saying you're a bit different from what I pictured. But then again, who can tell much from a letter?"

"True." She nodded. "It's only meeting face-to-face that one can ascertain certain things about a person."

"Indeed." He held tightly to her hand, and unspoken words seemed to travel between them.

From outside, one of the children hollered and Gene let go of Rena's hand at once. "Guess I'd better get out there and referee."

"And just when we were having such a good time." She gave him a little wink, one that sent his heart fluttering. Good gravy. Since when had a woman affected him this way? Even Jenny, as beautiful as she was, hadn't stirred his heart in such a manner.

"Gene, you're needed out here." His mother's voice sounded from the doorway. "Better hurry."

He sighed then turned in the direction of her voice.

Rena couldn't help but grin as she looked out the window at Gene and the children. He'd been summoned to scold Oliver but ended up dunking the boy into a pile of red-and-gold leaves. Then again, he always seemed to go easier on his own boys than the rest of the children. No doubt he felt sorry for them, losing their mother and all. The sheriff's disciplinary skills were unusual at best, but there was something rather lovely about the way he spoke to the boys and girls. It did her heart good.

In fact, there were a great many things about the man that did her heart good. After all, he could bake a heavenly pecan pie and wash dishes.

She watched him for a moment longer, her heart aflutter with joy, then returned her attention to the dishes.

Chapter Fourteen

....

Tips for Dealing with Unruly Young'uns—*Women have a deep God-given desire to nurture others. I felt that desire almost from childhood as I played with my dolls. My husband, Reuben, and I have parented one daughter, Sadie. But we also helped to raise Reuben's younger sister, Rena, who came to us at the vulnerable age of fourteen. If I've learned one thing about children, it is this: they respond to love. When all else fails...love.*

—Virginia Jewel, Gulfport, Mississippi

Gene spent the next couple of hours lounging on the broken-down sofa and gabbing with the ladies and Jonathan. At four o'clock his mother fixed a plate of food for Charlie and sent him packing. Though he hated to admit it, Gene didn't want to leave. He'd enjoyed his time with Jenny, sure, but he'd also shared more enjoyable conversation with Rena. Her embarrassed smiles and sideways glances had not escaped his notice. And he still couldn't get over the fact that she'd left a calm, quiet existence back in Gulfport to come here and tend to seventeen children. What a difference!

As he made his way back to the jailhouse, he thought about his boys and their behavior at the dinner table. He'd seen enough of their

shenanigans at home, naturally, but these battles they raged against each other had to stop, at least in public. How would he bring that about? A few moments of contemplation followed. Just as he reached the jail, a strange thought flitted through his mind: *"Love them."*

He swallowed hard and turned off the car.

"Love them."

At once he began to argue with himself. He did love them. He fed them, clothed them, gave them swats when they needed it.…

"Love them."

Ugh. There it was again, that…that nudging. Had he missed something, perhaps? Could it be that loving little boys involved more than an occasional hug or prayers at bedtime? Could he really love them with the kind of intensity necessary to turn their lives around?

Gene had no idea, but he was certainly willing to give the idea time to develop.

Later that night, the children finally settled down for Rena. The boys tumbled into their beds, exhausted from the antics of the day. Next came the girls. Callie and Josephine wriggled under their quilts right away, but Lilly took a little longer.

Rena paused to brush her beautiful curls and lifted a loose hair from the child's brow. "I always wanted curly hair," she said.

Lilly's nose wrinkled. "Not me. I want pretty, straight hair like yours." She fingered Rena's hair then leaned against her and whispered, "This was the best Thanksgiving ever." Her words were followed by a contented sigh.

Rena gave her a kiss on the forehead. "Really? Do you think so?"

"Oh, yes." Lilly giggled. "The very, very, very best!" She sat up in the bed, threw her arms around Rena's neck, and gave her a tight hug. "Thank you! Thank you!"

"You are so welcome, Lilly-Bear."

"Lilly-Bear?" The child giggled. "I like it."

Rena gave her a little kiss on the forehead and tucked her in. Then she turned her attention to the others, kissing Callie and Josephine on their foreheads.

"Miss Rena?" Josephine whispered from under the covers. "I... I love you."

Rena knelt next to the youngster's bed, her eyes now brimming with tears. "Oh, you sweet girl. I love you too." She gave her another kiss on the forehead, this one filled with far more emotion than the one before.

Minutes later, her heart quite full, Rena walked down the stairs to say good night to Jenny and Carolina, who were both resting in the parlor— Carolina on the lumpy sofa and Jenny in the broken wingback chair.

"Quite a day, wouldn't you say?" Jenny kicked off her shoes.

"Oh, it had its moments." Carolina smiled. "Right now, I feel about as broken-down as this old sofa. My joints are as twisted as these springs."

"I'm already working on that," Rena said. "I've sent a letter to my brother for the missions society. New furniture should be arriving over the next few weeks. Donated, of course, but I feel sure it will be a lot nicer than what's here now."

Carolina sat up suddenly and looked Rena's way. "Oh, that reminds me of what I was going to tell you earlier today. You're quite skilled at fixing things up."

"I do? What makes you say that?"

"Those centerpieces the children put together. And I, for one, am thrilled that this place is going to get a new look. It's such an eyesore in its current state—and dangerous, to boot. Renovations are much-needed and long overdue."

"I agree," Rena said. "I've sent a letter to my niece, Sadie. We've written several times over the past month about her upcoming trip to Daisy."

"She's coming here?" Jenny asked.

"She is. And I can't wait for you to meet her. Why, she's the prettiest thing you ever saw, and she has a knack—really, I can't think of a better word to call it—a knack for decorating. She's simply marvelous at it. I felt sure folks in Gulfport would hire her in a minute to fix up their homes, but she opted to go to college instead. I believe the timing of her trip to Daisy is perfect. She'll be such a help to me."

Carolina snapped her fingers. "Back to what I meant to tell you earlier. There's one other place in town in need of a woman's touch, and you're just the one to tackle it."

"Oh?" Rena settled onto the sofa, the springs stabbing her bottom.

"Yes." Carolina's eyes sparkled as she spoke. "The jailhouse."

"The jailhouse?" Rena sat up straighter. "You think we need to decorate the jailhouse?"

"Well, not decorate it, exactly," Carolina said. "Just clean it up…give it a bit of color and life. It's so dank and dreary."

"Isn't that what a jail is supposed to be?" Jenny asked.

"In theory, I suppose, though I daresay a criminal would stand a better chance of reforming if you offered him a bit of color instead of those drab gray walls." Carolina gave Rena a closer look. "Which reminds me—you look radiant in that blue skirt. Don't know if I mentioned it."

Rena smiled, overcome by such kindness. "Thank you so much."

"I feel sure one fella noticed," Carolina said, winking.

Rena couldn't be sure if she meant Jonathan or Gene but decided that a change of subject was in order. Before long, they were talking about the rest of the day, laughing over the wooden mouse and bragging on the taste of the pumpkin pie.

"I never really learned to cook," Rena admitted. "Just one more thing I missed out on, losing my mama at such a young age. Anyway, I'm awfully grateful you've been teaching me."

"If you don't mind my asking, what happened to your parents?" Carolina asked.

Rena shifted her gaze to the fireplace and tugged at her collar. While she wanted to answer Carolina's question, the words refused to come.

"I'm sorry, dear. I've overstepped my bounds. Forgive me?"

"No, it's not that. Not at all." Rena felt the sting of tears. "I so rarely discuss my parents…. Reuben didn't like to talk about them, so I kept my words inside. Well, inside and on the page. I've often written down my feelings about what happened to them."

"Must be very cathartic," Jenny said.

"Yes. Though it doesn't take the place of real conversation." Rena paused for a moment. "And to be honest, I would enjoy talking about what happened to my parents. I don't often get the opportunity to share aloud."

"Then tell us anything you like." Carolina gave her a sympathetic smile.

"I was fourteen when it happened," Rena explained. "It was a day like any other. I'd gone to school in the morning. I distinctly remember wearing a blue dress and a matching ribbon in my hair. Midmorning, I heard the wail of a siren as the fire truck went by. As children are wont to do, it piqued my curiosity. I never dreamed…." She drew in a deep breath, suddenly feeling the pain of the moment afresh.

"Oh, honey…" Carolina shook her head. "I can imagine what you're about to say."

"All was lost." Rena brushed away tears. "Our home burned to the ground, and my parents…" She began to cry in earnest now.

"You poor girl."

Rena finally managed to get the rest of the story out. "My brother and sister-in-law had just married. They were living in a new home in Gulfport, not terribly far from Jacksonville, where I'd grown up. They came for me...." She paused, remembering the day they had arrived. "Thank God, they came. And they took me in. I've felt the security of their love and care from the beginning. I never felt like an outsider. Only..."

"Only what?"

"Only, after twenty-four years of living with them, I found myself feeling trapped. I'd so enjoyed the comfort of their home that I'd never thought of venturing out into the real world." She gestured to her surroundings. "This is the real world."

"Oh, it's quite real." Jenny smiled. "And depending on which child you're with, it can be more real than you've imagined."

"The children are a handful," Rena said. "And I must confess, there are times when I want to throw my hands in the air and declare defeat. But then I remember what I felt like that first day in Reuben and Virginia's home. I was a parentless child with no sense of security until they came for me. If you think about it, my situation was the very same as Josephine's. Only, I had a place to go and she did not. Do you see what I mean?"

"I do." Carolina squeezed her hand. "I didn't realize until this very conversation just how much you have in common with these boys and girls. No wonder your heart cries out for them. No wonder you put up with so much. You've walked a mile in their shoes and know what they're going through."

"To some extent, yes." She shivered. "Though I can't imagine what it must feel like to be here without any family members at all, as some of the children are. It has to be a terribly lonely feeling. That's why I must do what I can to make them feel loved. And special. They are special, even when they're naughty. They have great value—to me and to the Lord."

"You've done a wonderful job of conveying this to the children," Jenny said. "I have a feeling that Josephine and the others will all thrive under your care. I've already noticed a remarkable difference in her attitude at school, if that makes you feel any better."

"It does." Rena smiled.

"It all comes down to seeing ourselves through God's eyes," Carolina added. "I've told Gene this a thousand times."

"Gene? He struggles with feeling valuable?" Rena could hardly believe such a thing was possible.

"He does," Carolina said, "whether it shows to others or not. And it's spilled over to the boys. I've never met two needier children when it comes to worth. And I'm not talking self-worth, either. In and of ourselves, we don't have worth. Nothing we ever do—or accomplish—in this life will change that. But resting in God's worthiness is key."

"Amen to that," Jenny said.

Rena leaned against the sofa, thinking through Carolina's words. They stayed on her mind as the ladies took to chatting about the upcoming Christmas season. And they lingered still as Jenny and Carolina rose to leave.

Rena bid them good night and headed up the stairs. As she slipped into her nightgown, the feeling of exhaustion was so deep she wondered if she would make it to the bed.

This day had worn her out on every conceivable level. The children under her care had been taxing as always, but William and Jacob were the toughest of the lot. No one could deny it, not even Gene. The youngsters were filled with anger. Not that she blamed them. Oh no. Losing a parent would bring out all sorts of emotions.

Losing a parent.

The words flitted through her mind, holding her captive. In that moment, a wave of sadness swept over her and she was fourteen years old again, sitting in class with her best friend Abby at the desk next to her. Just an average school day in East Texas, unlike any other. She was working on her math problems—strange, that Rena even remembered the specific algebra problem—when Mrs. Linden, the principal, came rushing into the room.

Only three words stood out now:

Fire.

Parents.

Dead.

A cold chill swept over the room, and Rena tried to push back the emotions that threatened to follow this memory. In spite of her attempts, the tears flowed anyway.

She tumbled onto her bed without even pulling back the chenille cover, as the familiar feelings of emptiness and devastation overtook her. With her face buried in the pillow, the sobs came. They flooded over her with such intensity that she could barely catch her breath.

Oh, but how could she control such emotion? She remembered the terrible nightmares. The pain of losing her mama.

Mama!

Her mother's dear face came into view at once. That perfect china-doll face with the beautifully rounded lips and compassionate eyes. Her voice…that soothing, calming voice…silenced forever.

And Papa! That godly, heavenly man. His resounding laughter would no longer echo across the house.

The house.

Rena shivered, remembering the moment she'd laid eyes on it after the fire. A hollow, burnt shell of what it had once been.

Reuben and his new bride, Virginia, had come for her at once, of course. Those first few weeks at their house in Mississippi were strange and terrifying. She'd never felt so lost.

Strange house.

Strange bed.

Strange town.

Near-strangers caring for her.

Everything…strange and unfamiliar.

Oh, how terrifying it had all been. However had she survived?

Only one word came to mind, and it calmed her at once: *love*. The love of a brother and sister-in-law who had poured themselves out on her behalf. Their love had given her a reason to go on. And the love she carried inside of her was more than enough to share with those who needed it most, even those most difficult.

Rena paused and reached for her hankie to wipe her face. As she did, she thought of William and Jacob once more. Sure, they took their anger on each other. Well, who could blame them? They'd lost their parents and then their adoptive mother. It was a wonder they could still function at all. And Josephine…God bless that dear little girl! How sad, to go from everything to nothing all at once.

Rena sat up in the bed, suddenly invigorated. She would pour herself out for all of the boys and girls in Daisy…every last one. And they would be won by her love, a love so deep, so strong, that it would tear down walls and lift broken spirits.

With renewed hope, Rena rose, washed her face, and dressed for bed.

Chapter Fifteen

....

TIPS FOR DEALING WITH UNRULY YOUNG'UNS—*As Daisy's only
doctor, I'm fascinated by the scuttlebutt over the town's orphan
children. My wife and I raised six strapping boys. Six. Sure, they
gave us fits at times, but they're grown and married now with
children of their own. My method of dealing with the boys was
different from most: I reasoned with them. Sat them down and
talked with them, face-to-face, man-to-man. I won their respect
that way. Now that they're grown, I see them talking to their own
sons with just as much respect. Hopefully those grandbabies will
grow into fine, respectable citizens like their parents.*

—Doc Moseley, Daisy, Oklahoma

Rena spent the better part of the next week reworking some of her dresses
into usable clothing for the girls. With a bit of maneuvering, she turned
a woman's skirt into two darling pinafores for Lilly and Callie. She could
hardly wait to get started on their Christmas dresses. She'd chosen an
older red velvet dress passed down from Virginia. With a bit of lace, it
would be just the thing for festive holiday dresses for the two sisters.

Rena struggled a bit with the pedal on the old sewing machine
she'd located in the closet but managed to get quite a bit accomplished

in spite of it. Of course, she had to work at night so that the children wouldn't see what she was up to. This left her exhausted most mornings, but she felt sure it would be worth it, as soon as the girls saw their new Christmas dresses.

The following Saturday Rena made the decision to go to town. She needed to visit the general store so that she could purchase some lace and other trim pieces. Carolina agreed to watch the children, but Rena decided to take Lilly with her. The youngster's bed-wetting problem was still very much an issue, though they never discussed it. She might as well face the problem and take the child to the doctor just in case.

She managed to keep Lilly's fears at bay long enough to convince her to go alone with Doc Moseley and his nurse into his small inner office. Who could blame her for not wanting to go with them? It smelled of camphor and rubbing alcohol. The doctor emerged several minutes later, a concerned look on his face.

"I hate to tell you this, Miss Jewel, but Lilly has pinworms."

"Pinworms?" She shook her head, trying to make sense of his words.

"Yes. I daresay most of the children probably have them." He explained, in simple terms, how bed-wetting often occurred as a result, and Rena groaned.

"This is all new to me," she explained. "I'm such a novice. What do we do?"

"First, I would suggest getting rid of the dirt under the children's nails. But this next part won't be as easy. You'll need to feed them as much garlic as they can stand."

"Garlic?"

"Yes. You can make it into a paste to be swallowed or cook it up in sauces and stews. Either way, you'll need to use plenty of it."

Rena sighed.

He gave her a compassionate smile. "I know. It sounds awful, but it's necessary. Within a few days the pinworms will be gone and you should see a marked improvement."

"Well, that's a relief."

"Yes, but I must warn you, bed-wetting has now become a habit for Lilly. For that reason alone, I would suggest you keep her from drinking anything in the four hours before bedtime. She's still very young, you know. Sometimes little girls have a hard time, especially if they're of a nervous nature. If you can get her to relax, well, perhaps things will go better for her."

"I will do my best," Rena said. Still, she could hardly stop thinking about the garlic she would need to buy. How in the world would she manage such a thing?

"My nurse is still with her," the doctor explained, "but you can go in now. She didn't care much for the exam, I'm afraid, so she's shaken. But she will recover." He placed a hand on Rena's arm. "And just for the record, I think what you're doing for these boys and girls is admirable. I only wish the director before you had exuded such kindness and patience. The children will thrive under your care, I've no doubt about it."

"Why, thank you." She hardly knew what to say. His words bolstered her courage and gave her a renewed sense of purpose.

"I raised several boys myself." He appeared to lose himself in his memories for a moment but finally looked her way with a smile. "Seems like a lifetime ago. They're not young for very long, you know. They grow up all too soon. I'm proud to say my boys have turned out to be fine, upstanding citizens."

"Thank you so much for that reminder. It's hard to imagine what these children will be like when they're grown, but I pray they are wonderful, productive citizens like your boys."

"With you guiding the way, I'm sure they will be."

She couldn't stop the smile from turning up her lips at his encouraging words. Still, she had a teary-eyed child to deal with.

As they left the doctor's office—Lilly still bawling—Rena turned toward the general store. "Since you were a very good girl at the doctor's office, I'm going to let you pick out a special treat at the store."

"A treat?" Lilly gazed up at her and brushed away the tears. "Really, truly?"

"Yes." Rena knelt beside her. "Any candy of your choosing. How's that? And if you like, you can also pick out a piece for each of the boys and girls."

Lilly's eyes widened and her tears dried up at once.

They arrived at the store and Lilly went to work, looking over the jars of candy. She oohed and aahed over the licorice, the cherry sours, and the gumballs. In the end, though, she went with the lollipops, choosing a red one for herself and a multiplicity of colors for the other children.

Rena turned her attention to the fabrics but found herself distracted as Henry walked into the store. He shoved something in his pocket then moved in the direction of the comic books. Everything about his movements spoke of mischief.

"Henry, what are you doing in town?" Rena felt as if her heart had gravitated to her throat.

For a moment he looked surprised to see her. Then he smiled. "Miss Carolina sent me." He held out his hand to reveal several coins. "Said she needed carrots and peas." He gestured toward the street. "The farmers come to town on Saturdays with their wares. See?"

"I suppose." Still, none of this made sense. Since when did Carolina send the children to town alone? And why would she trust him with money? Besides, he didn't appear to have any carrots or peas in his possession.

"Guess I'd better get on back to the house." He turned toward the door.

Something suspicious caught her eye. She gave him a second look to make sure she wasn't imagining things. "Henry, is that a wad of chewing tobacco in your mouth?"

He did not respond, but his face now looked a bit ashen.

She lowered her voice to a whisper so as not to arouse the suspicions of the other customers. "Where in the world did you get that?"

A shrug followed.

"Don't lie to me. Where did you get it?"

Henry spoke around the wad in his cheek. "Mrs. Hannigan." He pointed to the woman at the register. "She sold it to me."

"You're telling me she sold tobacco to a child?"

"I'm not a child." Henry looked offended. He also looked a little sick.

"Still, you're not grown. There is no way Mrs. Hannigan would have done such a thing." Rena took a couple steps toward the register, but Henry took her by the arm.

"Aw, c'mon, Miz Rena. Have a heart. I stole it from Joe, the barber."

"W–what?" All the encouraging words the doctor had spoken over her fizzled away at this confession.

"He had it comin'." Henry's eyes narrowed to slits. "He's been really mean to us."

"Your thieving ways are inexcusable," she said. "And now you've put me in a terrible predicament. We have to go to the barbershop at once and make apologies. But first I have to buy a pouch of chewing tobacco to replace the one you stole. You can pay me back for it by doing extra chores around the house, starting with replacing the boards on the front steps."

He groaned and slapped himself on the head. "You gonna use me like a slave? That's what Mrs. Wabash usta do. She used me up and spit me out. Then she left. You gonna use me up and spit me out then take off when that new director comes in the spring?"

"No, but I am going to make you pay for what you took. In the meantime, come to the register with me. I need to buy more tobacco for Joe."

He shuffled along beside her as she made her way to the front of the store.

She drew in a deep breath and faced the store clerk. "Mrs. Hannigan, I know it won't make much sense to you—and please don't ask why I'm doing this—but I have to buy a package of…" She turned and looked at Henry.

He mumbled, "Red Man chewin' tobacco."

"Red Man chewing tobacco," Rena repeated.

Behind her, the sound of children's voices shook the place. Rena turned and was stunned to discover Oliver standing there with the twins at his side. The twins rambled on about the candies they wished they could purchase but spoke so fast that she could hardly make sense of their words through the heavy brogue.

Next to them, the three brothers, Mikey, Bubba, and Tree, were shoving each other and cursing. Mochni had taken to doing some sort of rain dance that included whooping and hollering. This, of course, had snagged the attention of other shoppers, mostly women who looked terrified.

Rena took a step in the direction of the boys. "W–what are you doing here?"

"We followed Henry." Tree wiped his runny nose on his shirtsleeve.

"Saw him in the barbershop," Bubba added. "Going through dumb old Joe's stuff."

"You snitch. I'll get you." Henry lit into Bubba and knocked him to the floor. This, of course, got Mikey and Tree riled up. They joined the fight on their brother's behalf, claiming they were going to take off Henry's head for messing with their brother.

Mochni stayed out of it, as did the twins, who were more interested in scouring the store for things to play with. In the meantime, Henry barreled back hard with his fist and bumped a shelf holding several jams and jellies. The shelf came crashing down on top of the boys, which instantly put an end to their fight.

Mrs. Hannigan stood at the register with her mouth agape. Several customers began to talk at once, many scolding the boys or attempting to shoo them out of the store. Rena hardly had a chance to collect her thoughts before the conversations turned ugly.

She leaned down and spoke to the whole group of them. "Boys—all but Henry—go on back to the house. Take Lilly with you. She is up at the counter near the candy jars. I'll be along shortly with my purchases."

"Yes'm." Bubba wiped his bloody nose, and Tree rubbed his shoulder.

Henry rose, albeit slowly, and limped his way outside the store, muttering something about waiting outside.

Moments later Lilly drew near, looking concerned. "Can I still have my lollipop?"

"Yes, but it's clear that several of the boys will not be getting any."

Tree groaned and slapped himself in the head. "Aw, shucks. Look what you done, fellas. Gone and got us in trouble again. And I wanted that candy too."

They grumbled all the way out the door.

A visible sigh arose when the crowd of children disappeared from view. The adults resumed their conversations, most about how unruly the youngsters had been. Rena couldn't help but notice their frustration with the children, but who could blame them? She could only imagine what Molly Harris would say, once word of this got back to her. Her "Fresh as a Daisy" campaign would get just the fuel it needed.

Oh well. She had no time to worry about that right now. Rena went to work at once, helping Mr. Hannigan right the shelf while Mrs. Hannigan looked on. Many of the jars of jams and jellies were broken, but the ones that weren't were stacked willy-nilly onto the top shelf. Rena fought the urge to cry as she looked around at the mess.

"I...I don't know what to say," she managed at last. "I will pay you for the damaged goods, naturally." She reached for her purse.

Mrs. Hannigan drew near. "Ordinarily I wouldn't ask that of you, but those jars were just delivered. Mrs. Ramsey worked for days to get them ready, and she really needs the income they bring. She's counting on it, in fact."

"Of course. I'll cover the cost when I pay for my merchandise." Rena walked to the register and gazed down at the candy. She'd wanted to surprise the children, but it all seemed so pointless now.

"Is there anything else I can do for you?" Mrs. Hannigan asked and then offered what appeared to be a forced smile.

"Yes. I need some trim pieces for the dresses I'm sewing. And several cloves of garlic."

"I have some beautiful bits of lace right here." Mrs. Hannigan reached under the glass counter and pulled out a tray. "Pick out what you like while I go fetch the garlic cloves." She disappeared into the back room, but not before making apologies to another customer for the chaos that had just taken place.

Rena kept a watchful eye on Henry through the store's large plate-glass window while she glanced at the lace pieces. Yes, there were quite a few here that might work. And some lovely buttons, as well. She could almost imagine the girls in their new dresses now.

Mrs. Hannigan returned with several cloves of garlic. "All right. Now, is there anything else you need?"

Rena had just started to respond with a "No" when something occurred to her. "Has the postman gone for the day? I need to check the mail. I meant to come by earlier in the week but have been so busy."

"He's already gone, but I can give you your mail," Mrs. Hannigan said. "You've got letters aplenty. I've been holding them for you."

Rena glanced at Henry once again. He'd started gabbing with one of the local merchants. She might as well look over the stack of letters here. Once she got home, the children would be too much of a distraction.

She glanced through them all, smiling when she saw one from Sadie.

Another one from Reuben caught her eye as well. Still, there was one envelope that stood out above all others, but not because of the sender. It smelled of honeysuckle.

"Wonder who this one's from." She ripped it open and unfolded the letter inside. Her heart skipped a beat as she read:

My Dear Miss Jewel,

Rarely do I think of your name without pondering that most precious jewel of all, the diamond. Each facet sets off its own glow—in much the same way you do, when you enter a room.

Rena's heart nearly stopped beating as she read those words. The letter began to tremble in her hand. Who had sent this? The words sounded like something Jonathan might say, but did he really have such feelings for her? She read on:

Our conversation in the kitchen has stirred something in my heart I've not felt in quite some time. And though I cannot bring myself to speak the words aloud, I now possess feelings for you that I have not felt since my dear wife passed —God rest her soul. If you would allow me to admire you from afar while I work up the courage to speak my mind, I would be overcome with happiness.

Truly yours, Gene Wyatt

The letter now vibrated so violently, she nearly dropped it.

"Are you all right, Miss Jewel?" Mrs. Hannigan's voice served as a reminder that she was still in a very public place, one where she couldn't fully absorb the words in this letter.

"I…I…" Rena couldn't manage anything else.

"Would you like me to add these to the cost of the jams and jellies?" Mrs. Hannigan held up her items, which she barely glanced at.

"Oh…what? I, well, sure. Wrap them up for me, please." She fumbled in her purse, coming up with the necessary money.

Henry showed up at that moment, and she shoved the letter into her skirt pocket. To have one of the children find the letter would be humiliating at best. Why, they would have a field day with this!

"We need to go now." She reached for the package, but Henry took it instead.

"I'll carry it, Miss Rena."

"Thank you." She fumbled with the other mail pieces, finally pressing them all into her pocket. "We've got to get home right away. No dawdling."

"But I thought you said…"

"Don't argue with me now, Henry. I've got to get home, and the sooner, the better."

"Yes, ma'am."

She wondered at the crooked grin that lit his face but didn't have time to ask about it. No, only one thing consumed her thoughts at the moment. Gene Wyatt had feelings for her. Feelings he'd openly admitted in the letter she now carried in her pocket.

Oh, wonder of wonders! Finally! At least one thing was going right today, one very important thing.

Her story was coming true. She could hardly wait to see what adventures the next chapter held. With her head held high, she marched out of the general store and began the journey toward home.

On the first Saturday in December, Gene stopped off at the newspaper office before heading home. He had some business to take care of with Jonathan Brewer. He found the newspaperman seated in a chair outside his office, which was just off the town square. Joe sat beside him, talkative as usual.

Gene greeted them with a nod.

"What brings you by, Sheriff?" Joe asked.

"Wanted to thank Brewer personally." Gene extended his hand and Jonathan gave it a firm shake.

"What are you thanking me for?"

Gene chuckled and withdrew his hand. "Guess it would be helpful if I told you. That article you ran about the bank robbery in Tushka helped county officials nab the other robber. Someone turned him in, based on your description."

"Well, it was the least I could do. Glad to be of service." Jonathan settled back into his chair and gestured for Gene to take the empty chair next to Joe.

Gene took the proffered chair and leaned back, exhausted after several days of dealing with paperwork. Though everything inside of him wanted to dislike Jonathan, he couldn't help but admire the man.

"Anything else, Gene?" The newspaperman gazed at him. "The reporter in me seems to think you've got something else on your mind."

"Guess I do." He squirmed in his chair. "I really wanted to come by and thank you for those pieces you're running each day on child-rearing. At first I wasn't sure they would help, but I get the point now. Several folks have told me that they're softening toward the children."

"Hope it sticks," Jonathan said.

"I'll confess, those kids are growin' on me," Joe said. He lowered his voice to add, "Like a fungus."

Jonathan and Gene erupted in laughter.

"I just wrote another article, one that's sure to set the mayor's hair on fire."

"What hair?" Joe asked. "The man's bald as a billiard ball."

This got another laugh out of the men. Jonathan passed the paper Gene's way.

Gene could hardly believe his eyes as he read the well-written piece, which shed light on the children's plight and the needs at the orphanage.

"This is brilliant, Jonathan. The perfect counter-position to Molly's 'Fresh as a Daisy' campaign, and one sure to turn the hearts of the towns-people to the children."

"Glad someone thinks it's brilliant," Joe said. "And by the way, Mayor Albright already read it this morning and he's fit to be tied. Says this article is an invitation to dance with the devil, and he refuses to dance."

"Hmm. Well, I daresay, we've been dancing with the devil all along," Jonathan said. "To my way of thinking, dealing with the problem head-on is a better solution than ignoring it or hoping it will go away."

Gene had just started to respond when Old Man Tucker approached, looking a bit winded.

"Howdy, fellas." Tucker tipped his hat.

"Howdy, yourself." Gene smiled. "What's new around town this Sat-urday? I always look forward to your reports."

"Well, let's see now. Donald Johnson has the shingles, and his wife, Maybelle, is down with the flu. I heard from Doc Moseley that we might have an epidemic of pinworms goin' 'round too."

"Any good news to speak of?" Jonathan asked.

"Well, not exactly good, but I have some interesting news about some goings-on at the general store less than an hour ago." Tucker leaned against the wall and shook his head. "A real mess."

"What's that?" Gene asked.

"Mrs. Hannigan tells me that Miss Jewel came in today. There was some sort of commotion with the children."

Gene groaned. "So soon? I'd hoped the children would keep things calm for a while."

"Well, that wasn't the real story." Old Man Tucker leaned in close. "Real story is about Miss Jewel. Katie Hannigan says Miss Rena Jewel bought a pouch of Red Man chewing tobacco from her."

"Chewing tobacco?" Gene and Jonathan spoke in unison.

"Yep." Old Man Tucker leaned back against the wall, as if he'd just delivered the best punch line in the world.

"I don't know what to make of it." Jonathan looked perplexed.

Gene shook his head. Something about this story seemed fishy. "You talked to Mrs. Hannigan yourself?"

"Well, no." Old Man Tucker scratched his head. "Not exactly. I heard it from Donald Johnson, who heard it from the mayor's wife, who heard it from Molly Harris. If'n you don't believe me, ask Mrs. Hannigan. She'll tell you. Miss Jewel bought a pouch of Red Man chewing tobacco just a short time ago."

"There's got to be some mistake." And then from across the street, he caught a glimpse of the very person they were talking about. Rena Jewel, looking quite fetching in a new dress.

"Well, there she is." Old Man Tucker let out a whistle. "And don't she look perty today? Don't look the sort to be chewin' and chawin', now, does she?"

"No." Gene took a couple of steps toward her but stopped, unsure of what he would say to her if given the opportunity. After all, the story he'd heard was just a rumor. Besides, Henry was with her. No point in dragging the child into the woman's sin…if indeed it was a sin.

Still, what kind of woman chewed tobacco? Certainly not a good, upstanding one…one who had claimed in her original letter to be temperate in every way. On the other hand, if she'd purchased the chewing tobacco for one of the boys, they had an even bigger problem on their hands, didn't they? Surely she would never do that...right?

Old Man Tucker gazed at Miss Jewel with a look of admiration in his eye. "I daresay there's a lot about that woman we don't know. She's a mystery, that one. But I aim to figure her out." He quirked a brow. "And speaking of figures, she's got a nice one, don'tcha think?"

Gene found himself too preoccupied to respond. Miss Jewel was, indeed, a mystery. Why would a woman—a genteel, Southern woman—be buying chewing tobacco?

He didn't have a clue. But he made it his mission to find out.

Chapter Sixteen

....

TIPS FOR DEALING WITH UNRULY YOUNG'UNS—*Folks 'round these-here parts call me Old Man Tucker. Ain't never understood the name, what with me only being sixty-seven and all. Don't they know "old" is a long way off? Guess some folks is ready to spit nails over my letter to the editor at that-there* Atoka County Register. *Cain't blame me. Jonathan Brewer brought up the subject of the children from the orphanage, and I just gave him my mind. What was left of it, anyhow. Said my piece. Folks 'round here know how I feel about the children, anyway. I'd be just as happy if Mayor Albright picked up that orphanage and moved it to another city. Then, for once, I could sleep at night without wonderin' what those kids was gonna do to me the next day.*

—James Tucker, Farmer

Rena spent the next twenty-four hours trying to come up with recipes that would include garlic…and trying to make sense of the letter she had received from Gene. Neither effort seemed to be paying off, particularly the issue of the letter. On Sunday morning before church she read it over and over again, just to make sure she had not misunderstood its contents.

No. There was no denying the obvious. The man had declared his feelings and would be waiting on a response. But how would she go about it? And what would she say? Why, she barely knew him, after all. Sure, they'd had that one conversation in the kitchen, but how could she declare her affections after one chat?

The children were quiet that Sunday morning. Suspiciously quiet. They came and went from Sunday school, their behavior better than ever before. Why this made her nervous, she could not say. She should be celebrating the fact but could not seem to relax.

Seeing Gene in church did little to calm her nerves, particularly when she noticed his anxious demeanor. He clearly had something on his mind. She could tell from the way he stared at her. The whole thing made her a bit uneasy. Thank goodness Jonathan and Jenny distracted him. Otherwise, she might've had to face him on the church steps in front of the whole congregation. She made it back to the house in time to serve the garlic-ladened stew, which the children hated. She felt so bad about it that she offered them sandwiches after the fact.

Just as the meal ended, a gagging sound startled her. She looked over to see Oliver hunched forward, clutching his belly. Rena rose and rushed his way just in time to see him lose the stew all over the dining-room carpet. She flew into action, racing for the kitchen to fetch dishcloths to clean up the mess. From inside the kitchen she heard the sound of children's laughter. A quick peek back inside the dining room clued her in to the fact that he wasn't sick at all. He'd hidden a hot water bottle under his shirt. The little stinker had planned the whole thing. He had perfect timing, considering the awful stew. She had to give it to him.

And give it to him she did. Rena handed him the dishcloths and put him to work at cleaning up the mess. Turned out he'd used last night's pea soup in the hot water battle. He claimed it tasted disgusting and looked even worse. She couldn't help but agree with him. Still, there

1912

was only so much a weary soul could handle. She needed rest, and she needed it now.

On Sunday night Rena reached under her pillow for her notebook, determined to write down her thoughts before dozing off. Surely she could process them on the written page. Her thoughts always came easier when she penned them.

Strangely, she couldn't find the notebook. Her heartbeat quickened as she thought about where it could be. Just as quickly, she reminded herself that she'd taken it down to the kitchen to copy down a recipe. She would have to remember to fetch it later. In the meantime, she would just have to process her thoughts in her head.

She fell asleep thinking about the words in Gene's letter. Her dreams, lovely and sweet, were the stuff fairy tales are made of. She wore a white gown—very princess-like. Her prince, dressed in a sheriff's uniform with a gun strapped to his side, met her at the altar, where he took her hand. The only thing odd about the dream was the one performing the ceremony—Mayor Albright, dressed as a coachman.

Rena overslept on Monday morning. The children, most of whom had already dressed, met her downstairs in the kitchen, where she fixed a quick pot of oatmeal. After a hurried breakfast, they lit off for school and she found herself in the house alone. She could have done any number of things: swept the kitchen floor, changed out the curtains in the dining room, painted the door trim in the parlor, telephoned Sadie to discuss her upcoming visit, composed another letter to Reuben to ask why the furniture had been delayed...yes, she could have done any of these things, but she chose not to. Instead, she got back to work on the Christmas dresses for the girls.

After adding lace to Lilly's dress, Rena realized she'd forgotten to check for her notebook in the kitchen. She scolded herself for being so out of sorts before going downstairs to fetch it. Oddly, she could not find it.

Thinking of the notebook reminded her of Gene's letter, which she carried in her pocket. All the way up the stairs she thought about the words in that precious letter. They were so dear to her now, so touching. How would she go about letting him know that she cared about him too? Not that she'd really had time to watch her affections grow, but she could no longer deny the obvious: she had feelings for the man.

I, Rena Jewel, have feelings for a man. After thirty-eight long years, I've crossed that bridge.

She practically waltzed her way into the bedroom to return to her sewing. Oh, but the task felt so much lighter, now that she had more exciting things on her mind.

Rena had just started the process of making up her bed when she bumped her pillow, knocking it to the floor. Underneath, she found the notebook, the very one she thought she'd left downstairs.

"For heaven's sake." She chuckled. "I must be losing my mind." She shook her head and chastened herself for being so flighty. If this was what falling for a man could do to a person, she couldn't afford such nonsense. She needed to keep her wits about her, after all.

Oh, but she didn't want to keep her wits about her. She wanted to grab the mop, make it her partner, and dance around the room with it. Would the neighbors think her nutty if they saw her through the window? Likely, but who cared? Let them say what they might; she had happier news stirring.

A knock on the front door roused her from such luxurious thoughts. It was probably Carolina, stopping by with another batch of recipes.

Rena practically floated down the stairs. She swung wide the front door, fully expecting to see Carolina on the other side, but almost fell over when she saw Gene standing there, dressed in his uniform. At once her face grew hot. "Oh." She smiled but tried not to look too obvious. "I wasn't expecting you."

He removed his Stetson and nodded. "Hope it's all right that I stopped by without calling first. I know you're very busy."

"The children are already in school, so I've got time to visit." Her words came out with a lilt, which she could not help. How could a woman in her situation speak without allowing her innermost joy to shine through?

"There's something I need to talk with you about." He reached for her hand and gave it a squeeze, gazing intently into her eyes. "Is it all right if I come in?"

"Come in? Why, of course. Please do." She gestured for him to come inside then closed the door behind him. She half wondered if Molly Harris or Mayor Albright were outside, spying on them. If so, she'd just given them plenty to talk about, hadn't she?

A nervous giggle escaped.

"You okay?" Gene asked as he took a few steps toward the parlor.

"Oh, I, uh…" She nodded. "I'm good. And you?"

"Well, I've got something on my mind, as I said."

"Yes, you do." She gave him a little wink. Where it came from, she could not be sure. Still, the words in his note gave her the courage to step out and live dangerously.

He took a seat and gestured for her to sit next to him. She was happy to oblige.

Gene tried to work up the courage to speak but found it difficult. How did one go about asking a woman if she chewed tobacco? A fella didn't just dive into a conversation like that, did he? Especially not with a woman who looked as if she might spring off the sofa at any moment and fly across the room. He'd never seen her so nervous.

Gene finally broke the silence with a question. "Rena, can I ask you something?"

"Well, sure." She batted her lashes.

"Okay. Now, please don't be upset, but I really have to know the answer. It's very important."

"Y–yes?" She inched her way a bit closer until they were almost touching. Odd.

"There's a rumor going around town about you. Just wanted to hear your response to it for myself."

"A rumor?" Her cheeks turned the prettiest shade of pink. "What are folks saying now? That I don't watch the children closely enough? Or maybe that I'm not feeding them the proper foods?"

"No." He shook his head. "Nothing like that."

"Then what?" Her lips curled down in a pout. A cute pout. He almost lost his thoughts for a moment as he analyzed it.

Gene finally managed to get to the point. He cleared his throat, looked her in the eyes, and let her have it. "They're saying you chew tobacco."

"I—I w–what?" She gasped and her mouth dropped open in a most unladylike fashion. Her entire demeanor changed. She went from being a gentle lamb to a lion, in a split second. Her voice grew more intense. "Why in the world would they say a ridiculous thing like that?"

He rose and paced the room, stopping in front of the fireplace. She remained on the sofa, still looking perplexed. Angry, even.

Looked like this wasn't going as well as he'd hoped. Still, he must forge ahead. "Did you, or did you not, buy a pouch of Red Man chewing tobacco from Mrs. Hannigan yesterday?"

"Oh my gracious." Rena buried her face in her hands. "I did. But to be honest, I'd forgotten about it until this very moment. You see, something happened yesterday when I was at the store to, well, to distract me." Her lips curled up in a coy smile, but he couldn't make heads or tails of it.

"Distract you?"

"Yes." A nervous giggle followed. "It's the silliest thing, how I could've forgotten about the tobacco, but I guess I must have. Would it help to know I didn't buy it for myself?"

"I can only hope you didn't buy it for one of the boys."

"No, no." She put her hands up. "Certainly not. I bought it to replace the pouch that Henry stole from Joe."

"Ah." *Well, that makes sense, I suppose.* "I see. So where is it now?"

Her smile faded at once and she paled. "I…I…I wish I could remember. I was at the store with Henry. I bought the pouch. Then I checked the mail…" Her face flushed. "And then…" She shook her head. "Heavens. I truly don't know what I did with it. I don't recall seeing it with the candy and the lace I purchased." A look of terror crossed her face, and she rose. "Oh, Gene…"

"So, we're missing a pouch of chewing tobacco, then?"

"I guess so." She took a few steps in his direction, her brow knitted. "To think that folks have been talking about me behind my back makes me feel just awful."

"Folks around here have precious little to do but gossip," he said. "So this is nothing new. And I, for one, am extremely relieved to hear that you do not chew tobacco. That's all we need, what with Molly on the warpath. That 'Fresh as a Daisy' campaign of her is big news around town, and this would only add fuel to her fire. I can't tell you how glad I am to hear of your innocence."

"Tell me you didn't really believe that." She drew near and put her hand on his arm. "You…well, you know me better than that."

"To be honest, I don't really know you well at all. I enjoyed our conversation in the kitchen on Thanksgiving and learned a lot, but I'm sure there's a lot more to learn."

"Y–yes."

He paused. "I–I'd like to get to know you better." He swallowed hard, stunned at his own words.

"You would?" She smiled. "So that you can report back to the missions board about my poor behavior?"

"No." He laughed. "If I'm going to report anyone's behavior, it will be Molly's. Or maybe the mayor's. Or James Tucker, who wrote a negative letter about child-rearing in today's paper. But not you. You're nothing but a shining example of what grace looks like."

"Well, thank you." The sweetest expression followed, followed by more eyelash-fluttering. "Very kind of you to say."

"You've forgiven me for accusing you of chewing tobacco, haven't you?" For whatever reason, he felt compelled to reach over and brush the loose hair out of her eyes. Should he do so?

"I suppose. If you will forgive me for losing the chewing tobacco." She gave him a shy glance.

"Oh, I doubt it's lost," he said. "In fact, I'm pretty sure Henry's hidden it away in some secret place." Gene couldn't take it anymore. Still clutching the Stetson in his left hand, he reached with his right to brush the lock of hair out of her face. Afterward, his hand lingered against her cheek. She glanced up at him and smiled.

A comfortable silence rose up between them. Gene lifted his hand from her cheek and fingered the brim of his hat. "Well, I have to get on back to the jail now. My prisoner's being transported to the county seat later today."

"I see." She paused and appeared to be thinking. "Well, thank you for stopping by. Again, I apologize for my oversight. I do hope all is forgiven."

"All is forgiven." He flipped the hat onto his head, gave her a curt nod, then headed for the door.

After Gene left, Rena did her best to make sense of what had just happened. Instead of declaring his undying love, he had accused her of... chewing tobacco? Did the man really think for one moment that she would buy tobacco for herself?

She paced the entryway, her thoughts now jumbled. After a few moments, it all made sense.

"He just used that tobacco story to stop by. He needed an excuse to see me." In that moment, she felt sure she'd figured out the problem. "He's too shy to express his feelings in person. That's why he has to write them down in letters."

If anyone understood that, she did. Wasn't she the one who kept her secrets hidden away in a notebook? Yes. And surely the man cared about her. She wasn't just dreaming this up. Hadn't he gone out of his way to rest his hand against her face?

A nervous giggle followed. "We do have our secrets, now, don't we?" Indeed, they did. And she would play along, no matter how long it took. They would make a game of it, no doubt. Cat and mouse. Gentleman and lady. But in the end, she would win the game, take the prize, and live happily ever after.

Chapter Seventeen

....

TIPS FOR DEALING WITH UNRULY YOUNG'UNS—*Sure, I chew tobacco every now 'n again. What boy don't? And yeah, I been known to steal a little 'a this and a little 'a that from the locals when their backs 'r turned. How else am I gonna get the stuff I need? It ain't like anybody 'round here's giving me the time 'a day, anyway. Most 'a the folks in Daisy would sooner ferget I even exist. So I just give 'em even more reason to wish it. Besides, I'm nearly fifteen. I'll get out of this stinkin' town soon—run away and take care of myself. So, go on and try to "fix" me. Ain't gonna work. I ain't no child, and I don't need rearin', so you can put that notion right outta yer head.*

—Henry the Fearless, Age Fourteen

Rena spent the rest of the morning walking from room to room, her thoughts a jumbled mess. She tried to busy herself with chores, but her mind would not be stilled. She needed to talk to Henry as soon as he arrived home from school, but she would have to broach the subject carefully. Otherwise, her words might send him packing. He suffered from wanderlust. She could see it in his eyes.

Carolina arrived at three o'clock and Rena ushered her inside. "I'm headed into town and will be stopping by the general store. Do you need anything? Figured you weren't quite ready to show your face just yet till this tobacco story dies down."

Rena groaned. "So you've heard."

"Who hasn't?" Carolina patted her arm. "Honey, I don't believe a word of the gossip. But you should be aware that Molly has already gone to both the mayor and the reverend and is doing what she can to stir up trouble. She's called one of her infamous meetings, of course."

"O–oh?"

"Yes. Now, don't fret over it. I'm only telling you so you know. That whole 'Fresh as a Daisy' group—mostly women with nothing better to do—will be meeting to discuss a plan of action."

"Plan of action?" Rena had to take a seat at this point.

Carolina sat next to her. "Yes. They plan to write to the missions society about your so-called addiction to tobacco and your inability to control the children. Apparently Mrs. Hannigan was quite upset by the scene the boys caused at their store."

Rena started coughing at this news. "But surely they don't really think... I mean, honestly? They believe I purchased that tobacco for myself?"

"Who knows what they think." Carolina patted her knee. "They're just gathering ammunition to be used against you and the children's home. They see this as a major victory in their camp."

Fear took hold of Rena's heart. "Oh no! Well, I have to tell them. Surely they will understand that it's all a big mistake if they hear it from me. And as for the scene Henry created at the store, I paid for every last jar of jam. No one lost any money."

"You know how it goes." Carolina released a slow breath. "They hear what they want to hear and do what they want to do. The mayor is with them, of course. But that doesn't scare me. They would have to convince both the county officials and the missions society that you are unfit as a caregiver before anyone could demand your dismissal."

"My...dismissal?" Rena felt a lump grow in her throat, and she could not speak above it.

"Well, there I go, getting the cart ahead of the horse again." Carolina sighed. "Didn't mean to alarm you. Just trying to be strategic by thinking of the what-ifs. You've got a great support team, honey, and we're not going to let you down. Gene told me what really happened. I know that tobacco belonged to Henry."

"Actually, I purchased it for Joe." Rena fidgeted with the torn fabric on the arm of the sofa, her nerves affected by this conversation. "Only, now I don't know what became of the tobacco, which means I really need to go to town to buy more. We still need to pay Joe back for what Henry stole."

"Nasty habit, chewing." Carolina's nose wrinkled. "I say we skip buying any tobacco at all and just give Joe the money to replace his original pouch."

"Good idea." Rena's gaze shifted to the floor. "Would you...I mean, would you mind going by Joe's shop and dropping off the money for me? I don't think I can face him now, what with folks gossiping and all."

"I'll be happy to. But you'd better talk to Henry to find out what's what. We need him to admit what he's done—not just to save your hide, but because confession is good for the soul. And while we're on the subject of confession, I might as well speak my mind."

"O–oh?"

"Yes." She gave Rena a warm smile. "I was a little nervous when I heard that Mrs. Wabash was leaving, to be honest. Didn't think bringing in someone new was the best plan of action. Molly and her crew had almost won me over to their way of thinking." She gave Rena such a penetrating look that unspoken words seemed to travel between them. "But bringing you here was the best decision my son ever made. Well, since Brenda…" Carolina paused. "Anyway, he made the right decision. And so did you, by coming. If you ask me, he's happy about that, as well."

Rena did her best to hide her embarrassment but wondered if Carolina could see past it. Did she know about the letter her son had written? If so, how did she feel about it?

Carolina rose, straightened her skirts, and looked Rena in the eye. "So, back to my original question: anything you need from the general store?"

Rena stood and nodded. "I have a list in the kitchen. Hold on a minute and I'll get it for you." Her heart felt as heavy as lead as she made her way into the kitchen. She scribbled a couple more things onto the list, including several yards of fabric for her sewing projects, and reached into the canister for some change to cover both her purchases and the missing tobacco. Passing them off to Carolina, she sighed. "I'm so grateful you're on my side, Carolina. I honestly think I would've packed my bags and left already if you hadn't treated me so kindly."

"Sweet girl." Carolina wrapped her in a motherly embrace. "I love you. And I love what you're doing for the children. They need you, and on some level I think you need them too."

Rena felt the sting of tears and wiped her eyes with the back of her hand. "Thank you."

At that moment the front door swung open and the children poured inside. Henry was the last to enter. Carolina took one look at him, gave Rena a nod, and made an announcement. "Tell you what, Rena. I could use some help in town. What say I take most of these children off your hands for an hour or so?"

"W–what? Are you sure?"

"Sure." Carolina gestured to Henry. "I figured you and Henry are due for a little chat." She glanced at the boys. "Isn't that right, Henry?"

"Um, I, well…" He shrugged. "Ain't sure what we got to talk about, but I guess so."

"Mm-hmm." Carolina ushered the other boys and girls outside, and their happy voices grew faint as they moved down the lane.

Rena drew a deep breath and turned to face Henry. "She's right, you know. We do need to talk."

" 'Bout what?" He dropped his books on the end table and plopped down onto the sofa.

"About what happened the other day at the general store."

His gaze shifted to the ground. Then out the window. "Don't know what yer talkin' 'bout."

"You know very well what I'm talking about. After I caught you with the chewing tobacco, I bought another pouch to give to Joe. But then…" She paused and took a seat next to him. "Well, we never made it to the barbershop, did we? I got distracted."

"Ain't my fault that stupid letter made you forget."

She felt her cheeks grow warm. "Well, yes, I was reading a letter, but that's not my point. The point is, we left the store in a hurry and I forgot to stop by the barbershop. Then, when I checked my packages later, the tobacco was missing."

The tops of Henry's ears turned red and his eyes widened. His mouth opened, as if he planned to say something, but then closed again. He returned his gaze to the window.

"Henry, what happened to that pouch of tobacco I bought?" she asked, a sense of dread coming over her. "It's important that I know the answer."

He hung his head.

"Tell the truth. I take part of the blame, since I forgot. Does that make you feel any better?"

Henry pursed his lips but eventually nodded. "If'n I tell ya, you gonna punish me?"

"I haven't decided that part yet," she said. "I just know that I won't be able to sleep, knowing I've corrupted you further."

"Shoot…" He chuckled. "You ain't corrupted me, Miz Rena. No way, no how. I was already plenty corrupted before you got here. So, rest yer mind about that."

"Where is the tobacco, Henry?"

"I gave it to Joe."

"You…you what?" She reached to take his chin in her hand and turned his face up to hers. "If you're lying to me, I'll be able to tell by looking into your eyes. It's a special gift I have, knowing when folks are lying."

He gazed directly into her eyes. "Then tell me what you see. 'Cause I put the pouch of tobacco on Joe's desk, the very spot where I stole the other one."

"Did you apologize?"

"Nope." Henry shook his head. "He didn't realize I stole the first one, so I figgered it was kinda pointless to sorry up fer something he didn't know I'd done."

"But the Lord knows. And it's always good to let Him know you're sorry for the wrong things you've done."

Henry did not look convinced. "Don't know 'bout that."

She shook her head. "It's true. Besides, I've probably stirred up more trouble by sending Carolina to town with money for Joe. And Molly Harris is all worked up over this as well. She and the mayor will use it against me. They want to see me gone."

"Well, shoot." Henry gave her a pensive look. "That's the reason I gave the tobacco back, Miz Rena. You don't need more trouble." A downcast look came over his face. "Never meant to drag you into this. I just wanted to try the tobacco to see if I liked it."

"And did you?"

He shook his head. " 'Tween you and me, it made me sick."

"I figured." She rested her hand on his arm, suddenly overcome with emotion for the boy. "Henry, we've never really had a good talk, you and me. I regret that. I want to know you better. Want to know what makes you tick."

"What makes me tick?" He laughed.

She looked him in the eye. "What I'm really wondering is, why do you do it?"

"Do what?"

"You know." She locked him in her gaze. "Why do you act up? Get in so much trouble?"

As he stared at the ground, an uncomfortable silence grew between them. After several awkward seconds, he tugged at his shirt collar. "Gettin' hot in here," he managed.

"Yes, but you didn't answer my question. Why do you act up? What's the point of it all?"

"Just trying to get attention, I guess," he muttered.

"Why?"

His next words came out sounding strained. "My ma passed when I was only four. And my pa…" He rolled his eyes. "Well, he had big dreams. Maybe too big. He was always fond of the bottle, but he said he was gonna build a big tavern in town."

"A tavern? I don't recall seeing one," she said.

"Nah. He never sobered up long enough to build it. But he did build a still out in the woods, east of town. That's how he ended up in jail. Sheriff found the still and arrested him."

Rena thought carefully before responding. "I'm so sorry to hear that, Henry. I didn't know. Had your father struggled with alcohol for long?"

"Fer as long as I can remember, he's had a bottle in his hand." Henry smiled. "He's been out of jail for years now, but he has a wanderin' eye. Moves from state to state." A lengthy pause followed and Henry's smile faded. "You know, Pa's a stubborn, mule-headed old coot when he's sober, but he's lots of fun when he's liquored up. I always did like it when he was drinkin' cause I knew he would be in a good mood."

"Oh my." She hardly knew what to say in response. Perhaps it would be better to let him keep talking.

" 'Course, Pa never stuck around for long. When he took off I stayed with my grandpappy for a while, but he said there weren't enough money in the world to keep me underfoot fer long. Guess he thinks I'm a handful." Henry paused. "He said I'm too much like my pa, that the apple don't fall far from the tree."

"Just because your father has faced challenges doesn't mean you have to go through the same thing," Rena explained. "You can ask the Lord to give you a different sort of life."

"Ask the Lord?" Henry raked his fingers through his hair with a perplexed look on his face. "Miss Rena, sometimes you say the derndest things. It's like you think I could just sit down and talk to God like He was my pa or sumpthin."

"Actually, it's easier than that to talk to the Lord," she said. "With your pa, you'd have to work up the courage. But with the Lord, all you need is a still, quiet moment. No one needs to tell you what to say or what not to say. You can just be yourself."

"Be myself?" He snorted.

"Yes." She reached to take his hand. "Haven't you ever had anyone that you could just be yourself around?"

"Well, a couple of the boys. Oliver and Mochni, mostly. I can be myself around them." He paused and gave her a scrutinizing look. "What about you?"

"W–what?"

"Anyone you can just be yourself around?"

"Yes." She couldn't help the smile that followed. "My niece, Sadie. She's coming next week to spend the Christmas holidays with us, so

you'll get to meet her and see for yourself."

"Is she perty?" Henry offered a mischievous grin.

Rena chuckled. "Yes, very. But get your mind off that subject right away. She's much older than you."

"I'll be fifteen next month."

"Indeed." Rena gave him an admiring look. "And I would guess you're long overdue for a birthday party. Ever had one?"

"Me? A birthday party?" The very idea appeared to render him speechless. "You...you would do that for me?"

"Well, of course. Special days are worth celebrating, and so are special people. And just for the record, Henry, the Bible says that God is a father to the fatherless. So the next time you're disappointed in your real father, look to the Lord. He'll never leave you or forsake you, and that's a promise."

A look of shame washed over him. "Miz Rena, I'll tell 'em what I did. I'll tell the sheriff, and Joe too."

"That would be great, Henry. Confession is good for the soul."

He nodded and rose. After grabbing his books, he turned to face her. "Might as well confess something else too, while it's on my mind."

"Oh? What's that?"

"I, um...well, I'm the one who put that poo-poo cushion on yer chair during Thanksgiving." A pause followed, and then came a quiet, "Forgive me?"

She rose and gave him a hug. "There's nothing to forgive. Now get on upstairs and do your homework. You're a smart boy, Henry. You're going to go far in this world."

He squared his shoulders, gave her a genuine smile, and bolted up the stairs.

"What'd the kids do to land themselves in jail?"

Gene looked up as he heard Charlie's voice. His deputy gestured to the jail cell, where several of the boys and girls from the children's home had locked themselves inside.

He laughed. "Well, it's like this…my mother came to town to do some shopping and brought the children with her. Not sure why. She stopped by here on her way to the store, and a bunch of the kids locked themselves in the cell." He gestured toward them. "They're having so much fun in there that she decided to leave them."

"Who's got the key?" Charlie asked.

Gene lifted the key ring, gave it a jangle, and dropped it onto his desk.

Charlie laughed. "Gonna keep 'em in there forever?"

"Nah. I suppose it's time to free the prisoners. Besides, my mother's due back in a few minutes and she'll probably panic if she finds them still locked up."

He walked over to the jail cell just in time to hear Josephine ask the others a question: "Why do you suppose Miss Rena never got married?"

"Yeah, is she an old maid?" Oliver asked.

Gene rattled his keys to warn the children of his approach. They looked his way.

"Sheriff Wyatt," Josephine said, "can you help us solve a riddle?"

He peered through the bars at them. "If it's a riddle involving a certain children's home director, the answer is no."

"So you don't know why she's an old maid, either?" Wesley asked, brushing a dirty blond hair back with the sweep of a hand. "Figures. Men can never figure out the female sex."

Josephine's eyes widened. "He said *sex*."

"There's nothing wrong with saying a person is of a certain sex," Gene explained as he stuck the key in the lock. "And maybe you're right. I've never claimed to know anything about women." A rush of emotions ran through him at this statement. Brenda, he had known. Brenda, he had figured out. Well, mostly, anyway. She had perplexed him on occasion, but he'd always managed to understand her in the end.

"I think Miss Rena had her heart broken," Callie said, a knowing look on her face. "She just looks like a woman who's pining away for a man in her secret heart of hearts."

Gene pushed the cell door open. "If she's pinin', she's mighty quiet about it."

"I think she should marry Mr. Jonathan," Callie said. "Wouldn't that be romantic? He's so handsome, like a storybook character."

"Storybook?" Gene snorted as he took a step inside the jail cell. "Miss Jewel's not the sort to read fanciful stories, so you can put that notion right out of your head."

"Yer wrong, Sheriff," Oliver said. "She loves stories."

Several of the boys shot him a warning look, and Gene knew at once they were up to something.

"What do you mean?"

"Oh, well...nuthin'." Oliver hung his head.

"The boys were snoopin' in Miss Rena's room," Lilly said. "They found her storybook."

"Storybook?" Gene stopped himself before asking more. His first response should have been, "Snooping?"

"She's a writer!" Callie whispered. "She writes the most romantical stories you ever did read. We stayed up all night long reading them. Heroes on horseback. Men with cowboy hats. Damsels in distress. You name it, she writes it."

Gene did his best to shush them immediately. Talk about a misunderstanding! Boy-howdy, would the townspeople get worked up if they heard this nonsense. It would likely be a juicier piece of gossip than that chewing-tobacco debacle.

"You've got to be mistaken," he assured them. "Likely she's carrying someone else's writing tablet or reading a story written by a friend. The Rena Jewel I know would never contrive make-believe stories. She's far too sensible for that."

Oliver snorted and repeated a few words: "She's far too sensible for that!"

"That's what you think." Josephine nodded, and the funniest little smile lit her face. "Just wait."

"Yep, that's right," Mikey added. "One of her stories is about a Texas Ranger named Gerald. What do you think about that?"

Gene bristled. "You must be joking."

"We're not," all of the children spoke in unison.

"What do you think of that, Sheriff?" Josephine asked.

"I think you've been writing those stories and putting them in her book to make it look like she's a writer when she's not." He rose, completely disgusted with them for setting her up like this. "And frankly, I've had it with all of you. First you let the townspeople think she chews tobacco, and now this? What's next?"

He saw a couple of the boys glance at each other and realized there might be more yet to be revealed. Still, this was all he could handle for one day.

"You will one day have to repent for the awful things you've done to your directors. You know that, don't you? And I'll be honest and say I won't have a moment's pity on you when folks react to the news. You'll deserve every bit of tongue-lashing."

"But, Sheriff, honest and true, she's a writer," Josephine said. "We couldn't make up something this big."

"Sure, you couldn't. And my name isn't Gene Wyatt, and I don't live in a town called Daisy, Oklahoma."

In that moment, he almost wished he *didn't* live in Daisy, Oklahoma, for life here was growing more complicated by the day.

Chapter Eighteen

....

Tips for Dealing with Unruly Young'uns—*I'm not a parent myself, but I've spent enough time around children to know what they respond to. Children, even in the midst of tantrums, long to be held and loved. They want someone older, wiser, and calmer to lovingly step in and offer assurance that things will be all right. Never is this more important than when a child is out of control. Even the most rebellious youngster will respond to a loving embrace. His tantrum will vanish as a heartfelt "I love you" is spoken. This I know from personal experience, having so recently been a child myself.*

—Sadie Jewel, College Student and Visitor to Daisy

On the second Saturday in December Rena fussed with the house, getting the new furniture pieces in place. The donations weren't quite what she would have chosen, but she made the best of things.

Overnight, a light snow had fallen, taking her by surprise. Living on the Gulf Coast for so long had scarcely prepared her for the winter wonderland. Thank goodness most of the snow had melted. Otherwise, traveling to town to fetch Sadie would have been difficult. Not that it really mattered just yet. She still had plenty of work to do inside the house before heading to the train depot.

"I think that sofa would look best over here, under the window." She pointed, and Henry and the other boys moved it to the new location.

"What about this new end table, Miss Rena?" Callie pointed to a beautiful mahogany piece. "What should we do with this?"

Rena glanced around the parlor. "I think it will fit nicely next to the sofa."

She spent the better part of the next hour shifting and re-shifting pieces and even hung two new pictures on the wall, which Virginia had sent as a special gift. When all was said and done, Rena stepped back and admired their work.

"It's bee-you-tee-ful!" Josephine let out a squeal and flopped onto the sofa. The other children piled in around her, and before long they were all laughing and talking about the transformations inside the house. Rena couldn't help but notice the transformations in the children as well, though she never mentioned it.

The hall clocked pealed eleven times. Rena glanced into the hallway mirror and realized she must tidy up before heading to the station. She could never let folks in town see her in such a disheveled state. They already had their doubts about her sanity. If she showed up looking like something the cat dragged in, they would surely make more of it than necessary. She headed upstairs to fuss with her hair and change into a proper winter dress.

At noon, Carolina arrived with Jacob and William at her side. The boys were quarreling, naturally. Nothing new there. Still, they erased their battle lines as soon as they saw the new furniture. Minutes later, they took their seats amid all the other boys and girls in the newly decked-out parlor.

"Now, you children keep that room clean while I'm gone," Rena said. "I want to make a good first impression on Sadie."

"Unlike the first impression they made on you when you arrived a couple of months ago?" Carolina gave her a wink.

Rena chuckled. "Exactly. Promise me you won't leave them alone for a minute while I'm gone. I'd hate to see them play some sort of prank on Sadie. She's the dearest thing in the world and the last person who deserves to be the brunt of a joke."

"I promise." Carolina nodded toward the children. "Did you hear that, all of you? We're going to treat our company with the utmost respect."

The girls looked their way and smiled, but the boys had taken to wrestling on the new Persian rug. Rena took her winter coat from the coatrack, slipped it on, and buttoned it up, readying herself for the trek outside. She glanced out the window, wondering what was keeping Gene. After a moment she looked back at Carolina.

"Thanks so much for keeping an eye on everything while I've gone to fetch Sadie. I'm so excited to bring her here." She looked around the room with a sigh. "I'm just tickled pink that the furniture arrived before she did. Really livens up the place, doesn't it?"

"Yes, it's wonderful. But if she's half the decorator you say she is, she'll take what we have and whip it into something extra-special," Carolina said. "Besides, she's family. She'll feel at home no matter what the place looks like."

"True." Rena threw her arms around Carolina's neck in an impromptu embrace. "And you're like family to me too, Carolina. I want you to know that. I'm so grateful for all you've done since I arrived."

"You blessed girl. I've loved every minute." Carolina gave her a tight squeeze. "Now, how are you getting to the station? Surely you're not walking."

"No, Gene is going to be along shortly to pick me up."

A now-familiar feeling of contentment settled over her as she spoke

Gene's name. In the week since receiving his letter, she had begun to entertain thoughts of courting him. All in due season, of course. And speaking of seasons, Christmas was nearly upon them! Why, in just a couple of weeks they would celebrate together.

"Gene, eh?" Carolina smiled. "Well, isn't that nice."

"Yes." Rena did her best not to sigh aloud, though her level of contentment grew daily. She'd fallen in love—with Daisy, with the children, and possibly with the sheriff. Not that she knew what love felt like, exactly, but she did have some idea.

Strange, that he'd never acknowledged the letter he'd sent. One of these days she would work up the courage to broach the subject. Today she had other things on her mind.

Gene's car pulled up a few minutes before noon. Rena stepped out onto the porch and gave a little wave. Her happiness dissipated as Charlie stepped out of the car to meet her.

"Sorry," he said. "Not exactly who you were looking for, I'm sure. But Gene's up to his eyeballs in paperwork and couldn't get away. Do you mind?"

"Mind?" She offered what she hoped would look like a convincing smile. "Of course not. I'm happy for the ride. Thank you for coming to fetch me."

"Of course." Charlie chattered all the way to the depot, filling her in on the goings-on in town. Turned out Mrs. Hannigan had a ruptured appendix, Joe the barber was thinking of taking a trip to Texas, and Old Man Tucker had his eye on Molly Harris.

That last bit of news made Rena nervous. In fact, everything about Molly made her nervous. She did her best to squelch any concerns, however. This was a day for celebration, after all. Sadie would arrive on the 12:45 train and spend four glorious weeks in Daisy. Oh, Rena could hardly wait!

Charlie pulled up to the station and turned off the car. He came around to open the door for Rena and she emerged, giving a little shiver.

"I hope we don't have to wait long."

"Nah. The twelve forty-five is never late." Charlie wiped the snow off of the bench outside the depot and gestured for her to sit. She eased her way down, her teeth now chattering.

The train arrived right on schedule, whistle blowing and steam billowing into the air in white clusters. Seconds later, Sadie emerged in a lavender chiffon dress.

"Aunt Rena!" She offered a joyous wave and then came bolting toward her just as she'd done hundreds, if not thousands, of times before. Rena's heart danced for joy. She wrapped Sadie in her arms and the two began to squeal in much the same way Lilly and Callie might have, if they'd been separated for any length of time.

"Oh, I've dreamed of this day for months." Rena reached to touch Sadie's face. "And here you are, you beautiful girl! But where's your coat?"

"Coat?" Sadie laughed. "When I left Gulfport, temperatures were in the seventies." She shivered. "Never even thought about it, to be perfectly honest. Guess I will now."

"Allow me, miss." From beside them, Charlie slipped off his coat and draped it around Sadie's shoulders. She gave him an admiring look.

For a moment, no one said anything. Then Charlie cleared his throat. Rena noticed the look of interest in his eyes and quickly made introductions.

Charlie's gaze lingered on Sadie's blond hair and beautiful face before saying something about the weather. Then the poor fellow fumbled all over himself as he attempted to fetch her bags. This, of course, got Sadie tickled. She reached out to help him, and when she did, their hands met. Rena looked on in amusement as the two gazed at each other, neither saying a word.

If their how-do-you-do was any indication, this was going to be a very special Christmas visit. Very special, indeed.

Gene looked up from his work as he heard the door open. Rena brushed through the open doorway. Behind her came an unfamiliar young woman. The stranger appeared to be dressed in—what was that, Charlie's coat? Charlie stepped inside behind the ladies, his cheeks blazing red. Odd. Had he caught a chill, perhaps? He didn't look like himself at all.

"Gene." Rena took several steps in his direction, the smile on her face so engaging that he found himself captivated. "We're headed back to the children's home, but I wanted to stop by so that you could meet Sadie."

She stepped aside, and the young woman came into full view. She was a beautiful blond with bright blue eyes and a smattering of freckles on her nose.

"How do you do," she said with a nod, her Southern accent shining through loud and clear.

Gene extended his hand. "Gene Wyatt."

"Gene, meet my niece, Sadie." Rena's face beamed. "She's here at last. I've told her all about the town, of course. She's read every letter. But she wanted to see it all for herself. Every square inch. This is our first stop."

"Of all the places in Daisy you could have gone, you came to the jail first?" Gene grinned. "Well, I'm honored."

"Oh, we simply had to." Sadie removed Charlie's coat, revealing a fancy purple dress underneath. "For weeks I've heard of little else but this jail. I hear you're wanting to redecorate." She rubbed her hands together then looked around. "My, we have a lot to do. Well, at least I've got several weeks."

Gene groaned. So that's what this was all about. His mother was up to tricks again. "Well, I suppose you could...I mean..."

Rena and Sadie lit into a lively conversation about drapes and paint colors, and he did his best to act interested. Charlie, on the other hand, didn't seem to have any trouble paying attention. No, his gaze was riveted to the beautiful Sadie, who carried on with great animation.

"We must shop for fabrics." Sadie clasped her hands together. "No better time than the present. Is there an adequate fabric selection at the general store?"

"There is." Rena nodded. "Though the weather has surely limited recent deliveries. Shall we take a peek since we're in town anyway? I'm sure Carolina won't mind if we take a bit longer, if it's related to the work she's commissioned me to do."

"Mm-hmm." Sadie turned, now standing nose-to-nose with Charlie, whose face glowed brighter than the taillights on Gene's car. "Well, you seem to be the helpful sort. Would you mind escorting us?"

"M–mind?" Charlie shook his head and offered her his arm.

Gene looked on, fascinated. Rena glanced at him and gave a gentle smile. "I don't suppose you would have time to slip away for a few minutes, would you?"

"Slip away?" He looked down at the mounds of paperwork on his desk and wondered if he dared.

"It's nearly Christmas, after all." Her voice had a melodic lilt to it, one he suddenly couldn't resist. Darned if he knew what had come over the woman in recent weeks. Still, he couldn't shake the idea that spending a few minutes with her—even looking at fabrics—would be far more pleasant than plowing through paperwork.

The happy foursome ventured out into the cold, making the walk to the general store. Sadie chattered on about fabrics and such, but

Gene didn't pay her much mind. His thoughts were affixed to Rena, who seemed to be wearing her hair differently today.

They arrived at the store just in time for Mr. Hannigan to greet them with hot chocolate and a cheerful "Merry Christmas."

"Ooh, I love Daisy already." Sadie took a mug of chocolate, a contented look on her face.

The ladies went to work at once, looking at the fabrics. Gene milled about a careful distance away. He knew nothing about fabrics and such. A few moments later, Molly Harris entered the store dressed in a heavy winter coat. She grumbled about the weather and claimed her rheumatism was giving her fits.

The cantankerous woman paused in front of Sadie and crossed her arms. "What have we here? More do-gooders?"

Gene watched as Rena faced Molly and offered a strained smile. "Molly, this is my niece, Sadie, from Gulfport. She's visiting for the holidays."

"Hmph." Molly scrutinized Sadie's dress then began to spew her usual venom. "Just like your aunt, no doubt. You plan to flip everything upside down with your so-called goodness like she's done?" Molly gestured to Rena, whose eyes widened.

"My *goodness*?" Sadie looked perplexed. "What do you mean?"

"Do-gooders, all of you. You're more trouble than you're worth." Molly pushed her way through the ladies and headed to the canned goods.

Gene wanted to interject his thoughts but didn't dare. Rena was a do-gooder, no doubt about it, but not in the way that Molly was implying. She genuinely cared for the children and had their best interests at heart.

Charlie cleared his throat and offered Sadie his arm. "What do you say we look at fabrics another day? I daresay a cold wind just blew through. Likely it's much warmer outside."

"Indeed." Sadie took his proffered arm, her lips curling up in a delightful smile. "I'm sure there's much more to see, anyway." She gazed at him, her eyelashes now fluttering.

"Oh yes." He cleared his throat. "Much more."

The two stared at one another, clearly seeing all they cared to at the moment. Gene looked on, unsure of what held him more spellbound—Sadie's relaxed attitude toward Molly Harris or Charlie's apparent infatuation with the Southern belle on his arm.

On the other hand, perhaps neither held him captive like Rena now did. The emotion pouring out of her eyes clued him in to the fact that Molly's words had stung. Well, then, he would be the salve on the wound.

Offering her his arm, he said, "Ladies, your carriage awaits."

Heads high, they all marched through the door.

Rena did her best to brush off the pain caused by Molly's sharp words back at the general store. She wanted Sadie's visit to be perfect. Nothing would get in the way of that. Gene—God bless him—seemed to pick up on her concerns. He closed up shop at the jail and drove them all back to the children's home, where the boys and girls greeted Sadie in their usual boisterous way. Thank goodness they didn't pull any pranks, though they delighted in telling the story of how they'd greeted Rena on her first day.

Sadie responded with laughter and smiles, which only served to endear her to the children. Before long, she was telling all sorts of stories about Rena, stories that brought Rena a bit of embarrassment in front of Gene.

They enjoyed a wonderful dinner together, followed by Sadie's favorite dessert, cherry pie. Afterward, the children followed on Sadie's heels as she made her way into the parlor, Charlie still following at a comfortable distance. Gene offered to help Rena clear the dishes from the table, as always. She enjoyed their playful banter as they worked and wondered if he might sneak in a word or two about his feelings toward her. He did not, but she felt—on at least one occasion—that he would have, if not for his mother's occasional presence.

Once the table was cleared, Gene offered to help his mother in the kitchen so that Rena could spend time with her niece. She thanked him and made her way to the parlor, following the sound of the children's laughter. Once there, she found all of the girls marching across the parlor with books on their heads.

"What have we here?"

"She's teaching us to be real ladies, Miss Rena!" Josephine's book slid off and landed on the floor with a *thump*. "Ladies like her."

"And what about me?" Rena asked. "What am I?"

"A lady too, of course." Callie smiled.

"Ooh, but Miss Sadie is young and pretty and such a fine lady and…" Josephine clamped a hand over her mouth. "I'm sorry, Miss Rena. I didn't mean to be rude. You're very pretty too, of course."

"No offense taken. Sadie is lovely, isn't she? I've thought so from the time she was a little girl." Rena paused and signaled for the children to draw near. She sat on the sofa and slipped her arm around Lilly's shoulders. "When Sadie was little, I would teach her the same things she's now teaching you. Manners, posture, sewing…oh, we had such fun."

"That's right," Sadie said. "Aunt Rena taught me how to set the table, how to speak to adults, and how to fix my hair. I learned so much from her."

"Why didn't your mama teach you?" Lilly asked. "Is she dead like my mama?"

Sadie paused, deep tenderness in her expression. "No, honey. My mama lives in Mississippi."

"Then why didn't she teach you those things?" Callie asked. "I mean, that's what mamas do, right?"

"Sometimes mamas are too busy," Sadie explained. "My mother was in charge of several committees—at the church, the women's society, the missions society.... Why, it's because of women like my mama that this children's home exists. She wanted to make sure you were cared for."

"But not you?" Lilly asked, her eyes wide with innocence. "She didn't care about teaching you to cook and sew and other lady-stuff?"

Sadie sighed and shifted her gaze to Charlie, who hadn't taken his eyes off her from the moment she started talking.

"She did teach me quite a few of those things. I was just saying that Aunt Rena was a big part of my life too. My point is that sometimes the Lord uses other folks—besides our mamas, I mean—to teach us what we need to learn."

"Is that why He brought you here, Miss Rena?" Callie asked. "So you can be like a mama to us?"

"That's right." Rena felt an inexplicable joy fill her heart.

"And you too, Miss Sadie?" Josephine asked.

"Why, I suppose so. Though I'll be leaving in a few weeks to go back to college." She paused and the girls sighed. "But let's not worry about that just yet. Let's enjoy the time we have together, all right?"

"Yes." Rena rose as she heard the teakettle whistling from the kitchen. "And let's start right now, with tea. Carolina's been kind enough to prepare it. Sadie, would you like to show the girls what I taught you about serving tea and cookies to guests?"

"Who are our guests?" Josephine asked.

"Ooh, I know!" Sadie rose and called for the boys to join them. By the time Rena returned from the kitchen with the tea tray and cookies, the boys were seated around the dining table once again, all smiles.

Rena leaned over to whisper her thoughts into Sadie's ear. "You've come just in time. How can I ever thank you?"

Her niece swung around, a mischievous look on her face. "I can think of one way," she whispered in response.

"Name it."

Sadie's lips curled up, revealing her dimples. She nodded toward the young deputy and whispered, "Invite Charlie to Christmas dinner?"

Rena looked back and forth between them, suddenly very aware that sparks were flying. She could only hope neither would get burned.

Chapter Nineteen

....

Tips for Dealing with Unruly Young'uns—*My Christmas memories are fuzzy from the age of fourteen on. I'm pretty sure I blocked out many of them after the death of my parents. That's why I feel so strongly about giving the children of Daisy the best Christmas ever, because I know the pain of facing the holidays without a mother or father. They deserve a carefree holiday filled with good cheer and wonderful gifts. My tip for dealing with unruly children during the holidays? Share the real reason for the holiday and give them memories that will last forever.*

—Rena Jewel, Director of the Atoka County
Children's Home

The final days before Christmas were spent decorating the house, visiting with Sadie, preparing food, wrapping presents, and sewing outfits for the children. Many times Rena would sew well into the night with Sadie at her side, pinning and pressing the various dresses or slacks. They giggled and talked until exhaustion set in. Then they tumbled into bed, slept a few hours, rose…and started the whole thing over again. All in preparation for the big day: Christmas.

A host of gifts arrived the week before Christmas—many from the missions organization, but a handful from some old friends Rena hadn't thought about in a while: the trio of sisters from the train. Along with a substantial monetary gift, they sent toys in abundance and a note saying that they were praying for the children and thinking often of Rena. Rena responded with a lengthy letter, updating them on the goings-on around Daisy. She left out the part about Molly, of course. And the mayor. Thank goodness, neither had presented much of a problem since that awful day at the general store when Sadie first arrived.

On Christmas morning, Rena awoke with butterflies in her stomach. Before they could attend the morning service, the children would open their presents. Chief among them were the outfits she had made.

Rena woke the boys first. She'd no sooner said "Merry Christmas!" than they were up, jumping on the beds, raring to go. The girls sprang to life at Sadie's joyous "It's Christmas morning!" proclamation. Minutes later, still dressed in their night attire, the children gathered around the tree in the parlor. Sadie served up hot cocoa and shortbread—an unusual breakfast for the children, but one they would never forget.

"Ooh, Miss Rena!" Lilly gazed up at her from the floor, eyes wide. "There are presents under the tree?"

"When did those get here?" Henry asked. "There were no presents last night."

Rena stifled a yawn and thought about how late she and Sadie had stayed up and how many trips they'd made up and down the stairs with wrapped gifts in hand. She had added to the donations with a few presents of her own, which made for quite a stack.

Before long, wrapping paper was flying and children were squealing. Tree was delighted with his wooden train, and the girls loved their rag dolls. The other boys had a wonderful time with their marbles, checkers, and dominoes. Henry's eyes grew wide as he opened the new pocketknife, and Oliver jumped for joy at his copy of *Oliver Twist*, which he claimed had been written just for him.

Finally the moment came to open the new clothes. Rena thought she would burst with excitement. She started with Lilly, who ripped open her package. The beautiful red dress complete with white lace was prettier than anything store-bought. The child held it up and primped.

"Oh, Miss Rena, it's beautiful! Is it really for me? Really truly?"

"Really truly. You can wear it to the Christmas service at church." Out of the corners of her eyes, she caught a glimpse of Callie looking on. "Now it's your turn, honey."

Callie opened her package and began to squeal with delight as she saw a dress in the same red velvet but with a slightly different design. "Ooh, we match!"

Josephine's dress nearly brought down the house. The crushed green velvet was beautiful, of course, but the antique ivory lace added just the right touch. The youngster looked up at Rena with tears in her eyes. "Oh, Miss Rena! This reminds me of a dress my mama bought for me when I was little."

"Does it now?" Rena smiled. "I'm so glad. You're going to look like a princess when you wear that dress to church."

The boys opened their packages one by one, revealing new slacks, buttoned-up shirts, and socks. Most were overcome with joy, but Henry grew silent as he gazed at the coat and trousers Rena had made him. She drew near and whispered, "Do you like them?"

He nodded. "Never had anything like 'em."

"Now it's your turn, Miss Rena." Josephine tugged at her hand.

"Oh?"

"We made you something." The little girl gave her a crudely wrapped gift, which Rena opened right away. Inside, she found a little plaque, hand-carved, that read "For I was an hungred, and ye gave me meat: I was thirsty, and ye gave me drink: I was a stranger, and ye took me in: naked, and ye clothed me: I was sick, and ye visited me: I was in prison, and ye came unto me" (Matthew 25:35–36).

Rena felt the sting of tears as she clutched the plaque close to her heart. "Oh, you sweet, sweet children. Thank you so much. This must've taken weeks."

"Nah." Henry gave her a sheepish look. "I'm pretty fast at whittlin' and such. Didn't take no time a'tall."

"Still, it's beautiful. I will cherish it."

After a moment's pause, Josephine said, "Miss Rena, there's another gift for you too. We found it on the tree a little while ago."

"Yes." Oliver pointed at the tree. "See there? There's an envelope with your name on it."

"An envelope?" She grinned, realizing that the boys and girls must have written her a special note. She took the envelope in hand and opened it with care. Her heart raced the moment she unfolded the letter inside.

My darling Rena,

I hope you have the most wonderful Christmas ever. I know that mine will be perfect because I plan to spend it with you.

Gene

She shoved the letter back inside the envelope, doing her best to avoid Sadie's stare and the animated expressions on the faces of the children.

"What is it?" her niece asked, drawing near.

"Oh, just a note from a friend. Nothing important." Still, she could hardly stop the trembling in her hands. Rena glanced at Henry, who shifted his gaze back to his new clothes. "You children go on upstairs and get dressed," she said.

They gathered up their packages, and she did her best to stay focused. On the outside she managed a calm, quiet demeanor. On the inside she jumped up and down. Gene's letter had sent a delicious shiver through her. He was looking forward to spending the day with her. Oh, and she felt the same! She could hardly wait, in fact.

Up the stairs she went, ready to dress in her Christmas finest. No more practical clothing for Rena Jewel. No, ma'am. A special day demanded a special dress, and she had just the one—a red-and-black plaid with green ribbons, to boot. Quite festive.

After dressing, she fashioned her hair in the now-familiar loose upswept style. Then, remembering what Gene had said about her hair on Thanksgiving, she unpinned it and let it flow loose over her shoulders. Afterward, she took her hairbrush into the girls' room, stood the girls in a row, and braided their hair, joining in their giggles.

Once the children were dressed, they gathered in the parlor. Rena could hardly believe how wonderful they all looked in their new clothes. Of course, not everything fit exactly right, but most of her guesswork had been correct.

Henry tugged at his collar. "Dag-nabbit, Miss Rena. This collar is choking the life outta me. Can I unbutton it?"

Callie sashayed around the room, showing off her red dress.

"Look at Callie!" Oliver laughed. "What happened to yer dungarees, Callie? Yer all sissified."

"Miss Sadie is teaching me how to be a lady," Callie said. Then she gave him a shove.

At this, the boys erupted in laughter.

Rena got them quieted down, and before long they were bundled in coats and headed to the church. Sadie—God bless her—started a lovely rendition of "Silent Night," and before long all the children had joined in.

They arrived at the church, every last one of them looking peaceful, beautiful, and calm. Even Molly Harris looked stunned as the children filed in, removed their coats, and revealed the beautiful garments underneath. Mrs. O'Shea was so taken with the outfits that she oohed and aahed at length. The only one who turned up her nose at the children on this fine day was Calista, whose red-and-green dress paled in comparison to what Lilly, Callie, and Josephine wore.

Thank goodness, Lilly complimented Calista. Before long, the mayor's daughter was all smiles and even joined in and played with the other girls.

"If I hadn't believed in miracles before today, I would now." Gene's gentle voice came low behind her.

Rena turned, finding herself face-to-face with him. "I believe in miracles myself," she said. Oh, how she wanted to say more…to tell him how much his little note had meant to her. But with the first hymn playing, it would have to wait.

They enjoyed a wonderful Christmas service then headed back to the house for what she hoped would be the best holiday dinner ever. For days she, Sadie, Carolina, and Jenny had prepared food. Now to serve it to their hungry guests…

The men took their seats at the larger table and the children joined them, using their best manners. Rena would have to thank Sadie later for her work in that department. Before long they were all gathered 'round, eating sliced ham, turkey, and a host of other delectable foods.

Rena watched from the end of the table as Charlie looked Sadie's way. She noticed the twinkle in his eyes, and the flush on her niece's cheeks did not escape her, either. These two were smitten with one another, no doubt about it.

Thank goodness the boys and girls didn't seem to notice. Then again, they were far too preoccupied with one another to pay much attention to the adults in the room. The change in wardrobe had really transformed them, inside and out.

Gene could hardly take his eyes off of Rena during the meal. She'd never looked so beautiful, or so happy. A couple of times he caught her glancing his way, so he shifted his gaze to his plate. No point in looking like a schoolboy caught cheating on an assignment. Not that looking at her felt like cheating. Oh no. It felt just right.

To his left, Jenny's happy voice rang out. She asked him a question, but he didn't hear it. Everyone laughed. "Gene, are you with us today?" Jenny asked.

"Oh, um, yes. I'm here."

Yes, he was certainly here, and happy to be so.

After lunch everyone gathered in the parlor. He still couldn't get over the difference in the room with the new furniture and paint. Rena had really turned this place around. Then again, she had turned a great many things around. The children, for instance. He'd never seen them look—or act—so nice.

Jonathan clapped his hands. "Everyone take a seat," he said. "I've brought a special gift for the girls."

"Just for the girls?" Oliver asked, his lower lip jutting out.

"Well, maybe something for the boys too," Jonathan said. "But the girls get their gift first." He disappeared outside into the cold and then returned, covered in snow and carrying a large wooden crate. Gene couldn't help but wonder what he was up to.

Josephine's eyes widened in surprise. "What is it, Mr. Brewer?"

He pointed to the stamp on the box. "See that? New York, New York. This package came all the way from Manhattan."

They all began to talk at once. Gene could hardly make sense of this. Surely he would not have ordered something from across the country.

Jonathan pried open the wooden box. A series of gasps went up—

not just from the girls but from the boys too—as they laid eyes on an exquisite wooden dollhouse, complete with a multiplicity of rooms.

"Oh, Mr. Brewer!" Lilly ran to him and threw herself into his arms. "It's the most beautiful house ever!"

The girls began to play with it at once. Well, all but Josephine, who stood off in the distance, her eyes filled with tears.

Gene took a couple of steps in the child's direction. "Don't you want to join them, Josephine?"

The child shook her head. After a moment's silence, she pointed to the second floor of the dollhouse. "That used to be my room."

"What, honey?" he asked, not quite understanding.

Josephine sighed. "That room at the top of the stairs. It was mine. In my old house, I mean. Before..." A tear rolled down her cheek and she turned away, whispering, "Before Mama and Papa died."

From across the room, Gene caught Rena's gaze. He gestured for her to join them, and she drew near. Off in the distance, Jonathan handed the boys a large box to open, so everyone in the place was happy...except Josephine.

"Everything all right over here?" Rena asked, settling down onto the floor next to the tearful youngster. Josephine shook her head. "I don't want to play with the dollhouse, Miss Rena. Do I have to?"

"Well, of course not."

"It's too much like my real house, the one I used to live in before I came here." Josephine began to cry in earnest now.

Rena swept the little girl into her arms and covered her hair with kisses. Gene's heart felt as if it would burst as he looked on. "Oh, honey," Rena said, "I understand. I really do. My parents passed away too."

"They did?" Josephine looked at her, eyes narrowed.

"When I was fourteen. I lived in a home with my mama and papa, and they were both killed in a house fire."

"Same as my parents," Josephine said.

"Yes," Rena said. "I…I was at school at the time it happened."

"Me too," Josephine said, the tears now streaming.

Gene felt the strangest sense of compassion wash over him. He took a seat on the floor and listened.

"I went to live with my brother in Gulfport," Rena explained then gestured to the dollhouse. "In a house very much like this one. My room was upstairs too."

"I have an idea, Josephine," Gene said. "Why don't you pretend this dollhouse is the house you live in now? Miss Jewel has done a fine job in fixing things up, and I…" He paused. "Well, I'll be repairing the floors soon. And the broken cabinet doors."

"You will?" Rena gave him a hopeful look.

"Yes. I've got a whole team of men ready to come in here and work." He rested his hand on Rena's arm and whispered, "I'm sorry. I should've done it sooner. Forgive me?"

The smile she offered in return was so sweet it nearly melted him. "Of course."

"Wonderful!" He rose, feeling the joy of the season more than ever. Off in the distance the boys played with their gift from Jonathan— a bow-and-arrow set.

The gift Gene had brought would pale in comparison, no doubt. A hand-crafted checkerboard was hardly a dollhouse or a bow-and-arrow set. Still, he'd spent days making it and hoped it would fill the hours for both the children and Rena.

Rena.

He looked her way and smiled. Whether she'd meant to or not, the woman had grabbed a piece of his heart. What she would do with it, he had no idea.

In that moment, he was reminded of that ludicrous story the children had told him about her notebook. Did she really craft love stories? Were there heroes and damsels in distress? As he gazed at her and watched the light pick up the soft twinkle in her eyes, he had to conclude one thing: he would play the role of hero, both with the house and with these children. He wouldn't do it to fulfill some fairy-tale story. He would do it because it was the right thing to do. And if it brought a smile to the face of a certain damsel in distress…so be it.

Chapter Twenty

．．．．．．．．．．．．．．．．．．．．．

TIPS FOR DEALING WITH UNRULY YOUNG'UNS—*I have found, generally speaking, that children keep us young. Even when our joints are locked up, we still feel the urge to get down on the floor with little ones and play jacks or marbles. As a grandmother, I can attest to the fact that I am more lenient on my grandsons than I was on my son. Perhaps this is part of the reason they're so ornery. Still, I can't help myself. I've changed since my son was their age. Besides, after I load 'em up with spice cake and other sugary treats, I send 'em home to their pa, who gets to deal with them. Just doing my job, after all.*

—Carolina Wyatt

Rena couldn't remember when she'd spent a happier Christmas. Watching the children play with their gifts, listening to the sound of their voices raised in song, picking up on the subtle hints from Gene that he cared for her...she loved every moment.

Less than three days after Christmas, she'd picked up on another subtle hint—Sadie and Charlie were definitely falling for each other. She tried not to make too much of their lingering glances and flirtatious smiles, but the proof was in the pudding. They were goners.

Sure, Charlie was a bumbling fellow, but happy-go-lucky, and—were it not for the obvious differences—Sadie's sort of boy. Still, he was as poor as a church mouse and had little to offer her. Not to mention the difference in their education levels.

Rena tried to imagine what Reuben and Virginia would say, should they find out. Then again, how would they? In ten days, Sadie would be on a train, headed back to New York for her spring semester at Vassar. Once she boarded the train, Rena could breathe easy. In the meantime, she would keep a watchful eye on things.

On the Tuesday following Christmas, the ladies decided to gather in town to purchase fabrics and trims for drapes and pillows. Before leaving the house, Sadie offered to make up the bed she and Rena had been sharing.

"You finish getting ready," she said with the wave of a hand. "Let me help out around here for a change."

"Hmm?" Rena continued fussing with her hair, preoccupied by its unwillingness to behave today. She gave Sadie a glance. "Oh, sure. Thanks, honey."

Sadie pulled back the spread and knocked Rena's pillow to the ground. Rena turned away from the mirror just in time to see her notebook slide out of its hiding place and onto the floor below. She rose from her stool and sprinted across the room, but Sadie reached it before she could.

"What's this?" Sadie held it up. "Hiding something, eh?"

"Oh, no. Not really. I, um…"

"You never were very good with secrets, Aunt Rena." Sadie clutched the book close. "I can tell from the look on your face that there's something in here you don't want me to see. Might as well 'fess up. You know how I am. I can weasel a confession from a tree stump."

Rena sighed and sat on the edge of the bed. "If I tell you, will you give it back to me?"

"Of course."

"Sometimes—just for fun, mind you—I write things down."

"Oh." Sadie sat on the bed next to her. "You mean you journal your thoughts?"

"Well, that too. But sometimes a bit more. I…well, I write stories."

"Stories? Like dime novels?" Sadie's eyes widened.

"Well, not exactly." Rena paused to think it through. "Okay, actually they are a bit like that. There are heroes and damsels in distress…that sort of thing." She paused to seek out the expression on Sadie's face.

"Oh, Aunt Rena! My respect for you has just gone up by leaps and bounds. You're a romantic at heart."

"I suppose I am." Rena felt a flush of heat rise to cover her face. "I can't believe I'm sharing this with you. I've never told a living soul."

Sadie gave her hand a squeeze. "Your story's safe with me." She giggled at the pun. "Literally. Mum's the word, I promise." Her eyes lit up. "But I still want to know how you go about creating a hero for your story. Do you dream him up, or is he patterned after someone real?" She gave Rena a sly wink. "Someone you've got your eye on, perhaps?"

Rena began to fan herself. "Heavens, no. My stories are pure fiction. Nothing but."

"Oh, I see." The downcast look on Sadie's face reflected her thoughts on that news. "Well, then, tell me about this man. This fictional man, I mean. I can't wait to hear all about him. Is he suave? Debonair? Gallant?"

"I suppose he's all of those things, though not in the traditional way. I've written him to be kind and generous—very giving. That's his appeal, not necessarily his good looks."

Sadie wrinkled her nose. "Are you saying he's not handsome?"

Rena couldn't help the grin that arose. "Merciful heavens. Well, yes, he's handsome. To me, anyway. I cannot say if other women would find him equally as appealing."

Sadie's brow wrinkled. "I feel sure he's quite dashing. But you're sure you didn't pattern him after anyone you know?"

Rena shook her head, suddenly ready to put this conversation behind her. "This story was begun years and years ago, while you were still in primary school."

Sadie's eyes widened. "You don't mean to tell me you've been crafting the same novel all these years?"

"Well, yes." Rena paused. "I've been working on its various components. The plot needed work, you see. And the characterization left something to be desired. As I aged, I had to...well, I had to adjust the ages of the characters. And as my interests changed, I noticed that the story wanted to change along with me. So it has morphed over time into something quite different from what it once was." She sighed and looked out the window. "Anyway, let's don't talk about it anymore."

"I'll let it go on one condition," Sadie said. "You have to let me read it."

Rena gasped. "No. I mean, no one has ever..." She shook her head, suddenly feeling ill. "It's not for others. Not yet, anyway. Not until I've perfected it."

"After all these years, I'd say it's about as good as it's going to get."

Rena reached out to take it from her, but Sadie would not let go of it.

"Sadie, please. I'm terribly embarrassed already."

"No need to be. And please don't argue. I'm going to read it, if it's the last thing I do."

Rena tried to swipe the book from her again, this time tickling Sadie to get her to release it. The notebook flew from the younger woman's hands and shot into the air, and when it landed on the floor, a couple of loose pages fell out. Rena gasped as she realized that Gene's love letters, which she'd hidden inside the notebook, were now in plain view.

"What have we here?" Sadie rose from the bed, leaned down, and picked up the letters.

"No!" Rena tried to grab them but only succeeded in ripping off the corner of the one on top.

"'My dearest Rena…,'" Sadie read the words aloud. Well, the first few words, anyway. After a moment, her cheeks turned pink and she grew silent. Looking up, she said, "Oh, Aunt Rena…"

Rena buried her face in her hands.

Sadie folded the letters, shoved them back in the book, and handed the book to her without a word. When she did speak, her words were laced with emotion. "I…I had no idea. I mean, I had *some* idea, of course. It's clear when he looks at you that he's smitten. And Charlie tried to tell me that he felt sure something was afoot."

"He…he did?"

Sadie nodded. "Yes. But to think that Sheriff Wyatt could compose so beautiful a letter simply takes my breath away." She paused. "Not that it's my business. And now I feel just awful for reading something so private."

"You think *you* feel awful. I'm feeling downright sick. Never planned for a living soul to see those." Rena pressed the notebook under her pillow once more and then—with her stomach in knots—finished making the bed. That done, she turned to face her niece and released a slow breath.

Before she could say a word, Sadie gave her a little wink. "It will be our little secret," she said, crossing her heart. "I promise, I won't breathe a word to anyone."

Gene walked to the door of his office and looked outside.

"Looking for me?" His mother's voice called from the outer office.

"Oh, actually I was wondering what happened to Charlie. He went out a half hour ago to buy some coffee and never came back."

"I would guess he's gone over to see you-know-who." She grinned.

"Probably." The young deputy had been spending more time than usual at the children's home. Gene had his suspicions that it had little to do with the children.

"You have to admit, they're a darling couple," Gene's mother said. "Though it will surely break his heart when she leaves for New York in a couple of weeks."

"No doubt. Can't imagine what his frame of mind will be like when she goes."

"It's your frame of mind I'm concerned with right now," she said. "That's why I've come for a visit. Hope you don't mind."

"What's wrong with my frame of mind?" Gene asked.

"You've been acting a little odd lately. Are you feeling all right?"

"I'm in perfect health. Never better."

"And the boys?"

"They're as happy as larks. You saw them on Christmas Day. They're in fine form these days. They're with the other children today. Jenny and Jonathan have taken them all to the Wilkersons' farm to go sledding."

"Jenny and Jonathan, eh?" She pursed her lips. "Well, now, isn't that nice?"

"Mother, don't meddle."

"Me? Meddle?" She grinned. "I'm not. I just think it's sweet. Love is in the air. And you're right about the boys. They do seem to be making progress." She paused. "But that's not really why I stopped by. I just thought you'd want to know that Rena and Sadie are on their way over to measure the windows for drapes."

"Mother, honestly, I think we can forego the idea of changing up the jail. It's been perfectly fine like this for years, so I'm confident it'll go on being fine for years to come just as it is."

A rap at the door interrupted his impassioned speech about how fine everything was. Gene looked over to discover Rena standing there, holding fabric samples and looking enthused.

"Are you ready?" she asked.

After shifting his gaze to her beautiful eyes, Gene had to admit... he would paint the jail cell bright purple if she asked him to. How in the world could he say no to a wonderful smile like that?

As he helped her out of her coat, Rena rambled on about drapes. Behind her, Charlie carried in several packages for Sadie.

Gene hung Rena's coat on a hook and turned to his deputy. "There you are, Charlie. Took you long enough to get the coffee."

"Coffee!" Charlie groaned. "I forgot to buy the coffee."

"But that's all you went after," Gene said.

"You can blame me," Sadie said and then giggled. "See, we were in the general store making our purchases when Charlie arrived. I'm afraid I was a terrible distraction. I asked for his help in choosing fabrics. He does work here too, and I felt sure he would know which fabrics you might prefer." She flashed a smile Gene's way.

He sighed. "Guess I'll have to go to the store myself. Can't make it through the afternoon without coffee."

"Oh, before you go..." Rena gave him an imploring look. "I'll need to take measurements of the windows." She stretched out a measuring tape and took a few steps toward the east window. "We'll need to buy rods, of course. And paint. But getting the correct measurements is so important. I wonder if you would be so kind as to help me?"

She pulled a small stool over to the window and attempted to step up on it but nearly toppled in the process. He got there just in time for his hands to wrap around her slender waist, breaking her fall. She landed in his arms and the two stood face-to-face. He felt her breath on his cheek. Still, he did not release his hold. Not yet, anyway. Instead, he gazed into her eyes, his heart quickening. The sweetest smile lit her face, and he felt sure she had that same sense of longing that had so recently swept over him.

From across the room a giggle rang out. "Well, lookee there," Sadie said. "The hero sweeps in and saves the damsel in distress. That's a story worthy of publishing in one of those dime novels my mama reads."

Gene couldn't help but wonder at the glare Rena shot Sadie's way. Had he offended her by breaking her fall? Surely not. Perhaps the lingering gaze had been his downfall.

Rena's face turned red and he let go of her at once.

She handed him the measuring tape. "Would you...I mean, would you mind measuring it for me? I need height and width, please. And while you're doing that, I'll go fetch the coffee."

Before he could say "What did I do?" she disappeared through the door and into the cold.

Strange...it suddenly felt colder inside the jail than outside in the snow.

Chapter Twenty-One
....

TIPS FOR DEALING WITH UNRULY YOUNG'UNS—*I would like to offer a tip for dealing with undisciplined children: be consistent. If a parent establishes a daily routine—meals at a certain time, naps at a certain time, and so on—the child will feel safe. Children respond well when they know what to expect. As the parent, you must not only set the routine, but you must stick to it. This is never more important than at bedtime. A happy child is a well-rested child.*

—Virginia Jewel, of the Gulfport Jewels

The day before Sadie was set to leave for New York, Charlie went missing. Gene wondered about him all day and even made a few calls to search for him, but the young deputy could not be found. By early afternoon Gene had received word from Rena that Sadie was missing, as well. No doubt the two were sneaking in one last day before she had to leave town. He didn't blame them, of course, but Charlie should have mentioned it. This wasn't like him.

Late afternoon, Gene stopped by his mother's place to pick up Jacob and William. She met him at the door and ushered him inside.

"Hungry?" she asked.

"Starved."

He took a seat at her table alongside the boys, who were calmer than usual. They actually sat through the whole meal without punching each another. Strange. Must be something in the water.

After the boys finished eating, Gene lingered at the table to talk to his mother.

"You've got something on your mind?" she asked.

"Concerned about Charlie. He didn't show up today."

"Ah. I heard from Rena that Sadie was missing too. I'm sure they're off together on some last-minute adventure." She rose and began to clear the dishes. "I'll be honest…I'm worried about Charlie. When Sadie leaves tomorrow, he's probably going to fall apart. Likely you'll be the one dealing with the heartbreak on this end."

"I've already thought about that, and it concerns me. Not sure how he's going to recover with her so far away."

"Sadie's had quite an effect on him." She paused and set the gravy bowl back down on the table. "She's so much like her aunt, don't you think? Same kind, loving manner. They both have such a way of winning folks over."

Gene thought about what she'd said. "I guess you're right. Never thought about it."

"Speaking of folks who are being won over, I guess you've heard about Molly?"

"What has she done this time?"

"I think you might be surprised." His mother quirked a brow. "I saw this with my own eyes—otherwise, I'm not sure I would've believed it. She actually spoke several kind words to Rena at the general store this morning."

"Perhaps she's ill. Or maybe she's not in her right mind. Too much eggnog."

"No. She seemed perfectly normal. Only…kinder. Perhaps it's some sort of New Year's resolution to be a better person. Or maybe Rena's growing on her."

Like she's growing on all of us.

His mother picked up the dishes once again and disappeared into the kitchen. She returned moments later with the coffeepot in hand. She filled Gene's cup, and he reached for it before leaning back in his chair.

"I, for one, think it would be wonderful if Molly comes around. Perhaps if she grows close to Rena, she will eventually see the good in the children under Rena's care. Don't you think?"

Gene shook his head as concerns kicked in. "Actually, I'm more worried that the opposite might take place. Maybe Molly will sway Rena away from her post. Did you ever think of that?"

"Oh, surely not." Concern now etched his mother's face. "Rena's meant to be here with those children. It's quite obvious."

"To you and me, perhaps, but I'm not sure she's completely settled. At least, not to the extent I'd hoped. So I hope Molly isn't some sort of catalyst to drive her back to Gulfport before the new director arrives." For whatever reason, when he spoke the words "back to Gulfport," Gene's heart twisted. "If she goes away, it will change everything." He grew silent as his thoughts shifted.

After a moment, his mother cleared her throat. "I see how it is."

"W–what do you mean?"

Her brows elevated. "If she went away, it would change everything?"

He paused. "Well, with my boys, I mean. And the rest of the children."

"And you?" She gave him a pointed look, one he couldn't ignore.

Gene shifted in his chair then tugged at his collar. "It's been helpful to have her here, I must confess. She's very…" He paused and attempted to come up with just the right word. Truly, she was a godsend. Everything about having her here had been a blessing, right down to the way she had bonded with his boys. Of course, that beautiful smile didn't hurt, either. Neither did those pretty eyes. And those clothes she'd been wearing of late. All those colors did his heart good.

Stop it, man. Just be honest with yourself for a change.

Rena Jewel had been the one to fall into his arms the other day at the jail, but he was the one who'd fallen emotionally. Only, how would he tell her? Did she even feel the same way, or had he imagined the joy on her face in that wonderful moment?

"Um, Gene?"

He started back to attention and looked his mother's way. "Yes?"

"Son, there's no crime in admitting you're smitten. It's no sin. And I, for one, think it would be terrific for the boys to have a motherly influence."

"Well, I suppose that's what I was saying all along. Rena has already slipped into that role for all of the children."

"Yes, but I think your heart is hoping for a bit more with your two. Am I right?"

He shifted his gaze out the window and noticed Molly walking by. "I think perhaps we've deviated from the original conversation, Mother. We were talking about Molly's influence on Rena."

"Were we? I was sure we were talking about Rena's influence on Molly." His mother grinned then rose and took a step toward the door. "Though I must say, Rena's influence appears to have affected more than just Molly." She gave him a wink then pulled open the door and disappeared from view.

Gene leaned back in his seat, his thoughts now tumbling. Charlie had fallen for Sadie in just a few short weeks. Their feelings for one another were undeniable. Why, then, had it taken Gene so long to realize he had feelings for Rena?

He did, of course. And he could no longer deny it.

Now, to figure out what to do about it.

A wave of relief washed over Rena as Sadie came through the front door.

"Sadie, where in the world have you been? It's been hours. I've been worried sick."

"I'm so sorry." Sadie's cheeks flushed pink as she shrugged out of her coat. "I know I should have told you, but Charlie took me for a drive. We had the most wonderful day. He showed me the house he grew up in and then took me by the school. After that, we went to Tushka to see his mother."

"Tushka? You drove all the way to Tushka?"

"Mm-hmm. And then we went to Atoka. Oh, it was so pretty. Charlie told me all about the tornado in Atoka two years ago. Did you know that's how Gene's wife died? She had gone to visit her mother, who was ill."

"Gene doesn't really talk about it," Rena said. "He's very private."

"Yes." Sadie shook her head. "Such a sad story." After a moment, she smiled. "There's still snow on the ground in Atoka, would you believe it? It melted here in Daisy days ago." She fussed with the buttons on her coat, her hand fumbling over them. "Look at me. So silly."

"Sadie, are you quite sure you're all right? You and Charlie had us all in a tizzy. Gene and Carolina came by this evening to see if I'd heard from you. I didn't know what to say."

"Please don't fret, Aunt Rena. I promise we were fine." At this point, a look of desperation came over her. "But there's something important I have to tell you. Maybe you'd better sit down."

Rena's heart began to race. She took a seat in the chair and braced herself.

Sadie walked to the fireplace and fingered the mantel. "Aunt Rena, you know me better than most anyone."

"Yes. Of course."

"You know I'm not prone to flightiness. Right?"

"Right."

"And you trust my judgment."

"Until this moment, yes. But I have a feeling that what you're about to say is going to change that."

"Oh, Aunt Rena..." Sadie rushed her way and took the empty spot next to her. "I'm in love with Charlie."

"You're...you're in love with him? I knew you were infatuated, of course. But...love?"

Sadie closed her eyes and clasped her hands together. "Oh, yes. It's the most wonderful feeling I've ever felt. I highly recommend it."

"I see."

Sadie's eyes popped open, and she gazed at Rena. "Surely you can see my dilemma. I can't possibly be in love with someone who lives on the other side of the country from where I'm attending school. That's why I can't go back."

"Excuse me?"

"I can't go back, Aunt Rena. I simply can't. I've not been terribly happy at college anyway, but now..." A lingering sigh escaped and she leaned back against the sofa.

"But, Sadie, you can't be serious. You're the most studious girl I know. You would give up your education for a young man you scarcely know?"

"Oh, Aunt Rena, you know what it feels like to be in love. I saw those letters from Gene. Would you have me suffer in New York when my heart is here, in Daisy?"

"But..." She couldn't seem to come up with appropriate words.

"It's not just Charlie. Oh, I love him! I do. But it's the children too." Tears ran in rivers down Sadie's cheeks at this proclamation. "I love them so, and I can't bear the thought of leaving them. Or you."

A lump rose in Rena's throat, one she could not speak over. Not that she would've known what to say anyway. She joined Sadie on the sofa but remained silent.

Sadie gave her hand a squeeze. "I need you, Aunt Rena. I need you so desperately."

"Need me?" she managed. "What do you mean?"

A look of dread came over Sadie. "I need you to call Father and tell him for me. I—I can't do it."

"Surely you jest!" Rena felt ill at the very idea. "I would sooner face a den of hungry lions than tell your father you're not going back to college. He will be so upset. Your education means the world to him."

"But it doesn't to me. Don't you see?" Sadie erupted into tears, her sobs breaking Rena's heart. From up above she heard a stirring and realized that the children had awakened. Sure enough, Callie, Lilly, and Josephine appeared in the living room moments later, rubbing their eyes.

"What happened, Miss Sadie?" Callie raced to her side. "Did someone hurt you?"

"N–no." Sadie swiped at her eyes with the back of her hand and sniffled. "I'm—I'm sorry I woke you girls up. I didn't mean to."

"Are you all right?" Lilly climbed into her lap and leaned her head on Sadie's shoulder.

"Y–yes." Another little sob escaped. "I just love you! All of you. And I don't want to leave."

"We don't want you to leave either, Miss Sadie!" Josephine began to cry, and before long the other two girls joined her.

Rena looked on with a sigh. She managed to get the girls calmed down, and before long Sadie rose and took the children by the hand. "I'll get them tucked in," she said, sniffling again.

"You should go on to bed yourself," Rena said. "I'll be up in a minute."

She waited until Sadie and the girls were long gone to think about a plan of action. How could she possibly call Reuben and give him this news? Why, he and Virginia would be on the next train to Daisy, no doubt about it.

Then again, maybe that would be for the best. She would even encourage his visit. He would arrive and set things aright with his daughter. And while he was here, he could see the children's home, as well. Yes, her brother could surely fix all of this.

Chapter Twenty-Two
....

TIPS FOR DEALING WITH UNRULY YOUNG'UNS—*When a father speaks, he must command the full attention of his children. He should never have to repeat himself. He must love his children, naturally, but never allow them to lose respect for him as the authority figure in the home. Too often I have seen fathers give in to the whims of their children and pay a heavy price when they're grown. As the father of a bright, levelheaded young woman, I can attest to the fact that fatherly authority has made all the difference. Even now, my daughter would never think to go against my wishes.*

—Reverend Reuben Jewel, Director of the Hope Pointe
Missions Society

Rena's telephone conversation with her brother went exactly as she expected. He did not respond well to the news that Sadie planned to stay in Daisy. In fact, he fussed and fumed and insisted upon a trip to see her at once. He and Virginia would arrive on Tuesday, the fourteenth of January, to talk some sense into their daughter and, hopefully, put her on a train to New York.

On that dreaded Tuesday, Rena asked Gene to drive her to the depot to pick up her brother and sister-in-law. Her nerves were so badly affected that she could barely speak a word to the man as he drove. He looked a little nervous too. No wonder. He still hadn't confessed to writing those letters. Perhaps his shyness would go on presenting problems. Maybe he would never speak his mind.

Well, this wasn't the day for that, anyway. Today she had other issues to contend with. First, pick up Reuben and Virginia. Take them to the children's home for a tour and private conversation before the children arrived home from school, and then have a heart-to-heart chat with Sadie, who was probably hiding out at the jail, locked in a cell so that her father couldn't get to her.

They arrived at the depot just as the train pulled in. Gene looked Rena's way and released a slow breath. "Think you're up for this?"

She shook her head.

He came around to her side of the car and opened the door for her. Then he took her hand to help her out. It wasn't until a couple of minutes passed that she realized he was still holding her hand.

Well, so be it. She needed someone to hold her hand today. Facing Reuben would be tough. Gene's presence would steady her.

A couple of passengers exited the train, but Reuben and Virginia were nowhere to be seen. Then, just when she'd given up on them, they appeared. Virginia looked none-the-worse for wear, but Reuben...well, Rena had never seen her brother look so upset.

She hiked up her skirts and took off running in their direction, leaving Gene behind. Rena hugged Virginia first, whispered a soft, "I'm so glad you're here," then turned her attentions to her brother. His hug didn't carry the same tenderness, but she tried not to read too much into it.

"Reuben." She stepped back and took his hand. "I'm so glad you've come."

"Had no choice." He fingered the nose of his spectacles, pushing them into place. "One of us has to talk some sense into that girl."

Rena did her best to swallow her fears. "Yes, well, let's go and find her, shall we?"

"Find her?" Reuben paled. "You're not insinuating that she's run off with that fellow, are you?"

"No, no. Put your mind at ease." Rena patted his arm.

The porter appeared with their luggage and Gene drew near. Rena made quick introductions and silently praised the Lord that her brother treated Gene civilly. Then again, as head of the missions society, he had his reputation to uphold, didn't he? Yes, surely he would be kind to everyone. Well, everyone but Sadie and Charlie.

A shiver ran down Rena's spine as she thought of Reuben's upcoming encounter with the young deputy. Likely it would not go well for either one.

All the more reason to pray and trust the Lord. If He had orchestrated all this, surely He could handle an angry father and a lovesick daughter.

Gene made light conversation all the way back to the children's home. When they arrived, Reuben's expression shifted slightly. He stared at the outside of the house for a moment without saying anything. When he finally spoke, his words were laced with concern. "Rena, I thought the home had been through renovations."

"Mostly internal," she said. "Though Gene has painted the exterior."

"Well, yes, but look at those rotting boards. And the stairs are a shambles."

"Oh, they were much worse. Henry has replaced several of the boards already."

"Dreadful," Reuben said.

As they exited the car, Rena did her best to keep the mood as cheerful as possible. Thank goodness Gene played along. He joined in with heart-felt bantering, even carrying in Reuben and Virginia's luggage. Together they showed off the children's home, taking their guests on a tour—first of the parlor, then the kitchen and dining room. Lastly, Rena ushered them upstairs, where she offered them her room for the duration of their stay.

"We can't take your room, Rena," Virginia argued. "Where will you sleep?"

"There are extra beds in the girls' room. Sadie and I will stay in there during your visit."

She'd no sooner spoken the name *Sadie* than Reuben's face contorted. "Where is that daughter of mine, anyway? I wish to speak to her."

"I…well, we thought it would be best to give you some time to settle in before talking with her." Rena took Reuben's hand. "Could you give me a few minutes, brother? I want to speak with you on her behalf."

"On her behalf?" He did not look pleased.

Virginia slipped out of her coat and laid it across the end of the bed. "Likely she's too scared to talk to you, Reuben. Remember what we discussed. You won't overreact. Calm, cool heads. That's what's needed in situations such as these."

"Yes, I agree completely." Rena gestured to the stairs. "Now, please come back down to the parlor. I've got coffee and pie waiting. I'm sure you're hungry."

She led the way downstairs. Before long, her brother and sister-in-law were seated in the parlor and she was in the kitchen, with Gene at her side, slicing the pie Sadie had baked only this morning, while a pot of coffee brewed nearby. Though the two worked in silence, the conversation inside Rena's head was more than sufficient to keep her preoccupied.

Before carrying the refreshments out, Gene looked Rena's way. "Guess this would be a good time for me to head back to the jail to fetch the victims. Want me to send both of them or just Sadie?"

She sighed. "We'd probably better start with just Sadie. But tell Charlie not to fret. I'm sure this will all work out."

"Hmm." He offered a little smile, one that brought her hope. "Well, I'll be praying. I know you will too." He paused and gazed into her eyes. "You know, I once read that true love always wins out."

"O–oh?" She couldn't help the smile that followed. "Well, I do believe that's a biblical promise, so I will cling to it now as I face my brother. And thanks for those prayers. We're all going to need them."

Minutes later she found herself seated in the parlor with a slice of pie in hand. Reuben and Virginia sat on the sofa, picking at their slices of pie but not really eating them.

Rena decided to break the silence. "Reuben, I feel I must start by apologizing."

He looked her way. "For what has happened with Sadie, you mean?"

"Honey, we don't hold you responsible for that." Virginia placed her plate on the end table. "Honestly, we don't. She's young and these things happen."

Reuben did not look convinced. Rena could almost hear the thoughts going on in his head: *If you hadn't chosen to come to Daisy, none of this would have happened.* Those words were true, of course, but she didn't regret coming. Not one iota.

Rena's pie plate began to tremble in her hand. She set it aside on the small table to her right. "My apology is twofold. Yes, I feel I've somehow let you down because of what has happened with Sadie. But I also want to apologize—specifically to you, Reuben—because I never really took the time to understand your work at the missions society before."

He looked stunned at this news. "What do you mean?"

"I didn't really invest myself in the people of Gulfport. In the projects, yes. I could knit. I could sew. But I hadn't truly given my heart to the people we were ministering to. In fact…" She paused. "I must confess, I simply didn't take the time to get to know them. Not really. I just handed them a scarf or a cap and went on my way."

"Ah." His brow wrinkled and he took a sip of coffee.

"And now?" Virginia gave her a curious look.

"Now I understand. I'm invested. I couldn't leave these children if my life depended on it."

"I see. So I suppose talking you into returning to Gulfport is out of the question." Her brother pursed his lips and shifted the coffee cup to the other hand.

"It is. I love these children and they love me."

Virginia smiled. "'Greater love hath no man than this, that a man lay down his life for his friends.'" She paused and then added, "Or a child."

"Or many, many children." Rena grinned, her heart now feeling lighter. "Though I wouldn't go so far as to say I've laid down my life for them."

"Oh, but you have." Virginia dove into a lengthy speech about caring for those in need, and it greatly encouraged Rena. She had to wonder about Reuben's silence, though. Likely his thoughts were elsewhere—on Sadie.

The nervous young woman arrived moments later, entering the house alone. Rena silently thanked the Lord for that. Charlie would have his moment with Sadie's father, but not yet.

Virginia stood and rushed to her daughter's side. "You beautiful girl. We've missed you so much."

"I missed you, too, Mama." Tears covered Sadie's lashes.

Rena looked on as Reuben rose and took a few steps in his daughter's direction. "Father!" The color drained from Sadie's face as she looked his way. "You've come all the way to Daisy to talk with me."

"I have." He gave her a stern look. "But to clarify, I've come all this way to talk some *sense* into you."

"I see." She began to twist the handkerchief in her hands. "Would you like a cup of coffee? A nap? A slice of pie? I baked it myself. Or maybe some hot cocoa? I'll just have to run to town to fetch some chocolate from the general store. Won't take long."

"I've already had a cup of coffee, and Rena offered me a slice of pie, though I had no idea you'd baked it. Since when do you bake?"

"Since I moved to Daisy." She drew near and slipped her arm through his. "It's this town, Father. There's just something about it that makes me want to be better at everything I do."

"Interesting you should say that. I've come to talk with you about bettering yourself."

"Oh, I'm better already." Sadie grinned. "Feeling better about life every day, in fact." She beamed then plopped down on the sofa.

"You're missing the point." Her father took the spot next to her, and Rena sat back down in the wingback chair, a quiet observer.

"Father…" Sadie took his hand. "I need you to hear what I have to say. I've enjoyed my semester at Vassar, but…" She paused and a little shrug followed. "I've not felt at home. In fact, I've not felt much of anything except frustration. It's not what I'd hoped, to say the very least."

"But we've planned for your college education since you were a little girl." Her mother took the spot on the other side of her. "Do you know how many girls would move heaven and earth for the opportunity to attend a school like Vassar?"

"I do. And I don't want you to think I'm ungrateful. I think what you and Daddy did was the second-kindest thing a parent could do for a child."

"Second-kindest?" her mother asked. "What's the kindest?"

A lovely smile lit Sadie's face. "Trusting that she's grown up enough to know her own heart."

The silence from Reuben was deafening.

"What are you saying, Sadie?" Virginia asked after a moment.

"I'm saying that I'm in love with Charlie Lawson. And I'm saying"—her face lit up in a smile and she began to bounce up and down on the sofa—"I'm saying that we're married!"

Gene took long strides across the jailhouse with his heart in his throat. From his spot behind the desk, Charlie grinned. "C'mon now, Gene. You had to know this was coming."

"I didn't."

"But I love Sadie and she loves me." Charlie rose and took a few steps in his direction. "This is what people do when they're in love. They get married."

"So...so, that's where you were when you disappeared on us that day?"

"Yep. Drove to Tushka to introduce Sadie to my mother, then on to Atoka, where we got married at the courthouse. All legal and proper."

Gene thoughts began to tumble. "And then?"

"And then...is none of your business." A gleam in Charlie's eyes clued him in that this particular conversation was over.

"Ah." Gene couldn't think of anything else to add, so he shut his mouth and leaned against the desk. Charlie. Sadie. Married. Rena was going to have a fit. And Reuben! What would he do? Likely kill Charlie Lawson, first thing.

Charlie didn't look worried. He slapped Gene on the back. "Aw, c'mon, now. This is really all your fault, anyhow."

"My fault? How could this be my fault?"

"Sadie never would've had the courage to follow her heart if she hadn't read those letters you wrote. They were something else, my friend."

"Letters I wrote?" That certainly got his attention. He rose and looked Charlie square in the face. "What letters?"

"The ones to Rena, of course. Sadie said they were the most heartfelt words she'd ever read." Charlie gave him a playful wink. "Didn't think you had it in you, to be honest. I mean, you've always been such a down-to-earth fella. Never would've figured you for a romantic."

"Romantic?" Gene shook his head. "Wait a minute. Would you mind telling me what you're talking about? What letters?"

"Your love letters to Rena, of course. Don't tell me they've slipped your mind." Charlie's brow wrinkled.

"Slipped my mind?" Gene raked his hand through his hair. "No. Nothing has slipped my mind. If anyone's losing his mind around here, it's you. Running off and getting married without telling anyone? But I can absolutely assure you, I never wrote any love letters to Rena Jewel."

"You—you didn't?" At this news, Charlie eased his way down into the chair again. "You're sure? I mean, maybe you wrote them in a fit of passion and don't remember."

"I don't have fits of passion," Gene said, suddenly feeling a pulsing in his neck. "And I don't write love letters."

"Hmm." Charlie leaned back in the chair and stared him down. "Well, then, I'd say that pretty much changes everything."

Chapter Twenty-Three

······················

TIPS FOR DEALING WITH UNRULY YOUNG'UNS—*My son, Charlie Lawson, is a deputy sheriff over Daisy-way. He's been living on his own since he turned eighteen, just two years ago. You never met a prouder mama than this one. When I see him, all grown-up and as happy as a lark with that new bride on his arm, my heart just wants to sing for joy. Oh, it wasn't always sunshine and lollipops. He gave me plenty of trouble as a boy. My solution? I spoke positive words over him. Told him that he was going to do something with his life when he grew up. Planted big dreams inside him. Now I'm watching the fulfillment of those dreams, and let me tell you…there's nothing more satisfying.*

—Linda-Lou Lawson, Tushka, Oklahoma

The morning after Sadie broke her news, Rena received another love letter from Gene. This one had been slipped into her Bible, which she had left in the parlor on the end table. She opened the note with haste, her heart in her throat.

Darling Rena,

How I wish I had Charlie's courage! He has been motivated by love to do the very thing I can only think of doing. How will we ever spend our lives together if I cannot summon up the courage to share my heart? Oh, what a fool I am. What a coward! How long will I wait before the words cross my lips? I adore you. I have, from the day we first met. And I will— heaven help me—speak it plain as soon as I am able. In the meantime, I am fondly yours.

Gene

She clutched the letter to her chest and practically danced across the room.

"Rena?" Virginia put down her needlework. "Has something happened?

She thought about holding back, thought about keeping it to herself. Instead, she thrust the letter into her sister-in-law's hands and began to waltz around the room. "Nothing is wrong, Virginia! Everything is right. Never more right, in fact."

Virginia read the letter then looked over at Rena with tears in her eyes. "This is from the sheriff?"

"Yes." Rena took the letter back, skimmed it once more, then folded it and put it back in her Bible. "He's been sending them for weeks now, but I've never had the courage to respond. This time…" She grinned and held the Bible close. "This time I'm going to do it. I'm going to write the loveliest letter you've ever seen, one that fully shares my heart. I will not leave him guessing any longer."

Virginia wrapped Rena in her arms and gave her a tight squeeze. "You precious thing! I'm going to help you."

"You are?"

"Indeed. Let's craft a letter so beautiful that it gives him the courage to speak his mind in the open. What do you say?"

Rena giggled and then nodded. "We have to hurry. The children will be home from school in a couple of hours, and Reuben will be back sooner than that."

"He and Charlie have a lot to discuss," Virginia said. "I daresay he will be with that young man all afternoon and into the evening."

"Perhaps. But I must think of a way to deliver this letter once it's written."

"Oh, that's easy," Virginia said. "We'll walk to town and hand-deliver it to the jailhouse. That's where Reuben and Charlie are meeting, are they not? We can claim we need to tell them something."

"I suppose." Rena snapped her fingers. "Yes, this is the perfect day. Gene has gone to Atoka to deliver an inmate to the county jail. He will be gone most of the day, I think."

"Perfect." Virginia's cheeks glowed.

The ladies spent the next hour penning the most exquisite letter known to mankind. Rena felt giddy as she read it aloud the last time:

Dearest Gene,

Oh, how long I've wanted to write to you, to confess my truest feelings. Your letters have brought me a joy I've never before known. They've lifted my spirits on the darkest days and given me hope to think that we might one day be as happily matched as our young Sadie and Charlie. Please don't fret over not having the courage to share your thoughts aloud. I, too, have trouble with expressing my heart. Writing things down has always been my way of sharing my deepest feelings. Perhaps one day soon we will have a heart-to-heart discussion. In the

*meantime, please know that I return your sentiments—
totally, fully, and joyfully.*

> *Yours truly,*
> *Rena*

"What do you think?" Rena's voice trembled as she spoke.

"I think it's heavenly," Virginia said. "And I also think we should deliver it before you change your mind. Are you up to a walk to town?"

"I—I suppose."

"Good thing it warmed up a bit today. Let's go quickly, shall we?"

The butterflies in Rena's stomach almost convinced her to back out. However, the joy she felt as she remembered Gene's most recent letter bolstered her courage. She would speak her mind through this note, and she would speak it clear. How he responded would be up to him. Oh, but how she hoped he responded by sweeping her into his arms and sharing his affections face-to-face! Wouldn't that be lovely?

Rena and Virginia giggled all the way to town. The skies overhead were bright and clear, which matched their mood. They arrived at the jailhouse and Rena drew a deep breath. "How should we go about this?" she asked.

Virginia paused. "I know. Give me the letter. You go on over to the general store and wait. Pretend to shop."

"I really do need a few things from the store."

"Perfect." Virginia grabbed her arm. "I'll go inside the jail and check on Reuben. He won't be suspicious at all, particularly if I tell him he needs to come home for dinner at a certain time."

"Yes, and please invite Charlie to dinner too," Rena said. "I think it's a good idea, since it's your last night here."

"I will." Virginia released her hold on Rena's arm. "Now, the big question is, how do I get the letter onto Gene's desk?"

"Oh, that's easy." Rena smiled as the idea hit. "Tell Charlie that I need my fabric samples back. They're on Gene's desk in the back office. You can bring the samples to me and leave the letter in their place." She reached into her pocket and pulled out the letter, wishing she had sprayed it with perfume. Oh well. Surely Gene would love it, regardless.

Virginia took the letter and disappeared into the jailhouse. Rena's nerves nearly got the better of her. For a moment she considered following behind her sister-in-law and putting a stop to the whole thing. Then she remembered Gene's words, and they gave her the confidence to move ahead.

She practically danced her way into the general store. Once inside, she gave Mr. Hannigan a cheerful hello, asked how his wife was feeling, and filled her basket with all sorts of items for the children's home. She found herself singing "'Daisy, Daisy, give me your answer, do'" and had to chuckle at the irony of the words. Wasn't she waiting on an answer from the man she loved? Yes indeed. And perhaps—if all went well— she would soon need a bicycle built for two.

Rena rounded the shelves at the back of the store, headed up to the register, when Sadie stepped in front of her.

"Aunt Rena!"

"Sadie, what are you doing here?"

"Hiding out from Father while he talks to Charlie." She shivered. "I can't even imagine what they're doing over there, but it's taking hours."

"We'll know soon enough," Rena said. "Your mother just went inside to check on them." She hesitated about saying more, though she knew she could trust Sadie. Instead, she continued to shop, filling her basket to the very top.

Rena took her purchases to the front counter, where Mr. Hannigan packaged them. By the time she finished, Virginia had swept into the store in a flutter. She pulled Rena and Sadie to the side and giggled.

"Oh, Rena! I did it. I really did it. And I got away with it too. You were right. Gene is gone to Atoka."

"Got away with what?" Sadie asked, her brow wrinkled in confusion. "Something to do with Charlie and Father?"

"No, sweet girl." Her mother patted her arm. "Something completely different." She gave Rena a wink.

Rena felt her cheeks grow warm as Mr. Hannigan looked her way. She took her packages, thanked him, and moved toward the door.

"Wait." Sadie grabbed her by the arm just as she stepped outside. "What are you two up to? What aren't you saying?"

Rena giggled. "Oh, Sadie, you might as well know. I got another letter from Gene today."

At once, Sadie's face paled. She released her hold on Rena's arm and shook her head. "Oh dear, oh dear." She began to pace the walkway outside of the store, finally turning to face them.

"What is it, Sadie?" The joy Rena had been feeling only moments before suddenly dissipated at the look of horror on her niece's face. "Tell me. Please."

"Oh, Aunt Rena. I hate to be the one. Charlie told me just this morning that it would be best if you didn't know, at least not yet."

"Know what?"

"Those letters...the ones you've been getting from Gene?"

"Y–yes?"

"They're not from Gene at all."

Rena suddenly felt ill. "O–of course they are. Why, they're signed with his name."

"Yes. I know that. But, Aunt Rena, trust me...Charlie spoke with Gene himself."

"How did Charlie even know about the letters?" Rena glared at Sadie, knowing all too well how he must have heard about them.

"I'm sorry, Aunt Rena. I really am. I told him in confidence. But I can also tell you with complete confidence that the letters you've been receiving were not penned by Gene Wyatt. Absolutely, unequivocally not."

Rena now shook all over, but she could not blame it on the cold. This news was simply too much to take. "Then...who?" she managed.

Sadie shook her head. "I haven't a clue." She paused. "Well, I have my suspicions but no hard evidence. I had planned to talk with you about it when I arrived home."

"I see." Rena released a slow breath, feeling as if all of the life were draining out of her. So Gene didn't care for her at all. He hadn't written those letters. He wasn't suffering from lack of courage. He probably didn't even know she cared about him. What a dreadful situation.

"Oh no!" She let out a cry, which caused Molly Harris—who was just entering the store—to look her way.

"What is it?" Sadie asked.

"I wrote a passionate love letter to Gene, and your mother just delivered it."

"It's sitting on his desk as we speak," Virginia whispered.

"Stay calm," Sadie said, putting her hands up. "I'll just go in there and fetch it. No problem."

For a moment Rena experienced a sense of relief. This was followed by the inevitable feeling of letdown at the realization that Gene did not care for her. Oh, what pain rippled through her. She felt it so intensely that she thought she might be ill. But there was no time for illness now. Not with a letter to be retrieved.

After a moment's pause, Sadie pointed herself toward the jail, took a couple of steps in that direction, and then turned back.

"I can't go in there," she whispered, tears beginning to roll down her cheeks. "What if Father and Charlie are arguing? What if I walk inside and discover my husband's dead body laid out on the floor?" She began to weep.

Rena slapped herself in the forehead. "Fine. I'll go in. But let's hurry. We don't have much…" She'd almost spoken the word "time" when Gene's car pulled up. He parked in front of the jail, exited the vehicle, gave them a wave, and then disappeared inside.

"Oh. Help."

Rena turned on her heel and began to run toward home.

Gene waved at the ladies then walked inside the jail. After a long day in Atoka with a particularly difficult inmate, he could hardly wait for a quiet evening. He walked in on Charlie and Reuben Jewel engaged in a heated conversation. Gene quickly excused himself and made his way back to his office.

Closing the door, he released a slow breath, ushered up a prayer for Charlie and Sadie, then walked over to his desk. As he took a seat behind it, he gave it a second glance. Something looked different, though he couldn't say what, exactly.

Ah, yes. The fabric samples had been moved. Likely Rena had come to fetch them. But what was that in its place?

He stretched his arm across the desk and fetched the gilded envelope. Odd. If his name hadn't been written on the front, he would have wondered who it belonged to. He reached for the letter opener and, moments later, had the letter unfolded in his hand.

To say that the words written there took him by surprise would be an understatement. To say they brought an unexpected thrill would be even more so. For, as he read the words Rena had penned, every feeling he'd had locked up inside over the past several weeks came rushing out.

1912

He rose and paced the office, only slightly aware of a stirring outside his door. Finally convinced that Charlie and Reuben must've gone to fighting, he folded the letter, shoved it into his coat pocket, and opened the door leading to the outer office.

Sadie stood just outside with her mother at her side. Behind them, Charlie and Reuben looked on, both appearing perplexed.

"I'm sorry, Gene," Sadie said, "but I must know. Did you...I mean, did you happen to find a letter on your desk just now?" He had barely started to nod when she added, "I believe it was left there by mistake."

In that moment, every hope he'd had drained away.

He reached into his pocket, pulled out the letter, and held it up. "This letter, you mean?"

He would've said more, but Sadie fainted dead away in front of him.

Chapter Twenty-Five

....

Tips for Dealing with Unruly Young'uns—*Sometimes kids just need to be kids. We don't mean to cause trouble...most of the time. Like that time Henry and Oliver talked me into writing those dumb love letters to Miss Rena and pretending they were from the sheriff. I didn't mean to make her cry! Guess I was hopin' she and Mr. Gene would really fall in love. Henry bought the stationery at the general store, and I used my very best handwriting. The funniest part of all was figuring out how to come up with those bee-you-tee-ful words! Shh! That's my little secret. Well, mine and Henry's.*

—Josephine Collins, Age Eleven

Rena arrived home overcome with emotion. She swung wide the door of the house and was startled to see that the children had already arrived home from school. Adding to the chaos, Jonathan was there as well. He took one look at her and rushed to her side.

"Rena, are you all right?"

"No." She shook her head. "I'm not."

"Should I fetch the doctor?" He put his palm on her forehead. "You don't feel feverish. Do you have the flu?"

"I wish." She dissolved into tears. "What I have is...fatal!" She began to sob.

"I'm going for the doctor right now. Whatever you do, don't move. Just rest until I get back."

She tried to speak but could not. He shot through the door, his face ashen.

The children gathered round, looking terrified. Rena tried to stop the flow of tears, but they would not cease.

Josephine looked on, her eyes growing large. "Miss Rena, what happened? Did somebody die?"

"N–no!" Rena drew a deep breath and tried to calm down. She hadn't intended for the children to see her like this. Still, what could she do?

Josephine and the other girls grabbed her by the hands and pulled her inside. Seconds later, they were all seated at the dining room table, bawling.

"W–why are we c–crying?" Lilly wailed at long last.

"I—I don't know!" Callie sniffled and wiped her nose on her sleeve.

Rena did her best to calm down so that she could alleviate their fears. Still, she must confront them. Surely these little monsters had done this. They had written those letters, or her name wasn't Rena Jewel. Then again, she wasn't sure what her name was right now. Mud, from the looks of things.

By now the boys had joined them. Most looked terrified to find her in such a state. They gathered around, and Henry asked if he could do anything to help.

"Yes." She sucked in a breath and said, "Tell me who wrote those awful letters, and don't lie to me!"

What happened next was proof positive they'd done the deed. She'd never seen a room clear so quickly. In seconds, the only two who remained were Henry and Josephine—and Josephine now wailed louder than ever.

Rena, horrified to learn the truth, rose from her chair and headed upstairs. She needed privacy. She needed time to think. Moments later, she was closed in her bedroom with the door locked. She flung her body onto the bed and began to cry in earnest.

She heard a rap on the door and ignored it.

"Miz Rena," Henry's voice sounded. "Please. Can we talk to you?"

"P–pretty p–please, Miss R–rena," Josephine added between sobs.

"No." She paused to blow her nose. "Not now."

They would not go away. One of them—Henry, likely, judging from the knock—was persistent. She finally relinquished and opened the door. Josephine stepped inside the room first with Henry right behind her.

"Miss Rena..." Josephine grabbed her hand. "Oh, please forgive me. I didn't mean to make you cry. I never ever thought you would cry. We just thought..."

"What did you think?" she asked, her harsh words laced with anger. "That you would humiliate me in front of people I've grown to care about? That you would get me so upset I would actually want to leave this town and never return?"

"But you cain't leave Daisy." This time it was Henry who spoke. "You just cain't. Those letters weren't s'posed to get you to leave. They were s'posed to make you stay!"

"Well, they've done just the opposite. I want to pack my bags and head back to Mississippi, where I can still show my face in public. Because that's one thing I'll never be able to do around here again."

Henry leaned against the door, his eyes now misty. "I–I'm so sorry, Miss Rena. Please don't go."

"Please!" Josephine cried. "You're like a mama to me! If you go away, I don't know what I'll do!" She dissolved into tears.

Rena tried to gather her wits about her. She looked back and forth between the two youngsters, a mixture of emotions rushing over her.

If what Henry had said was true, they weren't trying to hurt her. They thought the letters would make her want to stay put. But why had they done it? What had they hoped to accomplish? And how had they managed to write such convincing letters?

"A new director is coming in May, remember?" she said. "Surely the sheriff can look after you until then." She took a seat on the edge of the bed and swiped her eyes with the back of her hand. After a few moments her breathing steadied. She hoped her voice would do the same. "One thing I simply must know."

Josephine sniffled. "W–what?"

"However did you write such grown-up letters? Your choice of words was so convincing, so educated. I understand the beautiful handwriting. Miss Jamison has often bragged on your penmanship, Josephine, but however did you choose the wording?"

"Oh, that." Henry worried the carpet with the toe of his shoe. "We, um, well…"

She looked at the boy, knowing in her heart of hearts that he could not have composed those letters. But someone had done it. Who?

Before they could respond, Oliver appeared in the open doorway, followed by the twins, then Mochni and several of the others. Callie wormed her way from the back of the troop to enter, as well.

"I know how they did it, Miss Rena," she said. "They used the words in your stories."

"My stories?" A new wave of fear washed over Rena at this revelation.

"Yes." Callie reached under the pillow and came out with the notebook.

Rena grabbed it from her, horrified.

Josephine's little face lit up, though tears still glistened in her eyes. "Your stories are so romantical. Heroes and damsels in distress. And the way they talk to each other is so lovely." She appeared to swoon. "Ooh, so lovely! That's how we knew what to say!"

"Wait." Rena shook her head, confused. "You're telling me that you took my very words and used them in those letters?"

"Yes." Henry sighed. "It's true."

"Remember that line in the first letter?" Josephine asked. "The one where the sheriff said"—here, she put on a deep male voice—"'If you would allow me to admire you from afar while I work up the courage to speak my mind, I would be overcome with happiness.'"

"Y–yes."

Henry pursed his lips. "Heck. Ya gotta know I coulda never come up with words like that. Not in a month of Sundays. But Gerald the Ranger said that very thing to Rosalinda, the woman he rescued from the runaway train. Remember? He wanted her to know that he loved her but was afraid to say it out loud."

She'd been had, but not in the way she'd suspected. They had read her stories and used them against her. Only, it sounded as if they had really used them *for* her, in their own strange way. Their hearts were in the right place, anyway.

"When we read your stories, we put two and two together and figured…" Henry's words faded away.

"That's how we knew you were in love with the sheriff." Callie bounced up and down. "See? He's Gerald and you're Rosalinda." Her nose wrinkled. "Only, he didn't really rescue you from a train, did he?"

"Nah, silly." Henry gave her a shove. "But he did pick her up at the train station that first day, so I'm guessin' that's why she wrote all that." He gazed at Rena. "Is that right?"

She closed her eyes and silently counted to ten. This couldn't possibly get any worse.

Or could it?

She opened her eyes. "Let me ask you children another question:

Did you tell the sheriff about my stories? Stories with a Ranger named Gerald and a woman named Rosalinda?"

"Oh, sure. Told him awhile back." Henry chuckled. "But he said I must be lyin', 'cause the Rena he knows is far too sensible for that."

All the boys and girls started laughing, but Rena didn't join them. In fact, she suddenly felt the room spin as her emotions kicked in once more. She shooed the children from her room and started crying all over again.

A few minutes later, another rap sounded at the door. She hollered out, "Go away!" but the door opened anyway. Rena looked up to discover Reuben, Sadie, and Virginia standing there.

"Oh, you poor, dear girl." Virginia headed her way and sat down on the bed next to her. She attempted to slip her arm around Rena's shoulders, but Rena did not wish to be touched.

"We passed Jonathan coming into town," Sadie said. "He'd gone to fetch the doctor."

"Ugh!" Rena groaned.

"Don't worry," Sadie said. "I told him it wasn't necessary."

"Did you tell him anything else?" Rena asked.

"Of course not, silly."

"Good. Because that would just be too much to take." Rena blew her nose into her hankie and swabbed her eyes with the back of her hand. Then she reached under the bed for her suitcase and tossed it on top of the chenille spread. Opening it was a bit more difficult, but she managed, doing her best to avoid the stares of her family members.

"Are—are you going somewhere?" Sadie asked, eyes wide.

Rena nodded. "I have no choice. I can never show my face in town again." She rose from the bed, opened the top drawer of her dresser, grabbed her unmentionables, and tossed them inside the open suitcase. Then she went to work pulling dresses off hangers.

"Rena." Reuben's voice sounded strained.

She looked his way, though he looked a bit fuzzy through the haze of tears. "You were right, Reuben. I've learned my lesson. I'm going back home where I belong."

From outside the door, the cries of the children rang out. Sadie soon joined the chorus, tears streaming.

Virginia rose and walked to Rena's side. "You can't leave, Rena. You simply can't."

"I can, and I will."

"Rena." Reuben's voice came again. "Listen to me. Please."

She stopped packing long enough to glance his way. He offered her a half smile then gestured for her to sit on the bed. Defeated, she plopped down next to the suitcase. "Whatever you have to say, can't it wait until we're on the train? We will have a long journey to discuss all of this."

"There will be no journey for you," he said.

"There will."

"No." He shook his head. "This is your home."

She felt the sting of tears once again but willed them not to come. No, from now on, she would act the part of the grown-up. No more tears for her, no matter how much humiliation came her way.

"Rena, there's something I want to tell you." Reuben's expression softened.

She didn't respond over the lump in her throat.

He gazed at her with such love that it shook her to the core. "All those years, I limited you," he whispered.

"Limited me?" She shook her head, unable to make sense of his words.

He released a slow breath. "I gave you menial tasks when I should have been challenging you more. I never really considered the idea that you might need to be needed elsewhere. I just wanted to make your life easier. There's nothing wrong with a brother wanting the best for his sister, but somewhere along the way, I lost sight of the thought that you might have more to offer. And that life might have more to offer you. Can you forgive me for that?"

"F–forgive you?"

"I was content to watch you creep along, when, in reality, you were born to soar. You were born for more than knitting or any of those other projects I gave you to keep you busy. You were born..." He gestured to the doorway where the children had now gathered. "For this."

"It hasn't been easy," Virginia said. "And I daresay you will face more challenges ahead. But you've laid down the life you used to know and taken up another life, one God intended all along."

Rena closed her eyes to shut out the image of the children. But try as she might, she could not shut them out. Did she really want to?

Before she could give the idea more consideration, she heard a door slam. A familiar male voice rang out from downstairs. "Rena! Rena, where are you?"

Her heart quickened as Gene's voice grew louder. "No!"

"Rena. I need to talk to you," his voice called again, this time closer.

She shook her head, everything within her crying out against this.

"Talk to him, Rena," Virginia said. "It will do you both good."

The crowd cleared, and she saw him bounding up the stairs. By the time he arrived in her open doorway, she was up and packing once again.

Gene stopped when he saw Rena. He couldn't help but smile. In spite of the tears...in spite of the messy hair standing atop her head...in spite of the red nose and disheveled clothing...she was the prettiest thing he had ever seen. And he would tell her so, no matter how goofy the words might sound coming out of his mouth. No, they wouldn't match up to whatever she'd read in those letters, but he would give it his best shot.

Gene stood alongside the others at the entrance to her room, a sense of longing overtaking him.

"Rena, please come downstairs so we can talk."

"No." She shook her head, tears flowing. "I can't."

"I need to talk to you. Alone. Please."

"No. Don't you see?" She turned away, dabbing at her eyes. "I can't. I'm…humiliated."

"Humiliated? Why?"

She turned back toward him and shoved the letters in his direction. "Because I was convinced you had written these notes to me. That's the only reason I…I…" Tears erupted. "Oh, please tell me you haven't read the letter that was left on your desk."

"I read every word."

At this point, Reuben and Virginia eased their way out of the room. Sadie nudged Henry out, and Josephine followed. The others drifted away, out into the hallway, leaving the two of them alone to talk. He would have to remember to thank them later.

Rena sat down on the edge of the bed. "I was just responding to the letters you…I mean, the letters I thought you… Oh, never mind!"

"Do I dare ask what they said? These letters the children wrote on my behalf, I mean. I heard they were really beautiful."

"Here." She reached inside her notebook and pulled out several pages of crisp, white stationery. "Read them for yourself. I plan to toss them in the fireplace. I would have burned them already, only, I just found out they were forged."

He picked up the letters from the floor and opened them one by one. They were beautifully written and expressed every emotion he now felt, probably better than he could have expressed them himself.

"So the letter you left on my desk was in response to these so-called love letters?"

She waited a moment to offer a nod. "Yes," she whispered. "And I beg of you to give it back. It is irrelevant now. If you have any mercy on me, you will forget it was ever written."

At this, his heart twisted. "I can only hope you are speaking out of embarrassment and not from your heart."

She looked his way, her brow wrinkled. "W–what?"

"Rena…" He drew near and reached for her hand. "I've been the biggest fool on the planet."

She did not respond, so he figured she must agree with him.

"The children got it right," he whispered.

"Th–they did?"

"Every word." He lifted the letters and smiled. "I have felt all of these things for some time now but didn't have the courage to tell you. Never could've put it in such pretty words, though."

"R–really?"

"Really. Truly." He put the letters down on the dresser and pulled her to a standing position. Sliding an arm around her tiny waist, he pulled her close. Her breath was warm against his cheek, but she did not try to pull away, for which he was thankful.

His heart really went to town now. "I might not be the best with words," Gene whispered, "but I do know how to tell a woman when I care about her." He drew her closer still and planted tiny kisses along her hairline. She relaxed in his arms, her face now tilted up to his. Gene ran his fingertip along her cheek and gazed into those beautiful eyes.

"Oh, Gene." She buried her face against his shoulder and trembled.

He lifted her chin once more and pressed his lips against hers. Her arms gently wrapped around his neck, and she returned his kiss with such passion that it sent a little shiver down his spine.

Never in all his born days would he have expected Miss Rena Jewel, director of the Atoka County Children's Home, to have this sort of emotion buried beneath the surface. Not that he was complaining, of course. Oh no. A second kiss convinced him that she was definitely capable of composing a good love story—and a believable one, at that.

Outside the door, the children took to cheering. He didn't mind. Let them cheer all they wanted. He would go on celebrating right here, with his arms around the finest woman in Atoka County.

Chapter Twenty-Six

. . . .

TIPS FOR DEALING WITH UNRULY YOUNG'UNS—*Folks in Daisy often claim that I'm too softhearted to be a reporter. They say I should cover the hard-hitting stories. That's just not my style. Give me a local heartfelt piece any day. That's one reason I'm so keen on supporting the town's children. Speaking of which, the men of Daisy, led by our own Sheriff Gene Wyatt, will rally together this coming Saturday morning at ten o'clock to begin renovations on the children's home so the boys and girls will have a safe place to live. We hope you will join us for fun, fellowship, and great food, which the ladies have promised to provide.*

—Jonathan Brewer, Reporter

The cold days of winter gave way to the warmer days of spring. Rena found herself in a state of heavenly bliss…most of the time. Every now and again reality would stare her in the face—usually in the form of Molly Harris, who still had some biting things to say about the children. And in spite of his campaign for reelection, Mayor Albright hadn't quite given up on his idea to shut down the children's home. Still, Rena felt sure these people would not prevail. With Gene's hand in hers, she could conquer any foe.

Not that she wanted to consider Molly or the mayor her foe. No, indeed. For, the more she got to know Molly in particular, the more she saw a woman much like herself, one who had never experienced life to the fullest. Perhaps with a bit of love she could be won over.

In late March, just ten short weeks after Rena and Gene's first kiss, the weather had warmed enough to begin serious renovations on the children's home. She watched as the man she loved gathered his troops—Charlie, Jonathan, Joe, and even Old Man Tucker, the latter agreeing to the task with a sour expression on his face. They arrived on a Saturday morning, ready to work. The task of the day? Start on the exterior of the home, pulling down all rotting boards and shutters. Rena looked on, her heart so full she could hardly stand it.

Sadie watched too, though she shifted back and forth from the children's home to the little house she and Charlie had purchased just down the street. These past few weeks had brought about additional changes in her life too. Turned out she and Charlie were expecting. She'd sprouted tears of joy when Doc Moseley gave her the news, and she had easily shifted into her mommy-to-be role. Except for the nausea, of course. It kept her inside more often than not these days.

But not today. Today she stood side by side with Rena, Jenny, and Carolina, looking on as the men labored away. Off in the distance the children played on the overgrown lot next to the home. The boys joined in a rousing game of baseball, and the girls squealed with glee every time one of the boys got a hit. Josephine, in particular, seemed smitten with the game. The youngster had joined in like one of the boys.

Rena paused to watch the game a little more closely, and Carolina joined her.

"Those boys are something else." Rena nodded toward the overgrown lot.

"Especially Tree." Carolina pointed as he made a hit that went long across the field. "See there? He's really good. Might make the major leagues someday."

"I can't imagine a major-league player with a name like Tree." Rena laughed. "Never have quite figured out where that name came from, anyway."

Carolina chuckled. "The boys told me awhile back. They said that he was a stubborn little thing as a baby. Wouldn't move when his mama told him to move, so she called him Tree. Said his roots were planted deep."

"Roots planted deep," Rena echoed the words. She grabbed Carolina's hand and gave it a squeeze. "I like that. May all our roots run deep."

"Roots of stubbornness...or something else?" Carolina grinned.

"Maybe a little of that too," Rena said. "But I meant our spiritual roots. May we all be like trees, planted by the waters. Immovable."

"A lovely thought." Carolina turned back to watch Tree, who ran the bases—if one could call them that—and landed safely at home. "I'll never think of the boy's name in the same light again."

"Amen," Rena whispered. She kept a watchful eye on the overgrown field as Josephine took her turn at bat. For whatever reason, watching the little girl brought the happiest feeling of the day. How lovely, to see her enjoying life once more. That same motherly feeling swept over Rena as she watched Josephine hit the ball and run to first base. Oh, how precious, to truly love a child in such a way. Had she ever known such love?

Off in the distance Gene gave her a wave, and she realized she *had* known such a love. How very, very full her heart felt today. She prayed this feeling would last forever.

Rena and Sadie went inside around eleven to make sandwiches and lemonade while Carolina and Jenny kept a watchful eye on the children. By the time they carried the food outside to the picnic table at eleven thirty, one of the little girls had disappeared on them. Lilly.

"I don't know how she got away from us," Carolina said. "I just turned my back for a moment to talk with Gene about something."

Thank goodness, the youngster showed up moments later. She approached with a rosy color in her cheeks and extended her hand, revealing a beautiful daisy. "Miss Rena, I brung you a present."

"*Brought* you a present," Rena corrected as she took the flower in hand.

"Brought you a present." Lilly giggled. "Only, I didn't exactly bring it. I plucked it up from the ground."

Rena's curiosity got the better of her. She didn't want to scold but felt sure the child had been up to mischief. "Lilly, where did that flower come from?" Daisies didn't grow in the wild, did they? Surely not. She placed her hand on the little girl's shoulder. "Where did you run off to? You had us scared."

Lilly never had a chance to answer. From around the side of the house, Molly Harris came huffing their way, her face red and her lips pursed. She pointed at Lilly, and her eyes narrowed into slits. "I knew it! I chased that devilish child all the way from my house. She stole that flower from my greenhouse."

This, of course, caused the other ladies—Carolina, Jenny, and Sadie—to draw near. Likely they thought they would have to come out swinging. Rena had a feeling she could handle this one on her own, though. With the Lord's help, of course.

A lone tear rolled down Lilly's cheek as she looked on. "I…I know. But it was so pretty, and I knew Miss Rena would like it. She's always talking about daisies, and I thought…" The child's words faded away and her tears now fell in earnest.

Rena knelt down to Lilly's level. "It is pretty, and you're right…I do love daisies. But it belongs to Miss Harris. We don't go onto other people's properties and take things that don't belong to us."

"This isn't the first time," Molly said with a frown. "I've taken to growing flowers in the greenhouse because these awful children ravaged my garden last summer. They've wreaked havoc on my flowers and my nerves. I expect them to stay away this season. Do I make myself clear?"

Abundantly.

"I'm so awfully sorry." Rena rose and faced the older woman. "I can assure you, Lilly won't do this again. She was swayed by the beauty of your gerbera daisies. You've got lovely flowers, Molly. I've never seen such beauties. However do you get them to bloom so early in the season?"

The woman's expression softened. A little. "Well." A pause followed. "As I said, I grow them in the greenhouse. Daisies bloom year-around indoors. If I can keep the pests away." She glared at Lilly, who—thank goodness—simply smiled in response.

"Well, they're magnificent. That's all I have to say on the subject." Rena reached out and took Molly by the hand. "I do hope you will try to see this through Lilly's eyes. She saw something of beauty, and it captivated her. One can hardly blame a child for being swayed by such a lovely flower as this."

"Hmph."

"She did the wrong thing by taking it, but she's learned her lesson."

Rena turned to the child, who offered a firm nod. "I have. Oh, I have, Miss Molly. I won't mess with your flowers again, even though they're the prettiest in the county." The youngster spoke in earnest, each word punctuated with emotion.

Something that almost looked like a smile turned up the edges of Molly's lips. "The prettiest in the county, eh?"

"Oh, yes." Callie drew near and joined in the conversation. "You know how Mrs. Hannigan likes to gloat about her daisies? Well, they're nice, but they don't hold a candle to yours."

Molly rolled her eyes. "I'm sick to death of Katie Hannigan bragging about those gerberas of hers."

"We used to steal Mrs. Hannigan's daisies," Callie continued. "But they're hardly worth stealing."

This brought an unexpected smile to Molly's face. For a moment, anyway. "I do hope you're not saying you've made the permanent switch to my place," she said after a bit of a pause.

"I just love flowers so much." Lilly sighed.

At once, a marvelous idea came to Rena. She rested her palm on Molly's arm. "Would you consider...I mean, would you do us the great honor of helping me plant a flower garden here at the children's home?"

"What?" Molly looked stunned at this proposition. "Why, that's just ridiculous. The children would destroy it before we could bring any of the flowers to bloom. And you know perfectly well that I can't abide children."

"Oh, please, Miss Molly!" Callie cried out.

"I would love that so much!" Lilly added.

The boys and girls all began to talk at once, their voices layering like the petals on the daisy.

"I think it's a marvelous idea," Carolina added. "I'll even help. What do you say, Molly? With your expertise, we'll have the prettiest flower garden in the state." She gave her a wink. "I'll bet Jonathan will do a write-up in the paper about it too. Why, they'll probably run it on the front page!"

This certainly brought a smile to Molly's lips. "Well, I'll have to think about it. Not sure I'm up to working with these rapscallions."

Lilly slipped her hand into Molly's and gazed up at her with a smile. "Oh, but we want you to work with us, Miss Molly. Really, we do. We don't know how to grow pretty flowers like you do."

Molly pursed her lips. "Well, I'll think on it. In the meantime, stay out of my greenhouse, you hear?"

"Yes, ma'am," Lilly echoed. Then she did the craziest thing in the world. She wrapped her arms around Molly's waist and gave her a tight squeeze.

The older woman, stunned, stood frozen in place. After a moment she gave Lilly's hair a gentle pat. Lilly released her hold, looked up at Molly with the sweetest expression on her face, then skipped off to play.

Rena couldn't help but smile. Molly, on the other hand, seemed rather discombobulated. She stammered a few words and then stopped cold, her expression stiffening.

"Would you like to stay to lunch, Molly?" Carolina asked. "Rena has made the most delightful chicken-salad sandwiches."

"Heavens, no. Eat with these children? I should think not." Molly marched off, muttering something about children being a nuisance.

"Methinks she dost protest too much," Carolina whispered. "I daresay that woman is going to be won over to our way of thinking before long."

"That would be the best possible news." Rena's heart practically sang at this idea.

Carolina called out for the men to join them, and before long they were all seated at the table, sharing a wonderful lunch together. Rena took her seat next to Gene, as always. These days, she could hardly stand the idea of being away from him for more than a minute. She knew he felt the same, based on the words he so often whispered into her ear when the others weren't around. Who needed love letters when you had a fellow so happy to share his thoughts aloud? Yes, the Lord had done an amazing work all the way around. And she felt sure He would continue.

About halfway through the meal, a shaggy-looking dog approached. His coat was matted, but he had a pleasant disposition...as was evidenced when he began to lick Old Man Tucker's hand. Either that, or the mongrel wanted a bite of the chicken-salad sandwich. At either rate, James Tucker shooed him away.

"Get out of here, mutt."

The dog didn't leave. In fact, the words only served to make him happier. His tail wagged and he nuzzled up to Rena, who gazed down at him, perplexed.

"Well, who have we here?" she asked.

"Saw him hanging around town yesterday," Jenny said. "No idea where he came from. I don't think he belongs to any of the locals."

The children began to squeal with delight at this revelation. They took to the dog like flies to honey, most of them scrambling from their seats to have a closer look.

"Ooh, can we keep him, Miss Rena?" Lilly threw her arms around the muddy pup.

"Of course not. That's a ridiculous notion." Ridiculous, indeed! As if watching over seventeen children wasn't enough!

"His name is…" Lilly paused. "Daisy! Like the town."

"That's a boy dog!" Wesley hollered then laughed. "Yer gonna name him Daisy?"

"Trust me, son," Gene said with a smile. "He won't know the difference." He began to sing, "'Daisy, Daisy, give me your answer, do,'" and before long the children joined in, in multiple keys at once.

"Oh, please!" Wesley got down on his knees in a begging position in front of Rena. "Give us your answer, Miss Rena. Do! Can we keep 'im? Huh?"

She laughed. "Now, why in the world would we want a mangy mutt around here? He would be nothing but trouble."

The dog began to lick Wesley in the face, and before long the two were rolling around on the ground together.

"You have to admit, a dog would be a good companion," Gene whispered. He slipped his arm around her waist. "And I'd sleep better at night, knowing you had a watchdog."

"Watchdog?" Rena laughed as she glanced down at the playful mutt. "That dog couldn't shake off a flea, let alone a burglar."

"Sometimes looks can be deceiving." Gene gave her a wink. "He's probably vicious when the situation calls for it."

"Hmm." Rena looked on as the boys piled on top of Wesley with the dog in the center of the pack. "Hardly."

Still, as the children looked up at her with their wide eyes and pouty faces, her heart softened. By the time they asked again, she'd already made up her mind. They could keep the dog. Hadn't she witnessed transformation in all of the children and even in her own life? Surely this mutt would clean up just as nicely. She hoped.

Gene looked on with a smile. The boys and girls would do well with a dog around. Rena, on the other hand…well, she would forgive him later for suggesting they keep Daisy.

Daisy. He had to smile at the name the children had chosen. The scraggly-looking mongrel didn't look anything like a daisy, and he certainly didn't smell like one. Just the opposite, in fact.

"Tell you what," Gene said. "You children finish up your lunch, and then you can give this pup a bath while we keep working on the house."

They went back to eating, though he caught several of them sneaking bits of chicken salad to the dog. Not that he blamed them. The poor pup was awfully thin. Well, they would fatten him up over time, no doubt about it.

As he turned back to his meal, he half expected Rena to be angry with him. Instead, she looked at him with a smile. "Did you see that Molly was here earlier?"

"I caught a glimpse of her. Who's in trouble now?"

"Lilly. She stole a flower from Molly's greenhouse."

Gene sighed.

"You know, in many ways Molly reminds me of this pup," Rena said. "She's a mess on the outside. But I have a feeling she's a softy on the inside. We need to give her time. I think she'll come around."

Gene chuckled. "Well, pull out an extra washtub and we'll scrub her down next to the dog. Maybe she'll come out smelling fresh as a daisy." He had to laugh as he realized what he'd said.

"Fresh as a daisy." Rena smiled. "That's the name of her campaign. Haven't heard as many folks talking about it, of late."

"I think the scuttlebutt is dying down," Gene said. He gave Rena a little kiss on the cheek. "I daresay you've won them all over with your charm, Rena Jewel."

She blushed and swatted him away. "Gene, not in front of the children."

"And why not?" He looked at her, pretending to be offended. "If a man can't kiss the woman he loves in front of the children she loves, then what good is he?"

"What good, indeed?" his mother said, passing by. "What good, indeed?"

Chapter Twenty-Seven

....

Tips for Dealing with Unruly Young'uns—*I've never been one to abide children. I've found them to be noisy, dirty, and, in general, nuisances. So no one was more surprised than me when I found myself working alongside a couple dozen of them, planting a springtime garden of daisies. Wasn't sure my heart could take it, to be quite honest, but it turns out I'm not as put off by the idea as I once was. Not sure who—or what—put a spell on me, though I suspect one little girl with dark hair and a button nose. All I know is, I've somehow found myself knee-deep in soil and flowers, with young'uns on every side.*

—Molly Harris, Confused Citizen of Daisy

By the time the April showers lifted, Rena's concerns over the naysayers of Daisy had lifted, as well. Molly Harris showed up several days a week to help in the ever-expanding flower garden. Oh, she still grumbled. Still complained about the boys. But Rena had her suspicions that Molly had taken a liking to the girls, one in particular. It didn't hurt that Lilly had fallen head over heels in love with her former nemesis and practically hung on her every word.

On the first Saturday in May, Rena surveyed the garden, filled with flowers in bloom, and tried to quiet her racing heart. As she turned to face Carolina, Molly, and the children, tears welled up. "I can scarcely believe it. Who would have known that this garden would change the face of the property?"

"What?" Gene approached from the front steps and gave her a pretend pout. "What about all my work? New shutters on the windows. New roof. New front porch steps. The whole place is spiffed up."

"Oh, it's all beautiful. I especially love the gingerbread trim across the front of the house." Rena drew her hands to her heart, wondering if she could take any more. She turned her attention back to the garden, her emotions overflowing. "But there's something so special about flowers. They really liven the place up, and they require so little work on our part."

Behind her, Molly huffed. "Speak for yourself. I've spent a lot of hours on my knees in the dirt to get them looking like this. Or haven't you noticed?"

"I have, of course." Rena knelt beside her and slipped an arm around her shoulders. "And I'm so grateful. You've been such a godsend. Truly."

"Well." Molly shifted her gaze back to the dirt, clearly not ready for a heartfelt chat.

Lilly tugged on Rena's skirt. "Daisies in Daisy!" She laughed. "Get it, Miss Rena? We're growing daisies in a town called Daisy."

"With a dog named Daisy who smells anything but sweet," Gene said, reaching down to scratch the newest member of the family behind the ears. The dog—who'd turned out to be part spaniel underneath all his matted fur—wagged his tail. "Though, for the life of me, I don't think I'd be very sweet either, if someone named me Daisy." Gene gave the pup an endearing smile. "Right, boy?"

Daisy leaped up several times, begging to be held. When Gene headed off to the house to continue his work, the dog turned his attentions to Carolina. The mongrel gave her a nudge and she pushed him away.

"Down with you!" Carolina scolded. She rose from the garden, brushed the dirt from her skirt, and sighed. "I know you all love that dog, but no one ever said I had to."

"He'll win you over, Carolina," Rena said. "Watch and see."

"I just hope he stays out of the garden this time." Carolina sighed. "He did far too much damage the last time around."

"But he asked for forgiveness," Lilly said.

"The dog asked for forgiveness?" Molly looked up and brushed a loose gray curl out of her eyes. "And how, may I ask, did he manage that?"

Lilly pointed to the dog, who had reverted to the begging position. Even Molly laughed when she saw him—for a moment, anyway. Then her expression soured. "Well, tell him to take it up with the Almighty. God's quicker to forgive than I am."

Though there was some truth in that statement, Rena did her best not to laugh. Truth be told, Molly had turned out to be softer on the inside than she'd imagined. Not that the older woman had been completely won over. Still, great strides had been made in that direction.

Rena looked on as Lilly plucked one of the flowers from the soil and stuck it behind her ear. The youngster put a finger to her lips and whispered, "Don't tell Molly!" then skipped across the yard.

Carolina knelt again and started pulling weeds. "I've been a fan of daisies from the time I was a little girl. Used to pick them for my mama."

The saddest feeling swept over Rena as she thought about Carolina's words. She knelt beside her and reached out to touch one of the daisies. "It's strange, but I have almost no memories of myself as a little girl. Not with my mama, anyway. It's almost as if my life before the age of fourteen didn't exist."

Carolina paused and gave her a tender look. "Then you have more in common with these flowers than you know. Do you know the origin of the daisy?"

"No." Rena looked up from the soil and squinted against the sunlight.

"The word 'daisy' means 'day's eye.' The name was given to the flower because daisies open up at dawn just as the day begins."

Rena paused to think through what Carolina had said before responding. "That's beautiful. They open at the break of day, eh?" She giggled at her unintended rhyme.

"Yes. And I think you're a daisy." Carolina winked. "Want to know why?"

"Why?"

Caroline gave her a tender look. "Because this is a new day for you, Rena. You're not the same young woman who arrived on the train just six months ago. You've blossomed and grown, and you're in full bloom now."

"Is it that obvious?" Rena returned her wink.

"Yes, but I'm not just talking about the fact that you're in love with Gene. You've blossomed as a mother figure to the children, and you've grown in your faith, as well. You've taken all this town has dished out— much of it good, but some of it not—and you've dealt with it like a real trooper. You're not just a thing of beauty like this flower, honey. You're rooted. Grounded."

"Th–thank you." Rena hardly knew what to say in response. But as she heard the word "rooted," she thought about Tree. His name, funny as it was, served as a constant reminder that planting your roots down deep was a good thing.

Molly coughed but did not join in the conversation. She was listening, though. Rena was sure of it.

"So there you have it. This is the dawn of a new day," Carolina said. "And you're opening up to the sunlight."

"It's a new day, for sure," Rena said. "But, to be honest, I'm confused about something."

"What's that?"

Using the back of her hand, she brushed a hair out of her eyes. "Well, here we are in April. A new director is set to arrive next month."

"W–what?" Molly looked up, her eyes wide. "Are you leaving?"

Rena shook her head. "If you'd asked me six months ago, I would've said yes. In fact, back then I didn't think I would last the whole seven months. But now..." She paused. "Now I can't imagine leaving. Ever."

"Well, write to that new director and tell her not to come," Molly said. "You just stay put."

"I've thought about that from so many angles." Rena was unsure of how much to share. She wondered—though the words had never been voiced aloud—if she and Gene would one day marry. If so, would she stay on at the children's home or take on a different role?

"I think it would be best to let her come and meet the children and then decide," Carolina said. "We'll never know otherwise."

Rena nodded. "I think it's for the best. But if I don't stay on as director..." Her words faded away. "Anyway, I'm just confused. Don't know what to do."

"The Lord will show you," Carolina said. "Just as He shines down on those beautiful flowers, He will shine down on you and give you what you need when you need it. In the meantime, rest easy. Stay rooted."

"Rooted." Rena echoed the word. Pulling up roots would be too painful now. Not that she planned on doing so...but even thinking about it brought a degree of pain.

As she pondered the what-ifs, a voice rang out from behind her. "Yoo-hoo, pretty lady! Turn around and lookee who the cat dragged in!"

Rena couldn't quite place the voice. She turned and gasped as she saw the three sisters from the train approaching. "Oh my goodness!" Rising from the garden, she brushed the dirt from her hands. "I don't believe it! I simply don't believe it."

"Well, believe it," Mamie said, wrapping Rena in a huge bear hug. "We promised you a visit, and we never lie."

"We're a little late on making good on our promise this time," Amy added, "but we always come through."

"Oh, you ladies more than came through at Christmas," Rena said. "I could hardly believe your generosity."

"Think nothing of it." Jamie fussed with her hat, a large purple velvet number with tall pink feathers. "It was our pleasure."

Rena took Mamie's extended hand and made quick apologies for her appearance. "Well, you've made my day. But, please, forgive my dress. I've been working in the garden all morning with the children."

"My dear, you look positively radiant." Mamie fanned herself. "Make no apologies. Life in Daisy must agree with you."

"Oh, well, I…"

"Yes," Amy added. "Why, you're simply glowing. Not at all the pale, frightened young woman we met on the train. You're much more robust, and I think the color in your cheeks becomes you."

Rena didn't know whether to be insulted or flattered by the fact that she'd just been called a young woman. And robust, at that.

"The caterpillar has morphed into a butterfly," Mamie said with a smile. She gave Rena's hand a squeeze.

Carolina rose and stood beside them. She was soon joined by the children and Molly, who stood off at a distance.

Rena made quick introductions and the trio of sisters responded, going on about how much they'd grown to love Rena on their train trip back in October. Her heart swelled with joy as they lavished her with praise and kind words about her love for the children.

Lilly, Callie, and Josephine chimed in, sharing their love for Rena, as well.

"Well, of course you love her, you blessed girls." Mamie knelt at their level. "What's not to love?"

Josephine reached over to finger the little silk bird on Mamie's hat. "Ooh, pretty!"

"Do you like that bird, sweetie?" Mamie asked. When Josephine nodded, she added, "I've been trying to think of a name for him. What do you think?"

"I think he looks like…" Josephine paused and appeared to be thinking. "Polly!"

"Oh, it must be a girl bird," Amy said, drawing near.

"Polly it is." Mamie rose and straightened her skirts. She began to fan herself, her rosy cheeks now glowing.

"Could I offer you ladies some lemonade?" Rena asked.

"Yes, that would be lovely." Mamie fanned herself then glanced at the house. "So, this is the house, then?"

"Yes. As you can see, it's being renovated," Rena said. "I'm happy to show you around. Let's go inside and get some lemonade." She quickly dismissed the children to play then led the ladies inside. Carolina and Molly followed behind the sisters, who still carried on about their trip from Tulsa.

When they reached the front porch, Mamie turned to Rena and smiled. "We've hardly stopped talking about the orphanage since the day we met you on the train. That's why we're here, in fact."

"I can't believe you would come all the way from Tulsa just to see the children's home." Rena shook her head, still overwhelmed by their kindness.

"We wanted to surprise you," Amy said. "So we took a chance in coming without contacting you first. I do hope you're not put off by that."

"Of course not." Rena gave her a warm hug. "I'm just so glad you're here." She led the way inside, and before long the women were oohing and aahing over the parlor, with their glasses of lemonade in hand. From there, she led them into the dining room.

Jamie gave the room a scrutinizing glance. "I can see that much has been done in the parlor, but these dining tables are in bad shape."

"Yes, well, in due time we will get new tables, perhaps."

"Do you have a carpenter in Daisy?" Jamie asked. "One that you trust?"

From behind Rena, a familiar voice rang out. "James Tucker is a mighty fine carpenter."

She turned to discover Molly entering from the kitchen with her own glass of lemonade. "Really?" Rena asked.

"Yes. You should see some of the pieces he's done. Why, there was a time when he talked of opening a store in town. I've seen every hand-crafted piece in his home and they're lovely...all of them." The sweetest look crossed her face for a moment and then vanished. "Anyway, he's the best."

"I had no idea." Rena shook her head, still perplexed by this news.

"Well then..." Mamie crossed her arms over her ample chest and grinned. "It's all settled. We will commission this, this..."

"James," Molly said. "James Tucker." She took a sip of her lemonade.

"Yes, this James Tucker to build one large table, big enough for everyone to sit together." Mamie scrutinized the room. "And new chairs too. It would be our pleasure to cover any costs."

"R–really?" Rena could hardly believe it.

"On one condition." Mamie narrowed her gaze. "You must invite us for dinner once he's done."

At this, all of the sisters took to talking at once. Rena joined in, overjoyed. Out of the corners of her eyes she noticed Molly slipping out of the room. Seconds later, she heard the front door close. No doubt she'd gone back out to the garden, or perhaps she'd headed home for the day. Rena would have to remember to thank her later. In the meantime, she listened as Mamie, Amy, and Jamie filled her ears with ideas for transforming the kitchen. Heavens! What a blessed day this was turning out to be!

Gene approached the front porch, ready to head inside for some lemonade. He noticed Molly seated on the porch swing alone.

"You might not want to go in there." She gestured to the front door. "Rena's got some friends inside, and they're louder than the choir on Sunday morning."

"Ah." He joined her on the swing. "Guess I'll wait a few minutes, then." From inside, raucous laughter rang out. "I see what you mean. They sound like a fun bunch."

"They're enough to give a person a headache." Molly took a swig of her lemonade. "All that chatter was affecting my nerves."

"Ah." Gene wasn't sure how to respond. He looked her way and noticed a half smile. Was she teasing about the women inside? They sat together for a couple of moments until the laughter from inside the house died down.

"Think it's safe to go in now?" he asked.

"I wouldn't risk it."

He grinned. "Maybe you're right." Gene paused, feeling a strange prompting to say more. After thinking it through, he decided to give it a go. "Molly, I haven't taken the time to properly thank you."

"Thank me? For warning you about the women, you mean?"

"No." He chuckled. "I'm grateful for your help with the garden. It's lifted Rena's spirits so much, and I know the children love it."

Molly remained silent.

"I know it's a sacrifice to spend time with the children. They are a handful."

"That they are." She took another sip of her lemonade.

"Not a day goes by that I don't thank the good Lord for bringing Rena here. She's been wonderful with the boys and girls. They've come a long way."

"And have a long way yet to come."

"I'll be the first to admit, I haven't always done the best job with my own boys. I've been at such a loss. I guess you could say it was easier to do nothing at all."

"I think we can all see where doing nothing was getting you." She narrowed her gaze.

"True." Just one word, but he hoped she would see it as a peace offering.

Molly looked his way, this time with genuine kindness in her eyes. "Gene, you've said too little where the boys were concerned. But maybe I've said too much. I'm afraid my words haven't been very helpful." She paused, and then her voice intensified. "It's just been hard to hold my tongue with these children wreaking havoc." She sighed. "Not that I've actually held my tongue much. But there's a reason for that. I want to help. I really do." She paused and gave him a sympathetic look. "I think, maybe, that's all I ever wanted. To be needed."

His heart softened at once. "Molly, I do need you. I need everyone to band together to raise my boys."

"When Brenda was alive..." Molly paused and shook her head.

"What?"

"Well, she seemed to care about me. She never took offense when I offered suggestions."

Suggestions. Is that what you call them?

"Anyway, she seemed to lean on me for advice. But after she, well..."

"Go ahead."

"After she passed, I tried to keep on giving suggestions the way I always had, but you didn't receive them the same way. So I suppose I got mad."

"I had no idea you and Brenda spoke about the boys," he admitted. "To be honest, I didn't play a large role in their discipline while Brenda was alive, and I know it shows. The boys don't respect me as a disciplinarian because I never really taught them how to. But I suppose it's time."

"*Past* time."

"Yes, I suppose so."

Molly rose and passed her empty glass to him. "If you're going inside, would you mind taking this in for me? Don't think I can stand the noise, to be quite honest."

"I would be happy to." He reached to touch her arm. "And Molly..."

"Yes?"

"Thanks for sharing what you did about Brenda. I still miss her. Very much."

"Me too." Molly's eyes misted over for a moment. Then she turned away and headed down the porch steps, muttering, "Better get back out to the garden. Heaven only knows what those children have done in my absence." Moments later, she disappeared around the side of the house.

Gene decided to brave a journey inside the house. His mother and the trio of ladies sat in the parlor, talking. The moment she saw him, his mother stretched out her hand. "Gene, come here. We've got guests." She proceeded to introduce him to the three sisters. Gene wasn't sure which was the funniest—their outlandish hats or their rhyming names.

"So, you are that handsome fellow Rena's been bragging on." Mamie rose and wrapped him in a warm embrace. "Well, she didn't lie, now did she?"

"Heavens, no." Jamie fanned herself. "You are quite handsome."

Gene felt his face grow hot. "I, um, well, I came inside to get some lemonade."

"Looks like you've just had some," his mother said, pointing to the empty glass in his hand.

"Oh, this wasn't mine. It was Molly's."

"Rena's in the kitchen," Mamie said. "She's gone to fetch some cookies. Homemade too."

"Mmm. I'm starving." Amy wiggled her thinly plucked brows.

"I'll go check on her." Gene took several steps toward the kitchen, grateful for the excuse to leave. He entered the kitchen moments later and had to smile when he heard Rena singing, "'Daisy, Daisy, give me your answer, do.'"

"I'll give you my answer," he said from behind her. "The answer is yes. I would love a kiss." Gene set Molly's empty glass on the counter.

Rena spun around, her cheeks the prettiest shade of pink. "Oh, I…" With soapy hands, she attempted to fix her mussed hair. She ended up with bubbles on the edge of her face. Gene drew near and reached out his fingertip to brush the tiny bubbles away. Then, just for fun, he stole a kiss. She swatted him with a dishcloth. "Not in front of the company!"

"They're in the parlor. And I have a feeling they would be thrilled to know we're in here kissing. Want me to go and tell them?"

"No!" She swatted him again and then laughed.

"I'm not sure what's happening with all the women around here today." He reached for the pitcher of lemonade and a fresh glass.

"What do you mean?"

"I can't quite figure them out. There are several brightly dressed women in the parlor, one delightful woman singing in the kitchen, and a very subdued Molly Harris out in the yard tending to the garden." He took a swig of the lemonade, and the cold liquid quenched his thirst at once. "Speaking of Molly, I actually had a pleasant conversation with her just now. Is it just me, or is she changing?"

Rena chuckled. "We're all changing. According to your mother, we're blooming like the daisies in our garden."

"I guess that's one way of looking at it," Gene said with a smile. The woman standing before him now was not the same frightened lady who'd stepped off that train back in October. She really had bloomed.

Rena's eyes sparkled. "I'll give you another piece of news— Molly secretly adores Lilly. And Callie too. She's smitten. And I even caught her saying something nice to Henry yesterday."

"What has bewitched her?"

"Love, Gene." Rena giggled.

"Love?"

"Yes. Don't you see? She's been won by love."

She took a couple of steps in his direction, and he swept her into his arms. "Won by love." He repeated the words, unable to think of any other response.

"Isn't that how we're all won over?" she whispered. "Some people just need an extra measure of love. Molly's one of them. And Josephine too. I've simply fallen in love with that little girl, and she's responded to it in the most amazing way."

"If I didn't know any better, I would say you plotted all this in that book you're writing."

Her face turned red. "Oh, please...let's don't mention my book." She groaned. "I put away that notebook weeks ago and haven't seen it since."

"Well, get it back out," he whispered. "Because I've got a feeling there are chapters left to be written."

"O-oh?" Her eyelashes took to fluttering, nearly taking his heart with them.

Gene's heart filled with joy, and he leaned in to kiss her. Yes, there were certainly chapters left to be written. The very next one, he would pen himself. With the Lord's help, of course. However it panned out, Gene felt sure it would be a doozy.

Chapter Twenty-Eight
. . . .

TIPS FOR DEALING WITH UNRULY YOUNG'UNS—*A great deal of thought and prayer has gone into the raising of my young son, Daniel. He is a precious boy, though he does try my patience at times. Since his father passed away four years ago, I've learned to lean on the Lord and trust that He will—as the Bible says—be the father to the fatherless. Perhaps that's why I feel so strongly about coming to Daisy to work at the orphanage. In loving those boys and girls, I will be displaying the Father's heart to them and giving my son the family environment he longs for. I cannot say what lies ahead, only that I trust God to lead and guide every step of the way.*

—Janelle Bradford, Incoming Daisy Resident

Gene spent the next four weeks putting together a special plan, one that only he and Charlie knew about. Rena was so distracted by preparing for the new director's arrival this afternoon that she hadn't picked up on anything. Not that he could tell, anyway.

Every time he thought about the new director, Gene paused. Perhaps he should've written to her at Christmas, encouraging her not to come. Still, he had a feeling that her services would be needed, especially if he carried through with his current plan.

On the third Saturday in May Gene finally got word that the last piece to the puzzle had just arrived in Daisy. He could now move forward with this plan of action.

But he would need help. Who could he call on?

All morning Gene thought about it. Several different scenarios went through his head, but none of them felt right. Around noon his mother stopped by the newly renovated jail with a plate of food.

"Don't know what you're up to in here," she said. "But you've been working far too much lately. Thought I'd better bring some food by so you can keep up your strength."

"Where are William and Jacob?"

"Playing marbles out front. They're fine."

She had a point. They were fine. In fact, they'd been mighty fine, of late—both in behavior and attitude.

He pulled the napkin off the top of the plate and smiled as he saw the chicken and dumplings underneath. "Perfect. Just what I needed today— something to stick to the ribs. It's been quite a day."

"It has, at that." She chuckled. "You're not going to believe what— or, rather, who—I just saw sitting outside the general store eating ice cream together."

"Who?" Gene took a big bite of the chicken and dumplings, savoring its flavor.

"Molly Edwards and James Tucker. Sitting there, happy as you please, eating ice cream. And here's the kicker...Henry is with them."

"Eating ice cream?" Gene swallowed hard.

"Yep."

This stirred Gene to action. He rose and reached for his hat. "Are you sure? Perhaps she laced it with cyanide. Did you notice any unusual behavior from Henry? Sick stomach? Headache?"

"Unusual indeed! He was laughing and talking up a storm." His mother's eyes continued to widen and her voice grew more animated. "I wouldn't have believed this next part if I hadn't seen it with my own eyes, but Molly slipped her arm around Henry's shoulders and gave him a hug."

Gene paced the room. "Impossible."

"No, I saw it just now. I promise."

Gene tossed the napkin over the plate of dumplings and headed to the door. "This, I have to see." He sprinted across the front of the jailhouse, his mother lagging behind.

"Slow down, son. I can't keep up with you," she huffed.

His boys met him in the street. "What is it, Papa?" William asked. "Are you off to arrest someone for suspicious behavior?"

"Possibly." He slowed his pace as he drew near the general store.

There, in broad daylight, sat not just Molly, James, and Henry, but Jonathan and Jenny, as well. All five of them ate ice cream, laughed, and chatted with ease.

"Well, go figure."

Gene approached the others, and Jonathan gestured for him to take a seat in one of the large rockers. Gene complied, and his mother took a seat on the bench with the boys next to her.

"What brings you out today, Sheriff?" Jonathan asked. "We haven't seen much of you around town lately."

"I've been…busy." He couldn't help the smile that followed.

"Busy, eh?" Joe's voice rang out.

Gene turned to see the barber standing behind him. Apparently someone had called a town hall meeting. Or maybe everyone just felt like socializing.

Joe gestured for William and Jacob to scat, and he took the spot on the bench next to Gene's mother, who looked over at him with a coy smile. Gene's heart quickened. When had this happened?

Thank goodness he didn't have long to think about it.

"Tell us what's on your mind, son," his mother said. "You're up to something."

And so he told them. He shared every last detail, right down to the part where he asked for their help. The next several minutes were spent putting together a plan of action. A workable plan. One that Rena would fall for, no doubt about it.

When they finished, everyone grew silent. Finally Molly cleared her throat. "I've got something to say."

Uh-oh. Gene looked her way.

"I think it's a grand idea," she said. "And about time too. This will be the best thing that's happened to this town in a month of Sundays."

"You think?" Gene asked.

"I know." She smiled. "And I have something to add. I've been think-ing on it," Molly said. "And it's a pity for that big empty field separating my house from the children's home to sit empty and overgrown with weeds. I've owned it for years but never knew what to do with it until now." A smile turned up the edges of her lips. "What if we used it for a park? A nice big city park where all the children can play?"

"Are you serious, Molly?" Gene could hardly believe it.

"I'm serious." Her wrinkled cheeks flushed pink, and the crinkles around her eyes deepened as she laughed. "I heard Rena and those three rhyming ladies talking about the idea, and it settled into my heart. I've given it a lot of thought."

"If we plow down that field and turn it into a park, the children will have easier access to your property," Carolina said.

"Already thought of that." Molly's cheeks flashed pink. "But it won't be a problem. I'll have help."

"Help?" Gene couldn't imagine what she meant.

Molly grinned. "You all might as well know that I won't be living at my place alone anymore." Her gaze shifted to James, who slipped his arm around her waist.

"Sold my farm," he said. "Been meaning to retire in town for years. Just never had the courage to do it."

"Wait." Gene looked back and forth between them. "Are you saying…?"

"Saying we're gettin' hitched." James planted a kiss on Molly's forehead. "We're a couple of stubborn old coots, so we go together like bread and jam."

"Speak for yourself, old man." Molly elbowed him then started laughing.

Before long, they were all laughing, every last one of them.

"So there you have it," Molly said. "We'll be Mr. and Mrs. Old Man Tucker, and we'll live just beyond the park, not far away. If you need us, all you have to do is holler."

Everyone joined in the celebration except Gene's mother. She still looked concerned. "What about Mayor Albright? He won't like the idea of a city park."

"Pooh." Molly waved her hand. "What's he got to say about it? That property belongs to me. I can do with it as I wish." She smiled and pointed to the mayor's reelection poster, which hung on the door of the general store. "He's too busy getting himself reelected. He won't want to cross me or any of the other voters."

The laughter and conversation continued, but Gene had other things on his mind. They'd better get busy.

Rena spent the morning cleaning. By the time Molly, Jenny, and Carolina arrived in the early afternoon, she had the house in tip-top condition. And the children—well, most of them—looked presentable, as well.

She struggled with her thoughts as she worked. Why, oh, why hadn't she told Gene to send the new director packing? Rena didn't plan to leave Daisy—not now, not ever. So why bring in someone new to tend to the children? None of this made sense.

Her friends arrived in rare form—all laughter and giggles. She'd never seen Jenny so happy. Or Carolina, for that matter. Even Molly seemed in better spirits than usual. Surely they weren't tickled at the idea of replacing her with the new director.

"We've decided to walk to town," Carolina said as she slipped her arm through Rena's."

"B-but…" This made no sense either. "Gene is supposed to pick us up at two thirty to drive us to the depot."

"I thought we needed the fresh air and sunshine," Carolina said. "And besides, we can't fit all of the children inside the car."

"The children?" Now Rena was really confused. "I thought you and Molly were staying here with the children while Jenny and I went to town to fetch the new director."

"As she said, there's been a change in plans." Molly let out a whoop, calling for the children, who joined them in a hurry.

Rena barely had time to collect her thoughts before they pressed her out the door and into the street. As they walked toward town, everyone carried on about the weather, the garden, the renovations on the house… anything and everything except the obvious. Did they not see the heaviness of her heart at the idea of handing over the reins to a new director? Didn't anyone care…even a little?

The conversation took a turn, and before long she heard some news that shocked her.

"Molly, you're getting married?"

Molly nodded. "Yep. Ain't it grand? James and I aren't wasting any time, either. We're getting married next Sunday after church."

Off she went, talking about the wedding, their living arrangements, and the empty field she planned to donate to the children's home. Rena found herself so confused by all this news that her thoughts were in a whirl.

What an odd day this was turning out to be. Nothing like she'd expected.

When they arrived at the depot, Rena looked around. "Where's Gene? Is he meeting us here?"

Carolina shook her head. "No, he's really busy today. He did ask us to stop by the jail on our way back, though. He wants to say hello to Janelle. He hasn't seen her since they were youngsters." She laughed. "Oh, what trouble those two used to get into. Janelle's mama and I were best friends and spent hours together with Gene and Janelle playing at our feet. They were a handful, those two." She went on a tangent talking about Gene and Janelle. This only served to get Rena more depressed.

The three o'clock train arrived right on schedule. Rena looked on as a woman—a beautiful woman with blond, coiffed hair—stepped off the train. Behind her appeared the cutest little boy with blond curls and an impish smile. The woman turned to give the youngster a hug then exclaimed, "We're here, Danny-boy! We've arrived in Daisy."

The youngster let out a shout, scaring the porter.

Rena took a couple of steps in her direction, following behind Carolina. She hadn't imagined Janelle to be this lovely. In fact, she hadn't spent much time at all thinking about the woman's appearance.

Carolina swept Janelle into her arms and gave her a gentle kiss on the cheek. "You darling girl. You're the spitting image of your mama at this age."

"Do you think?" Janelle smiled. "What a lovely compliment."

Rena stepped up and introduced herself. "Welcome to Daisy, Janelle."

"I'm so happy to be here. I've had the strangest feeling from the start that God was drawing me here for these boys and girls." Her gaze shifted to the children, who approached—albeit shyly. Quite a difference from the way they'd greeted Rena just seven short months ago.

She didn't have time to think about it for long, however, because the sound of voices hollering behind them interrupted her thoughts.

"Rena!"

She turned to see Old Man Tucker doubled over to catch his breath. Her heart quickened. "James, what is it?"

"S–something's h–happened at the jailhouse. It's G–gene and the boys. They— they need you."

Without giving another thought to the new director or any of the people gathered around her, Rena hiked up her skirts and began to run. She raced all the way to the jail, friends and loved ones trailing along behind her. When she arrived, she flung wide the door and raced inside with all of the children on her tail. Then she heard Gene's voice calling out to her from one of the cells.

"Rena!"

"Gene!" She hurried to the jail cell and was confused to find him locked inside. "What's happening?"

He groaned. "It's those boys of mine. They locked me in and ran off with the key."

"W–what?"

"Yes." He turned to Jonathan, who had appeared at Rena's side. "Could you find Charlie? He's the only other one who can get me out of here."

"Sure." Jonathan took off for the door, with Jenny following.

Rena looked after them for a moment then turned her attention back to Gene. He looked through the bars and smiled when he saw Janelle. "Well, this is a fine how-do-you-do. Quite a welcome, I'd say. How are you doing, Janelle? Good to see you again."

She stuck her hand through the bars and shook it. "Gene Wyatt. Obviously you're still the same rapscallion I knew as a kid."

"Obviously."

"Nothing new there." She giggled.

"Some things never change, Janelle." Gene raked his fingers through his hair and sighed.

Rena couldn't be sure, but she thought he winked afterward. Of all the nerve! Why would he wink at another woman?

Gene gazed at Rena with a pout. "Hold my hand?" He extended his right hand through the bar.

She reached out to take his hand, more confused than ever.

At this point Carolina appeared with Jacob and William at her side. "Lookee who I found!" She extended her hand and revealed the key, which she used to open the door to the jail cell. A resounding cheer went up from the crowd.

Instead of stepping out, however, Gene gestured for Rena to join him.

"You want me to come...in there?" she asked.

He nodded, a smile curling up the edges of his lips.

Something was definitely amiss. Rena felt it. Still, the man she loved wanted her to join him inside the jail cell. In front of half the town, no less.

She didn't want to, but the crowd pressed her in. Seconds later, Rena found herself behind bars, locked inside with Gene. Nothing about this made sense. Out of the corners of her eyes, she caught a glimpse of Sadie and Charlie entering through the front door. Sadie's impish smile spoke of mischief, for sure. What were these folks up to?

Gene cleared his throat and Rena turned her attention back to him. He did a couple of little funny dance steps then extended his hand. She paused, wondering if, perhaps, he'd lost his mind.

"W–what are you doing?"

"Dancing," he said. "And singing." He lit into "'Daisy, Daisy, give me your answer, do…'" then paused. Gene took Rena by the hand and added, "I'm half crazy, all for the love of you."

Embarrassment swept over her, hearing him sing this in front of half the town. "Half crazy in love?" Rena asked. "Or just half crazy?"

He chuckled then dove back into the song. "'It won't be a stylish marriage—'"

"Speaking of weddings," she interrupted, excited to give him the news. "I just heard that Molly and James are getting hitched. Can you believe it?"

He put a finger over her lips and continued the song. "'We can't afford a carriage….'"

"I've been meaning to talk to you about that," she said, interrupting him again. "Did you know that James is selling his work truck? The one he used on the farm? I think it would be perfect for the children's home. Don't you agree?"

Gene put his finger over Rena's lips again, which only served to make her mad. He seemed to be oblivious to this, because he kept singing: "'But you'll look sweet upon the seat of a bicycle built for two.'"

At this point, the front door of the jailhouse opened. The crowd parted, and Jonathan and Jenny came inside riding on a…what was that? Rena gasped. "Oh, Gene! Is that what I think it is?"

He nodded and repeated the line, "'I'm half crazy all for the love of you.'"

"You—you said that." She giggled.

"Yes, I said it," he whispered. "But I've got a few other things to add." His voice now wavered as he sang, "'It won't be a stylish marriage….'"

At this point he stopped singing and dropped to one knee, which brought about a rousing cheer from the onlookers, especially Sadie and Charlie. Rena's heart nearly stopped as she pieced it all together. She'd been had…by all in attendance, from the looks of things. Oh, but what a lovely way to be duped!

The next few seconds were a blur. Through the whoops and hollers of the children she made out a few words: "Love. You. Marry. Me?" He gazed up at her with such tenderness that her heart took to dancing.

As she whispered, "Oh, yes!" he rose and swept her into his arms. Then, with the residents of Daisy looking on, she gave him a kiss he wouldn't soon forget.

Chapter Thirty

. . . .

TIPS FOR DEALING WITH UNRULY YOUNG'UNS—*A special thanks to the new editor of the* Atoka County Register, *Jonathan Brewer, for allowing me to post this special article, which will appear in print on my wedding day. If anyone had told me back in October that I would marry on a beautiful midsummer day in Daisy, I would've said they were crazy. But here I am, ready to become Mrs. Gene Wyatt. I write this article today to thank the people of Daisy, who have shown such grace and mercy to our boys and girls at the Atoka County Children's Home. When I think of how far we've come together, I can't help but praise the Lord. Things will be different soon, but God has been preparing my heart all along. I will no longer have seventeen children under my care. I feel sure that Janelle Bradford, the new director, will thrive in her role, particularly since she will be caring for only the boys. Turns out she's quite a wonder with them. Perhaps that's why they've taken to her like flies to honey. As for the girls, well, Lilly and Callie are simply beside themselves at the news that they are to be adopted by Molly and James Tucker. I've never seen children so smitten. And Josephine? That darling girl—who reminds me so much of myself as a youngster—has already picked out her room in our home. The idea of raising a daughter makes me giggle with joy. I will still dedicate several hours a week to the children's home, of course. How could I not? I've heard from so many of you, who are willing to share in the load of raising the children. The residents of Daisy will link arms and hearts to see that the task is done right. Together, we will raise these children up in the way they should go. And when they are old…well, we pray they will not depart from it.*

—Mrs. Gene Wyatt, Lover of Small Children and Blissful Daisy Resident

Gene stood on the front porch of the children's home, watching the children play baseball at the new park next door. James Tucker served as pitcher, with Jonathan taking the role of umpire. Molly looked on from the sidelines, cheering as each child hit the ball.

Glancing at his pocket watch, Gene smiled. Any minute now, Rena and the other ladies would appear from inside the house, dressed and ready for a wedding unlike any ever seen in Daisy.

Just off the porch, the dog—that crazy, playful mutt—ran amok through the bed of flowers Molly had worked so hard on. The ladies would have a fit, he knew, but it seemed rather ironic—a dog named Daisy, tearing up the daisies in a town called Daisy.

"Shoo, now!" Gene called out.

The pup bounded up the porch steps and tried to leap into his arms. He brushed him away. "Not today, Daisy. Go play with the kids. Get on out of here."

As the dog loped away, Gene began to hum the familiar melody to "A Bicycle Built for Two." He stopped when he saw Jonathan crossing the yard in his direction.

"You getting nervous?" Jonathan joined him on the porch.

"A little," Gene said with a grin.

"I'm watching your every move, you know." Jonathan leaned against the porch railing. "Since I'll be doing this myself in a couple of months."

"What?" Gene took a couple of steps in his friend's direction. "Are you saying—?"

"That Jenny and I are engaged? Yep. As of last night." Jonathan nodded. "We would've announced it sooner, but this is your day. Well, yours and Rena's. We'll let folks know soon enough."

Gene slapped Jonathan on the back. "Well, congratulations!"

"Thank you." Jonathan paused. "You know, it's funny…sometimes we miss the very thing that's been in front of us all the while. I was so caught up with the paper, the children's home, the fight for right, that I almost didn't see Jenny as the blessing she is. I see her now, though." His eyes twinkled. "And I like what I see. Love it, in fact."

Gene couldn't resist the grin that followed. "I understand, trust me."

"Have you been inside?" Jonathan gestured toward the front door.

"Are you kidding?" Gene feigned a look of terror. "With all those women in there getting ready? They would've had my head."

"No doubt." Jonathan laughed. "Better not risk it."

"Shouldn't be long now, anyway." Gene glanced down at his pocket watch once again. "Rena told me to be ready at ten sharp. We're getting married right here on the front porch. That was her idea."

"It's a good one." Jonathan squinted against the morning sunlight. "And I see the ladies have set up the cake and punch on the picnic tables in the park. Another great idea, to have it outdoors."

"Yes, Rena's a wonder when it comes to creative ideas."

The front door opened and Rena's brother stepped outside, dressed in his robe and collar. He looked at Gene and smiled. "I think it's about time. You want to gather the children? Rena is fretting over them."

"I'll do that." Gene walked down the steps and across the yard. When he arrived at the park, he found himself caught up in the children's ball game. Gene was completely taken aback by the sight of Calista, the mayor's daughter, standing on the sidelines next to Molly.

Josephine—that precious little girl who would soon become his own—tossed the ball into the air and then caught it. She turned to her one-time adversary and gave her a curious look. "Calista, do you know how to play baseball?"

"Baseball?" Calista turned up her nose. "Of course not. That's a boy's game."

"I used to think that too," Josephine said. "But then Henry taught me how to play. Now I'd rather play baseball than play with my dolls or anything else."

Calista did not look convinced. Still, she stood with an interersted look on her face. Rumor had it her mama and papa were far too busy with Mayor Albright's reelection campaign to pay her much mind these days. Maybe the children would fill in the gap and give the youngster the attention she craved.

Seconds later, a flurry of activity on the front porch caught everyone's attention. Gene looked up just in time to see all the ladies—well, all but Rena—step outside onto the porch. His heart quickened as he realized the moment had come at last. He clapped his hands and hollered, "Game over, everyone. Time to get down to business."

The children fell in line, and Molly tended to their appearance. She fussed over Henry's hair, brushed some dirt off Wesley's knees, straightened Timmy's collar, and retied Lilly's shoes. Then, convinced they were ready, she turned to Gene and smiled.

"Well? What are we waiting for? Let's get this thing started."

Rena stood inside the parlor with Sadie at her side. She waited for her cue to walk out onto the front porch, where the wedding would take place. For whatever reason, her thoughts traveled to her notebook and she smiled, remembering last night's entry. Rosalinda and Gerald would live happily ever after, no doubt about it. But they would no longer need her help. No, she'd tucked that notebook away in a place where it could rest. Right now she had more important stories to write...real ones.

Her brother approached, dressed in his ministerial attire. She'd almost forgotten how formal he looked in the robe and collar. Perfect for a wedding.

"You look beautiful, Rena," he said as he slipped an arm over her shoulders.

"A blushing bride," Virginia added, stepping into place alongside him. "When Gene sees you, his eyes are going to pop."

"Do you think?" Rena had never thought of herself as beautiful— not by a stretch—but today she almost felt so.

"Absolutely." Sadie giggled.

"Oh, honey..." Virginia's eyes filled with tears. "You have no idea just how lovely you are, do you?"

Before Rena could respond, Janelle appeared with a bouquet of daisies in her hands. "They've been in the icebox, just as you suggested. They've held up well."

"They're perfect." Rena held them close and sighed. She smiled at Janelle. "I'm so grateful to you. You do know that, don't you?"

"You've only told me a hundred times!" Janelle laughed. "But please don't start up again. Today is about you and Gene, not about the children or any of our plans for the future. God has all those things in the palm of His hand."

"He does." Rena smiled. "Oh, but I'm so excited for you. For all of us, really. You know I'll be here several days a week, but if you ever need anything, don't hesitate to call."

Janelle gave Rena a hug. "I know this sounds strange—we've only known each other two months—but I already feel like we're family."

"Honey, you're in Daisy," Rena said and then laughed. "Here, everyone is family."

"Yes." Janelle's gaze shifted. "And you will never know how much I've needed that." She paused. "Ever since my husband passed away, I've been bound up with grief. I've never seen my tomorrows as having any promise."

Rena took hold of her hand. "That last sentence sounds exactly like something I said to my brother less than a year ago, back in Gulfport. Isn't that right, Reuben?"

He nodded and smiled. "Yes. I remember it well. Things have changed a lot since then, to be sure."

Rena returned her attention to Janelle. "I couldn't imagine that my tomorrows would be any different from my yesterdays." She gestured to the front door, where she could now hear the children laughing and talking outside. Hopefully they were gathering on the steps as she'd instructed them. "But you know what? My tomorrows *are* brighter in every conceivable way. I feel like coming to Daisy has caused me to…" She smiled as the right word came to mind. "Bloom. I've come to bloom. To blossom, if you will. When I got here, I was like a little seed—in cold, hard ground, at that. But the Lord took that seed and grew it into something rather spectacular."

Janelle's eyes misted over. "Thank you for sharing that. I pray the same thing for myself every night when I rest my head on the pillow. Being here is like a new beginning for me."

The front door cracked open and Charlie peeked inside. "The natives are getting restless out here," she said. "You almost ready?"

"I'm ready."

Janelle scooted out the door and Rena slipped her arm through her brother's.

"Walk me to the altar?"

"The front porch, you mean?" he grinned.

"Yes." She grinned. "Trust me, it's an altar. I've made my peace with God at that altar many a time. You'll never know how many times I stood there praying."

"Oh?" He looked her way, his brow wrinkling.

"Yep." She giggled. "Praying for the courage to come back inside this house and live another day with seventeen children. But God met me at the altar and has answered all of my prayers."

"He has, indeed." Reuben gave her a little kiss on the cheek then opened the door and led the way out onto the porch.

Off in the distance all her friends and family members had gathered, including those three precious sisters from Tulsa. Rena's heart sang with joy as she took in the children, dressed in their Sunday best. She focused for a moment on the boys, honing in on Tree. She couldn't help but smile. *May your roots run deep, precious boy!* Gazing at the others, she grinned. She prayed that *all* their roots would run deep...and that the Lord would keep them all safely planted right here, in Daisy, for years to come.

Her thoughts reeled back to that day in Gulfport when she'd spied a vase full of daisies on the buffet table. Now, as her gaze traveled from one child to the next, she realized the truth of it: God had given her the perfect bouquet. Each of these children was a delicate flower. Together, they made up an exquisite arrangement. Not the kind she could put in a vase, but the kind to keep her on her toes.

Reuben placed her hand in Gene's. He wrapped his arms around Rena and whispered, "You're the prettiest flower in Daisy."

Rena grinned, planted a little kiss on his cheek, then turned her attention back to her brother, whose rich voice rang out: "We are gathered here today…"

Impassioned words followed. She'd heard them many times before—for so many other brides—but today they were spoken just for her. Oh, how they filled her heart with joyous song!

"Daisy, Daisy, give me your answer, do!" She resisted the urge to hum the familiar little ditty but found her toes tapping as her brother continued his speech. *"I'm half crazy all for the love of you."*

Nearby, the bicycle built for two leaned against the house. If Gene had his way, the two of them would ride away on it. How she would manage such a thing in this beautiful dress, she had no idea. Rena giggled, trying to imagine the write-up in the paper. No doubt they would be the talk of the town.

Then again, hadn't she been the talk of the town all along? Let people think they were crazy. Who cared, as long as she lived this crazy life surrounded by the people she loved.

To her right, a flurry of activity caught her attention. The dog was digging a hole in the flower garden, his paws flinging dirt every which way. Molly sprinted down the stairs and chased after him, both of them disappearing around the edge of the house. In front of her, several of the children squirmed and Oliver quietly mimicked Reuben's words. She gave him a look, and the youngster's lips clamped shut. William and Jacob stood beside their father, punching each other in the arms. Not far away, Josephine caught her eye and gave her a smile so sweet that Rena wanted to sweep the youngster into her arms. Standing directly in front of her, the man she loved spoke vows so deep, her heart nearly burst with joy.

Yes, all in all, it was a near-perfect day in Daisy.

"Daisy Bell"

....

by Harry Dacre, 1892

There is a flower within my heart,
Daisy, Daisy,
Planted one day by a glancing dart,
Planted by Daisy Bell.
Whether she loves me or loves me not
Sometimes it's hard to tell,
And yet I am longing to share the lot
Of beautiful Daisy Bell.

Chorus:
Daisy, Daisy, give me your answer, do,
I'm half crazy all for the love of you.
It won't be a stylish marriage;
I can't afford a carriage,
But you'd look sweet on the seat
Of a bicycle built for two.

We will go tandem as man and wife,
Daisy, Daisy,
Ped'ling away down the road of life,
I and my Daisy Bell.

When the road's dark, we can both despise
P'licemen and lamps as well.
There are bright lights in the dazzling eyes
Of beautiful Daisy Bell.

(Chorus)
Daisy, Daisy, give me your answer, do...

I will stand by you in wheel or woe
Daisy, Daisy,
You'll be the bell which I'll ring you know
Sweet little Daisy Bell
You'll take the lead on each trip we take
Then if I don't do well
I will permit you to use the brake
beautiful Daisy Bell

(Chorus)
Daisy, Daisy, give me your answer, do...

About the Author

....

Award-winning author Janice Hanna, who also writes under the name Janice Thompson, has published nearly eighty books for the Christian market, crossing genre lines to write cozy mysteries, historicals, romances, nonfiction books, devotionals, children's books, and more. Her passion? Romantic comedies! She has authored three previous LOVE FINDS YOU™ books, including *Love Finds You in Poetry, Texas*; *Love Finds You in Camelot, Tennessee*; and *Love Finds You in Groom, Texas*.

Janice formerly served as vice president of the Christian Authors Network (christianauthorsnetwork.com) and was named the 2008 Mentor of the Year by the American Christian Fiction Writers organization. She is passionate about her faith and does all she can to share the joy of the Lord with others, which is why she particularly enjoys writing.

Janice lives in Spring, Texas, where she leads a rich life with her family, a host of writing friends, and two mischievous dachshunds. She does her best to keep the Lord at the center of it all.

WWW.JANICEHANNATHOMPSON.COM

WWW.FREELANCEWRITINGCOURSES.COM

Want a peek into local American life—past and present?
The *Love Finds You*™ series published by Summerside Press
features real towns and combines travel, romance,
and faith in one irresistible package!

The novels in the series—uniquely titled after American towns with romantic or intriguing names—inspire romance and fun. Each fictional story draws on the compelling history or the unique character of a real place. Stories center on romances kindled in small towns, old loves lost and found again on the high plains, and new loves discovered at exciting vacation getaways. Summerside Press plans to publish at least one novel set in each of the fifty states. Be sure to catch them all!

NOW AVAILABLE

Love Finds You in Sisters, Oregon
by Melody Carlson
ISBN: 978-1-935416-18-0

Love Finds You in Charm, Ohio
by Annalisa Daughety
ISBN: 978-1-935416-17-3

*Love Finds You in
Bethlehem, New Hampshire*
by Lauralee Bliss
ISBN: 978-1-935416-20-3

Love Finds You in North Pole, Alaska
by Loree Lough
ISBN: 978-1-935416-19-7

Love Finds You in Holiday, Florida
by Sandra D. Bricker
ISBN: 978-1-935416-25-8

*Love Finds You in
Lonesome Prairie, Montana*
by Tricia Goyer and Ocieanna Fleiss
ISBN: 978-1-935416-29-6

Love Finds You in Bridal Veil, Oregon
by Miralee Ferrell
ISBN: 978-1-935416-63-0

Love Finds You in Hershey, Pennsylvania
by Cerella D. Sechrist
ISBN: 978-1-935416-64-7

Love Finds You in Homestead, Iowa
by Melanie Dobson
ISBN: 978-1-935416-66-1

Love Finds You in Pendleton, Oregon
by Melody Carlson
ISBN: 978-1-935416-84-5

Love Finds You in Golden, New Mexico
by Lena Nelson Dooley
ISBN: 978-1-935416-74-6

Love Finds You in Lahaina, Hawaii
by Bodie Thoene
ISBN: 978-1-935416-78-4

*Love Finds You in Victory
Heights, Washington*
by Tricia Goyer and Ocieanna Fleiss
ISBN: 978-1-60936-000-9

Love Finds You in Calico, California
by Elizabeth Ludwig
ISBN: 978-1-60936-001-6

Love Finds You in Sugarcreek, Ohio
by Serena B. Miller
ISBN: 978-1-60936-002-3

*Love Finds You in
Deadwood, South Dakota*
by Tracey Cross
ISBN: 978-1-60936-003-0

Love Finds You in Silver City, Idaho
by Janelle Mowery
ISBN: 978-1-60936-005-4

*Love Finds You in Carmel-
by-the-Sea, California*
by Sandra D. Bricker
ISBN: 978-1-60936-027-6

Love Finds You Under the Mistletoe
by Irene Brand and Anita Higman
ISBN: 978-1-60936-004-7

Love Finds You in Hope, Kansas
by Pamela Griffin
ISBN: 978-1-60936-007-8

Love Finds You in Sun Valley, Idaho
by Angela Ruth
ISBN: 978-1-60936-008-5

*Love Finds You in
Camelot, Tennessee*
by Janice Hanna
ISBN: 978-1-935416-65-4

*Love Finds You in
Tombstone, Arizona*
by Miralee Ferrell
ISBN: 978-1-60936-104-4

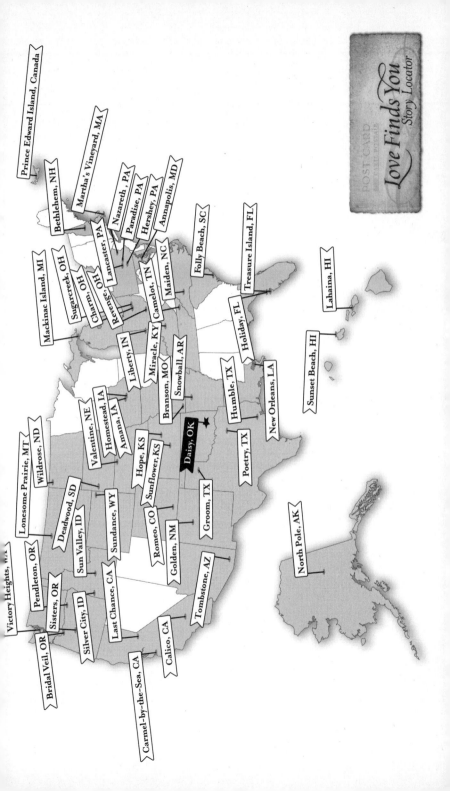